Praise for *The Detainees* by Sean Hughes

'Hughes is a comedian and the manner of his inspired stand-up observations is preserved in the text, with startling precision and depth'
GUARDIAN

'An angsty, black-comic novel about disease, drugs, drink and depression. The first Southern Irish contribution to a genre whose UK practitioners include Irvine Welsh, James Kelman, Martin Amis and Will Self: urban gothic. The strength of characterisation reveals the novelist's essential talent for observing the human animal and recording its noises'
INDEPENDENT

'One of the most important novels of this generation. The humour, which peppers the whole experience, is great but the pain and confusion is the main point. Sean Hughes has written the defining novel of this generation of bombed-out, pissed-off Irish internationals. It's funny because it's true and it's scary because it's true. It is also a searing indictment of a suburban Irish upbringing'
IRISH SUNDAY INDEPENDENT

'Hughes, an award-winning stand-up comedian, has produced a riveting thriller and blackly comic novel'
SUNDAY TIMES

'He is good at showing the lifeless reality of growing up in a working-class home in a dead-end Irish town, and the mixture of relief and self-disgust experienced on a daily basis by those who don't emigrate, or who choose to return. It's not the usual kind of gagfest you might expect from a comedian writing a novel. It's powerful stuff'
INDEPENDENT ON SUNDAY

Also by Sean Hughes
The Detainees

It's What He Would've Wanted

A novel about secrets, sex and bad weather

Sean Hughes

Scribner

First published in Great Britain by Scribner, 1999
This edition published by Scribner, 2000
An imprint of Simon & Schuster UK Ltd
A Viacom Company

1 3 5 7 9 10 8 6 4 2

Simon & Schuster UK Ltd
Africa House
64–78 Kingsway
London WC2B 6AH

Simon & Schuster Australia
Sydney

A CIP catalogue record for this book is available
from the British Library

ISBN 0-684-86029-5

Printed and bound in Great Britain by
Cox & Wyman Ltd, Reading, Berkshire

*For all those who continue to be part of the charade
and for the much missed Gavin Hills.*

Acknowledgements

Thanks to everyone at Simon & Schuster and to all those who helped with research and to anyone named Hannah.

Chapter 1

I wish I'd been born to different parents. They are decent enough folk, but . . . I guess it was the way they were raised. No, let me go further: I wish I'd been their parents. Let me introduce myself.

My name's Shea Hickson. Yes, I'm not too keen on it either. Dad was a bit of a revolutionary in his youth; Che Guevara being his icon of choice, he gave me a bastardized version of his hero's name. And maybe he'd substituted the traditional post-birth cigar with a jazz-woodbine, but early baby pictures show me wearing a beret. Cutesy Shea in his beret down to his nose remained on my parents' bedside cabinet for several years. Until it mysteriously disappeared. OK, seeing as I'm about to lay out big fat truths, here's confession number one.

I'm six, the house is burgled. Mum and Dad are devastated. TV, radio, jewellery, cash, all uninsured (Dad didn't like the system taking liberties with his cash). The cop comes for a statement over a cuppa and Mum asks me to check and see if any of my valuables are missing. I ask you, I'm six and I'm supposed to have valuables. It was the policeman's suggestion and Mum was very

1

impressionable when under stress. I skipped upstairs, delighted to be part of a burglary investigation, while keeping my fingers crossed that my Grand Prix Top Trump cards were still intact . . . Did I fuck! I was a crafty little fucker even then. I went straight into the folks' bedroom and snatched the beret photo. I thought that would be the end of it. I wouldn't have taken it had I foreseen the endless retelling of the theft: 'It's the sentimental things, what use would they have had for that picture?' blah, blah. I always used to imagine this down-at-heel family settling in for the night, watching our telly with my picture on the top of it. Hopefully using it as a reminder to their own kids that if they didn't behave they would make them dress like that too. It was a funny old day that, in total.

From that point onwards Dad eased his 'It's all about the redistribution of wealth, son' on pocket-money day from his pre-allowance speech. Oh – and I'm not being flippant here and I have tried to blank it from my mind, but – the stress of the robbery induced my little brother into the world five weeks early. Of course this little-boned attention seeker took all the adoration away from me but at least Dad made me feel wanted by giving my little sibling a stupid name as well. Welcome to the show: Orwell.

Me, I tend to look on the funny side of things. Not in a 'you've got to laugh' sort of way: if some bad shit is going down, I open my mouth and some sarcastic comment leaps out feet first. Some hit the bull's-eye; these usually come out in front of people who think I'm a bit of a laugh. Other comments inhale all the air in the room.

This happens in front of people who think I'm a bit of a prick. And then there's another bunch of people who think I just mumble.

So why am I writing this? Have I got a huge flag of a story to unfurl? Yes and no. There's a story all right, an extraordinary one, but it's not necessarily mine. I'm part of it just as we are part of many tales that we not aware of. We all have cameos in stories we are not conscious of. This story is really my dad's but he's dead now so he's not going to write it. I was toying with consulting him via the Ouija board but it would have taken us forever and when telling our own story, we all tend to embellish. I honestly believe my dad would have wanted me to do this, as the title suggests. I also figured if I was going to dig up my dad's old skeletons it might as well be for a reason, and I know this is a bit of a long shot, but believe me it does help you get over a death. If there is an afterlife, maybe Dad is looking up at me thinking I'm not a layabout after all, which is what he called me for the last five years of his life. This indubitably was preferable to Shea.

Chapter 2

It was Christmas Eve 1998. I don't really do Christmas so it was pretty much a Thursday for me. The relentless rain gave me a bad feeling. I found myself in a local pub ordering a Babycham. The bar was four deep, requiring the maximum allowable invasion of body space beneath a wave of £10 notes, brandished as bait for direct eye contact with the pourer.

'Pint of Bass and a Babycham for the cliché please.' I was bubbling under with drunkenness. I caught a quick glimpse of my reflection and was happy with the new crew-cut, less so with the loose hairs I could feel on my back or the battalion sticking to my hand every time I ruffled my barnet. I creaked my neck over at the Babycham drinker and was already regrettting the fact that I was going to try and shag her later on. But more pressing was trying to remember her fucking name. She had cut my hair earlier that day, or 'shaped it' as she was fond of saying. Before the reshape she had massaged my head, her chest brushing against my neck. Boy she was sexy. And while the session was punctuated with hairdresser-speak I checked out her body under the pretence of studying my hair. Black stockings, tiny skirt, small arse which looks big, one of those tops that bunched up in a knot below beautifully suspended breasts, blond messed-up hair, gelled in tight. Oh and her lips: round, red, full, perfect for blow-jobs. (I love blow-jobs, by the way. I know this in itself is not unusual, but I like to think that my conspicuously single-minded devotion sets me apart from the crowd.) She had the giddy laugh and bright eyes of the intellectually challenged. It is not lost on me that much to my eternal shame I've pretty much described a blow-up doll. What chance had demure, sophisticated ladies against this intrusion?

'There you go, doll, get that down you.'

'It looks very good from the side.'

'What?'

'Your hair, you nana!' Giddy laugh.

'Yeah, you did a great job.' Nana, for fuck's sake. 'I was curious about your name. Is that a made-up one for hairdressing purposes?'

'Ruth Austen? Oh, I get it: Ruth, Roots – very funny.' Her giddy laugh was starting to annoy me.

The things I do for sex. I'm thirty years old . When can I leave this phase of my life? I didn't even like her. I don't even like sex. I guess I just do it because I can, the ego needs refuelling. It's pretty much like climbing the highest mountain: because it's there. The real worry is, as I get older, I'll still be the same but only able to climb little hills. It's pathetic. I should have just finished my drink, thanked her for her company, gone home and had a wank. That would have been the adult thing to do.

6

Instead, I downed the rest of my beer like a teenager.

'My place then?'

'OK.'

I don't know what she saw in me, a bone-snapping moodist sauntering along in a layabout's body whose social skills amount to being on nodding terms with the rest of the race. And my cock's nothing to write home about either.

As we stepped out of the pub, the rain came down as if it had been lying in wait for us. We got home soaked and I was aware that my one clean towel smelt like an old dirty one. I helped dry her hair and clicked on the fire. I went to give her a little kiss on the cheek. She grabbed at the outline of my penis. This had me moving back half a pace. The kissing was full on but not passionate. Her tongue refused to budge even though mine was trying very hard to dislodge it. She stripped like a professional. The tits, free, were exhilarating. The vaginal hair sponged out akin to a perm released from a hat. I couldn't help myself and pointed to it, saying, 'Who does your hair?'

She grabbed my head and forced me to my knees whispering hoarsely, 'Anoint me.' I didn't have to mutter 'nutter' as my tongue swished away hair and tunnelled deep. I didn't enjoy this aspect of sex and it wasn't helped by her repeating, 'I want to see it coming out of my arsehole.' If she wasn't careful she was going to have a fanny full of puke. She grasped my hands and put them on her breasts with the order, 'Ripen them.' Oh for fuck's sake, surely David Lynch is going to come in now and shout, 'Cut! We've done the numb-tongue scene, let's reset for her point of view.'

Ten minutes later, as I caught my breath, she undressed me. I suddenly clicked that I was more turned on when she was clothed. Without warning, she bit hard on my right nipple. The pain had me pushing her away. I was nervous as she eyed my penis. She took it in her mouth in one. Her nose started making strange grunting noises. I was one step away from absolute pleasure because of my love for blow-jobs but the nagging presence that wouldn't permit relaxation was her teeth. She was going to bite through it and use it as a vibrator. My old chap was close to either coming or going. She stopped, got on top of the rug in the doggy position and shoved my penis into her vagina. It dawned on me that I was being raped. I felt a sensation new to me: puzzled, I tried to look down. She had stuck three fingers alongside my penis to jolly things along. I was being used and abused and enjoying every moment. Before long I was politely telling Ruth that I was about to come. I pulled out. She kept her three fingers in but took hold of my penis with her right hand and put it back in her mouth. I came straight away and remained in the same position for the next five minutes until she came herself.

I was enjoying that resting period but Ruth spoiled it by lying spread-eagled on the rug and staring at me while demanding that I urinate on her. This was the wrong side of acceptability for me and all I could muster was 'No, that rug was a gift from my parents.' There followed the usual silence caused by one person refusing to piss on another. Was this the same sweet girl who chatted about her sister in Bromley earlier today? This was my first threesome, me and the schizophrenic.

Dressed and back to mundanity, we small-talked until she left. We kissed, a little peck, at the door. It was still raining heavily. I was being nice but brisk.

'See you around, oh, and I nearly forgot . . .' looking at my watch, 'Happy Christmas!' One door closes; fuck I needed a drink. And regardless of the fact that she was a couple of eggs short of a fry-up, I knew it was going to be my masturbation fantasy for a while to come.

The doorbell rang. There would be hell to pay. I could sense my mood peddling down a couple of gears.

'Hi. Sorry about this, Shea. It really is pelting down. Can I wait until it eases?'

'Sure, come in.' The falsest smile remained transfixed on the not-so-happy face.

'Make yourself comfortable, I need to take a piss.' Open your mouth please.

Chapter 3

I had no idea how bad the weather was. My brother was stuck in his office. Orwell is a journalist. He had worked for the *Daily Angel* for two years and had been the company's golden boy. He had advanced so quick as to have an older assistant. The paper had tried to appease him with various editorial positions but freedom was what he craved. He had been headhunted by several monthly magazines until the newspaper created a new post especially for him, Head of Ongoing Investigations, but he refused it, and went freelance instead. This gave him an opportunity to chase whatever story he found interesting. It amounted to tabloid sensationalism but with better adjectives. The story he'd been sweating over lately was that of a prominent member of the British National Party, a closet queer who had ruefully taken up with some Moroccan boys on a holiday. Orwell had put out a good run of stories recently and the big cheeses were slapping his back for bringing circulation up a notch. His success meant that he had two tabloid journalists stalking his every move. Being only twenty-five he was resented around the office, especially as Dad had finagled him into his original position.

Orwell was supposed to be picking me up in the morning to whisk us down to Mum and Dad's for a family Christmas.

Mum and Dad, Jean and Terry, had settled into the slow lane of the New Forest. Deep breaths, no sighs, semi-retired. Jean, highly qualified, a degree in European Politics, had detoured off to the housewife's burial ground. Terry, who'd got a first in Meteorology, and had seemed destined to work at the cutting edge of his field, sadly had morphed into Terry the BBC weatherman. In her late fifties, Jean used her time to gather new skills – pottery, jam-making and appeasement; in his, Terry spent more time in his study than he had ever done in his working life, doing Lord knows what.

He surrounded himself with memories of his achievements, framed diplomas and snaps with notables, his favourite being one of him with James Hunt. Dad had helped James Hunt's racing team check out all-round weather effects on the cars. His perennial boast was of helping them up their lap time 1.2 seconds around the Silverstone circuit. Jean's pride lay largely in the food she served and the utensils that she carried it in. She had been the more ambitious of the two but once her two sons were created, a moment of clarity had prompted new agendas.

Terry was used to bad weather, secretly loved it. The lack of cover was a reason for buying the cottage. The challenge of facing the elements had been the spur to leave the street-lighting way of life. The forest was now a mere extension of his own back garden.

I wasn't looking forward to seeing them or my brother.

Christmas morning arrived. Five o'clock, the wind was still french-kissing the windows. I was wide awake and sickeningly tired. Feeling almost out-of-body, with the spirit trying to get back inside but not being able to fit. Beside me lay Ruth, her arm around my waist. She looked beautiful, clear-skinned, her curls placed delicately on her forehead, a silent princess, but all I could see was a mass of bones clamping my body. I would gladly have paid a fine to rid myself of this intrusion. I agonized over the immediate, hungover future, the hour or so of avoided eye contact before I could bid her goodbye. The rain was trying to gob on us and the thought of spending the day with my parents watching shit television engulfed me. My precious head-space settled on self-pity as the hangover kicked in.

Ruth moved on to her belly, loosening her grip. She's not dead then. I hadn't realized her nipples were so big. I had that semi-erection born of the early-morning horn and a full bladder. Without thought but with plenty of hindsight I cuddled up to her, running through the minimum two-minute grope before sticking my reluctant penis inside her, it slightly angling towards the bathroom door. A passionless quiet fuck which satisfied nobody had her awake. She went to the bathroom. I watched her out.

She had a beautiful body which was lucky for me as I have always had a problem with naked bodies. It may be a long shot but I think it stems from walking in, at an impressionable age, on a rubbery old couple having sex in a McDonald's toilet. I haven't been able to eat mayonnaise since. As for my own state of affairs I joined a gym last year after one too many penitential 'You're not getting any younger' sessions. I had done a deal for off-peak membership. Bliss, the whole pool to myself. But no, it was the truly hideous who shared my timetable. The experience just confirmed my fears as the bloated middle-aged made me more acutely aware of the ageing process: their faces old and distinguished but the bodies . . . keg-bellies, cushion-arses, protruding varicose veins, unsightly hairs, the dead-weight tits, and that was just the woman sharing the spa with me. I cancelled my membership that day.

Ruth interrupted my casually bitter meditations with 'Have you got a hairdryer?' I don't know why but I found this hilarious. Maybe it was the sight of this lovely lady with one towel wrapped around her body and another one around her head and knowing the one on her head had last been used to wipe down a friend's wet dog. To me this made her look more beautiful. A vulnerable lass stood before me and no I didn't want to protect her, I just love weakness in people; it makes me feel I fit in more, being all too aware of my own.

'No,' I smiled, 'but I can make you a cup of tea.'

I stopped off to relieve myself in the bathroom and spotted an open shampoo bottle. It was the dog's. Santa works in mysterious ways.

She kept asking me what was making me laugh which made me laugh even more. In the kitchen, I put in a call to Orwell to find out when he was coming but the phone line was dead.

When Ruth came downstairs, she looked distressed.

14

She kept on hollering, 'Have you called the police?'

'Why? What's happened?'

'You've been burgled! They've taken the telly.'

It took me an hour to explain why I didn't own a television.

Over breakfast she calmed down. We supped tea and ate toast politely, respectful of each other's morning rituals. I put the radio on, hoping the forecast would be better and that Ruth would be able to go. I was dreading Orwell coming and catching me with her; some of our weaknesses we should be left to deal with alone. The voice of GLR wasn't in its normal soothing register.

'Flash floods and gale-force winds are making all forms of travel hazardous. You are strongly advised to stay in your houses and forget plans for those Christmas walks. British Telecom are doing their best to restore fallen phone lines so you can wish your loved ones well. There is no sign of the storm abating.'

I'm sure Ruth was just as anxious to get home. One of her long curls flopped down to her mouth.

'I haven't come across this shampoo before. It's really nice, sort of coconutty with a shine too.'

I compressed my laughter. 'Yeah, it's some imported one. They warn you not to use too much though or your hair will start to moult.'

'I must watch out for it. Maybe I'll introduce it at the salon. What's it called?'

'Uh . . . Man's Best Friend.'

The day dragged. Each step shifting imaginary chains. Outside the huge outside darkened and claustrophobed, a dimmer switch on the side of my head I had no control of. Christmas: I felt happy for the kiddies, adult and standard, who were enthralled in their own spirit; their joy brought joy to me. I'm not anti-Christmas, it's just that I'm not any good at it. I would have been content just pottering round with my own thoughts for the day but Ruth kept chattering away like my mother, questions that didn't need answers all fucking day. I would have felt sorry for her but she didn't give me time to do so. I was on the verge of being extremely rude to give us a chance to strop off into our own separate corners. Come on rain, stop, come on Jesus, let her get back to the bosom of her own family. She just wants to celebrate your birth. The rain got heavier, blowing out all the birthday candles. The magnet hairdresser started stating blindingly obvious certitudes and I was beginning to think someone was pulling a string from her back as she showered me with doll-speak.

The rain eased at around seven. Well, I might as well be exact – 7.08 and away she went. My estimation of her went up when she didn't bother with the 'see you again' farewell routine. We both knew it had been a mistake. I cherished my solitude, for tomorrow it would be Pimms on the lawn with Momma and Poppa. My brother would no doubt collect me in his flash motor in the morning. Parents . . .

Dad was an Irish working-class boy whose parents scrimped and saved, even stopping their 'how to be posh' workshops so they could put their one and only through buggery school. Dad in turn didn't let them down. He got his first at Nottingham but unfortunately his parents didn't live to see him become officially posh or, should I say, become accepted by posh people. It would have made my grandparents' life complete had Dad driven down their road with his nose turned up and called them scumbags. But alas no, it was a slow process. My grandparents who I never knew but I believe led a very ordered life and didn't take each day as it came, regrettably both got run over by a bus, the only consolation for Dad being that they would certainly have been wearing clean underwear. It was a freak accident: the driver had a heart attack and veered into them. The saddest thing was that, after years of talking about it, they were about to move back to Ireland.

I love my family out of duty. If we were friends, we would have just drifted apart. But here we were, still trying to connect and failing and it's nobody's fault. Well, it's probably mine actually because I have no real friends; my parents have well-adjusted lives with loads of acquaintances with whom they have things in common. What are my interests? I like taking the piss out of everything I begrudgingly encounter. I like to sneer at the importance people place on life. I like to point out that the things that people think bring them happiness are dressed-up rituals and what they are actually experiencing is empty and formulaic. Honesty is dead and people are frightened of their own truths. I'm hardly the life and soul of the party.

If I went to see a shrink he would no doubt try to pinpoint the crossover moment from carefree flower of youth to miserable sod or, as I like to call myself, pursuer of truth. But I know when that moment came. I was fourteen years old. I was watching a black-and-white

17

alien movie and the earthling said, 'Take me to your leader.' This was a line that changed my life. OK, I'll point out that at this movement I was also having my first spliff. A gang of us had bunked off school and were havng a right laugh at the tackiness and primitive costumes. But then that line just hit me. The others continued laughing and I knew they were just morons.

'Take me to your leader' accumulated all these con-notations in my head. The fact that we all need leaders, whether it be God, government or child. The thoughts kept tumbling out: we aren't looking for something tangible, but need to know what to think; we have become a mass of people who need to be told what to do and then you look at all the means of communication and that's what they are doing, flooding us with how we should think; we are too lazy for individual thought and we just accept what we are given. The media try to be our leader and this is the only way democracy can work. That day I changed and there have been other days that have changed me. I questioned everything and because nobody else I knew shared my scepticism I was forced to withdraw into myself. So let's put that one straight: I didn't reject anybody, they rejected me. And any action I have taken since on this particular drive was never meant to hurt anybody. I understand we all need to be led but I will not rest until I have been taken to my leader.

Chapter 4

Orwell arrived early on Boxing Day and resembled Robert Downey Junior after a bender. He looked almost human. There's five years between us, which means we didn't share a childhood. He used to get my horrible hand-me-downs. Our folks were always about eight years behind fashion when dressing me, but by the time Orwell got the clothes they were enjoying a renaissance. It was a given that I took after my father and Orwell, my mother. But we did share a similar sense of humour and I always looked out for Orwell and probably gave him shitty 'I've been there' advice. Everyone in the family had a stubbornness of the bacon sarny proportion.

As adults, Orwell and I met once a week for a pint until Rebecca came between us. Rebecca, my ex; Rebecca, his fiancée; Rebecca who is expecting the folks' first grandchild; Rebecca who I still hanker for; Rebecca who's now very frosty towards me; Rebecca who really hurt me; Rebecca who I will never get over; Rebecca who gave great blow-jobs; Rebecca who is meeting us at the folks' later on. That Rebecca.

When we split, Orwell tried to comfort the two of us,

except he didn't try to fuck me. He had done nothing wrong and yet he had crossed an unmentionable line that only your brother has access to. We've never talked about it. I'll give him that – he understands my pain, even if he did cause it. She seems different when she's with him. She's certainly no one I ever knew. I wish I could be happy for them but I can't. I want them to break up. I want her to have an affair with my father, then the hurt would bring my brother back and I do want him back.

As we drove along I sneaked looks at him, his strong neck, baby-stubble face, widow's peak. It dawned on me that he hadn't smiled in my presence since the betrayal. I missed that smile, the nights of boozy mayhem. The shameful shared smile of the morning. I wanted him back. If there was something I could say I would say it but if there was a moment it is now gone and it's a terrible pity. We have the odd spark of ignition but that makes me even sadder. I know he goes over the same ground in his head. I hope she's worth it, I really do. In many ways I want it to be the dream romance because if it fizzled out it would make a mockery of the casualties.

I know I might be hiding the real pain, but the time I knew myself and my brother were finished was when he took me aside and looked me in the eye and, I'm not kidding you here, he said, 'All's fair in love and war.' You see, I knew my real brother would never have said that and if I'd had it in my power I would've enlisted him into the army there and then. That was the day he was taken to his leader and all the principles we had built together he simply knocked down. He had no choice but to accept his fate and play by the rules. Me, I developed a deep mistrust of the human race and a pervading inertia.

I felt a vibration which killed all reminiscences. It was my pager. The message read:

. . . LJ – a little task to do – RH . . .

That's the problem with secret organizations. You have to keep them secret.

The weather cleared the further we drove, as if directing us. A light breeze flapped debris from the storm. The sun glanced out, trying to enjoy the festive season. My parents' cottage came into view and it looked splendid. We imagined Mum sneaking peeks out the window as she tried to shoo-shoo the dust out of the house. The gravel forecourt made that beautiful sound as the tyres evened out their passage, the pebbles parting for the motorized Moses.

Mum opened the door, her smile so wide we felt like an embarrassment of brothers. Of course, Dad would be scuffling somewhere round the house. Mum tried to hug us but realized she still had the kettle in her hand. I excused myself to make a phone call from Dad's study and to let Mum enquire about Rebecca with Orwell. Dad's desk was remarkably tidy. I sat in the swivel chair and was a child again. I dialled the number, one of the three I knew off by heart. While I waited for him to pick up, I made a paper-plane from a loose sheet on my father's desk.

'Hello, LJ here. Shoot.'

I found out about my little task and was given a rather encouraging progress report. I do want to tell you what

I'm up to but most people don't understand the work we do. Put it this way: we are trying to make the world a more intelligent place and we use every means to get our message across. RH wanted me to sniff around a particularly pungent game-show host who apparently was having a dalliance with one of his daughter's school-friends. Why pick on him? Why indeed. Well, if he's going to play the family man, it's only right he should be one. It isn't a question of morals, it's the telling of the truth. A childish glee had me putting me down the phone, picking up my plane and doing the full 360-degree spin on the swivel chair to launch it. The room blurred past and I thought, for a moment, I'd seen the unthinkable. The chair continued on another, slower revolution – the vision passed before me again, demanding reason. My insides collapsed, adrenalin rose, pins and needles shot through my arms, normal sound ceased and was replaced by a ringing. My whole body went numb, then the shakes. I sat and stared. There, hanging from a light-fitting was my dad.

His head was lowered so I couldn't really see his face. The overriding image was that he was wearing his best suit and in his top pocket there was a carefully placed handkerchief. At no point did I try to cut him down. The orange flex left a bloodline on his neck. I was drained of all blood. Eventually, even though the image is etched forever in memory, hazy time lapses occurred. I screamed.

I don't remember much after that but Mum did all the practical stuff. The ambulance and police and, I assume, doctors and coroners and, inevitably, reporters, filled the house. And then the three of us, Orwell, Mum and myself, sat silently in the living room. I wanted to question Mum, thinking she would have answers. Of course, I apportioned some blame to myself. Some time before we attempted futile sleep I noticed Rebecca was also in the room and the three of them kept on passing a note between them. I snapped out of my limbo and Orwell handed me the smoothed-out paper-plane. I read what was no doubt his suicide note.

I am sorry. I have failed you. I have failed myself. Serendipity has been working in reverse. My bones were starting to ache and the future was only memories. Too many bad ones. Sorry, Jean. Your love is what kept me going and it is the thought of your love which gives me the strength to carry out this selfish deed. To my sons, you are fully developed. I have done all I can. Please don't let this shade your lives. I love you. I'm sorry.

Your husband and father, Terence

It's strange how the mind works but my first thought was how shit his handwriting was and that I couldn't really ask Mum to help me decipher it. I read it for at least half an hour and you'd be surprised how many connotations a simple note can have, especially when I don't have a clue what serendipity means. Again I felt I couldn't ask. I said I was going to bed. En route I looked up the word: 'serendipity *n*. the faculty of making happy and unexpected discoveries by accident.'

I went to bed to think it all through. Nothing was making sense and every time I closed my eyes I saw my father hanging. Where were my tears? I lay in bed scared and dizzy. I nodded off for a couple of minutes but awoke with a question pressing through the sleepy confusion. It wasn't 'Why did he kill himself?' I honestly don't believe people kill themselves, society kills them. It's as simple as that. If life makes living unbearable surely then it is to blame. If life could satisfy all there would be no suicide. Why did Dad think he'd failed us and himself? A series of clear perceptions marched through the haze: if only we could push society into accepting more of our own weaknesses, people wouldn't feel so inadequate; the cheap thrills and inanity the media force us to endure make some of us feel we are not suited; life should be challenging and full of opposing ideas; don't oppress the people by making them feel stupid.

A sudden urge had me in Dad's study. I wanted to find out more about the man. I knew he kept diaries. I heard a noise from the sitting room and went through and Rebecca was there drinking milk with the television on low. Orwell was in bed crunched up like my paper-plane. He didn't want Rebecca near him. That was the Hickson way, push those closest out of sight. I almost felt sympathy for her. She eased into a prototype comforting speech. She managed to annoy me within minutes with her 'It hits the youngest harder' patter. People with their goddamn assumptions. I didn't want to fight and I didn't consider her family so I gazed over at the television and there was Dad, a smiling Dad, and the newsreader feigning concern over the suicide of the beloved weatherman Terence Hickson. They showed a clip of him which I'd never seen before and my throat tightened. I could feel tears willing themselves out of my body. Tears mixed of realization of death and the annoyance of not knowing the man, guilt and intrigue, fatigue and loss, wonder and longing. Rebecca's proffered tissue never had a chance of containing the downpour.

The next two days the house filled with people I didn't know. I kept trying to catch moments with Orwell but could never get him alone. I kept to myself and tried long walks to break through the exhaustion that kept me awake at night. Every time I closed my eyes cruel hallucinations had me batting my eyelids to protect my mind from the macabre slide-show. I spent all my time in Dad's study collecting everything that would take me closer to him. On the day of the funeral I hit the jackpot and found a series of diaries he kept. I decided I wouldn't read them until I got home.

The funeral itself was eerie, mainly because Orwell and I had to wear Dad's suits as neither of us had brought appropriate clothing with us. I was similar in build to him but Orwell, being bigger-boned and four stone heavier, looked like the Incredible Hulk post-rage. The lowering of the coffin, I realized, is very undignified. I know it's to give us the memory to deal with the denial we all play with when someone close dies but you don't see that many people digging up loved ones just to be on the safe side.

I drank constantly but couldn't get drunk, the brain determined to take me to the edge. Mum aged visibly at the funeral. Christ! What was she going to do? Of course, all day I had drunkards pulling at me as if they were getting a final touch of Dad. People I didn't know told me stories about a man I didn't recognize, the more drunk the more exaggerated. I was spoken at, they all catchphrased 'you look just like your father'. Eventually I snapped – 'Yes, this tie is a bit tight.' I had my own space from then on as people avoided me. I guess I was bringing their buzz down. I slipped away to my room wondering did Dad also have this cruel streak? Regardless, it seemed to do the trick and I started to doze off. I awoke with a jolt but comforted. The hallucinations were turning my way. Maybe I was turning the corner with this mourning lark. I was accepting Dad's death. The sensation of being sucked off by an octopus was a new one. Whatever, I was certainly aroused and made a mental note to do more swimming. I kept my eyes closed as I put my hand under the duvet to inspect my jolly roger. It kind of freaked me that he'd grown a head of hair. I opened my eyes and pushed the head away. It was still dark and I heard moaning. As ever with sex, I fucked the consequences and continued with this very much needed experience. Look, I told you, I love blow-jobs. I know I'm not out on a limb here but I really do. If there was a blow-jobs organization I would be its chairman. I helped the motion with my hands on the head. I didn't recognize it from touch but I guessed it was Rebecca. It annoyed me that she had got even better at this. Then there came the thought that Orwell was getting this on a regular basis and then, of course, I thought of poor Orwell and the fact that we were doing the dirty on him. But I can't reiterate enough how much I adore blow-jobs.

Rebecca, for some reason, hated to swallow and she could always feel when the vein was about to splurt. I wanted this to last forever so I tried to put the event out of my mind. I couldn't get Orwell out of my head or Rebecca's head out of me.

I remember the time when myself and Orwell, totally pissed, gatecrashed an AA meeting. Orwell bounded to the front of the room, steadied himself against a nearby table and bellowed, 'My name is Orwell Hickson, this is my first meeting and it's taken a lot of courage and determination to get up here tonight.' The whole room erupted in applause. Orwell hesitated, took a deep breath and continued, 'My name is Orwell Hickson and I fucking hate hangovers.' There was a silence, just long enough for this childish prank to fall on its arse. I was cacking myself, which warranted its own attention. The group started hurling abuse at us and we were punched out of the room.

Rebecca sucked harder knowing I was just about to come and out of some warped sense of respect I gently started to lift her head but she went even tighter. Was this Rebecca's way of telling me she still loved me? It felt wonderful. I got carried away and as I jerked and pressed harder, I started whispering, 'I love you,' stroking her hair, 'I've never stopped loving you.' As the last few drops were being coaxed out, I decided that I was going to kiss her full on the mouth. That had been our gleeful pact, if ever I was to come in her mouth. I pushed her head up to mine.

Now either Rebecca doesn't look so hot without make-up or I'd been sucked off by a sixty-year-old man. I didn't know what to do but was pretty sure we weren't going to share a post-coital cigarette. He went to kiss me. I slapped him across the face. I saw some of my sperm fly out of his mouth. I got up, enraged, and asked him, not too hysterically as I didn't want anyone bursting in, like who the fuck he was. He smiled and said I could call him El Niño. With that, he picked up his false teeth from the dresser and blew me a kiss goodnight. I hoped I was still hallucinating but I wasn't going to ask him to pinch me for clarification. I didn't feel sickened, which was what I thought I'd feel. As with any new experience, it takes a while before you can get a handle on it. I know he was well out of order but it is hard to despise someone who has just given you the best blow-job of your life. And you know how much I love them. But I didn't sleep a wink for the rest of the night. In short, I knew I wasn't going to grow a moustache and hang out at Trade but I didn't bolt the door either.

It was almost impossible to bid farewell to Mum. During breakfast it was just the three of us. We all looked like we should have blankets over our shoulders and our feet in bowls of hot water. Mum insisted on a hearty life-shortening breakfast. I dreaded what was going on in her head. Throughout the ordeal her emotions hadn't flickered. Steady as a hollow rock. Mum was quiet at the best of times but Dad's death had lowered her volume further. She was now down to a mumble, an annoying mumble which had each conversation punctuated with 'pardons' and 'sorrys', or went unanswered. It became very frustrating trying to get her to repeat herself when the only answer her questions warranted was a 'yeah'.

Orwell wasn't much help as he was dealing with frequent outbursts of tears. I personally hardly ever cry at real life but can become unconsolable during movies. Maybe it's the music but it gets me every time. Even opening scenes can make my throat go lumpy. And I'm not just talking about the sad scenes either, the good guy getting away has the same effect. Maybe it's related to the size of the screen: the people are bigger so the emotions are more important. It's crazy really. Someone dies in a movie, I bawl; they show footage of dead people on the news and I can handle it. Real life is maybe too sad.

I look at my mum and the dice she has been thrown and I'm powerless to do anything for her. It goes beyond crying. I don't know what keeps her going. I fear she'll go soon too. You hear that all the time about older couples, one dying then the other in quick succession. The tricky nature of Dad's exit and the fact that we are supposed to be so alike also baffles me. Why did society kill him when surely he must have known that life is simply a bowl of grapes and the only fun to be had is to spit the pips at people?

Mum served our fry-ups. My appetite vanished as the sausage reminded me of El Niño. I looked to Orwell, who was steadfast with his breakfast, although his hands trembled. I offered to drive. He refused, determined as he was to cause a four-mile tailback on the motorway.

I had the diaries packed safely in the car and we both hugged Mum but didn't say a word to her. It would have belittled her to try and say unsayable things. She mumbled something. 'Yeah' and a shrug and we were off. I felt as redundant as a drummer in Ringo Starr's solo

29

band. Orwell started the car in reverse and nearly ran over Mum; she had to dive out of the way.

'I didn't know you were into euthanasia,' I quipped.

Orwell's 'There's a time and a place for jokes' brought about a ten-mile silence. His way of reopening the conversation was 'Do you wish you'd spent more time with Dad?' Now that's a tricky one, the obvious, guilt-drenched question. I had given it a lot of thought but I wasn't sure if Orwell was ready for the answer I had formulated. It was hard to concentrate with Orwell's erratic driving.

'The way I see it is, you have your relationship with your father so isn't it just as valid to ask, "Do you wish you'd spent less time with him?" You might have liked him less if you'd known him better. When the son and father are both adults, either you hit it off or you don't. There's a point of tolerance if you don't and you skirt around up to that point. There's never a break-through in conversation. Actions, yes, but not just by hanging out. Every moment I spent with Dad was forced and inarticulate because we had embedded memories of each other paired with our own ways of life. When I was with Dad, the idea of it depressed me. Being with him depressed me. Leaving him depressed me. We weren't right for each other. Now that he's dead, I want and aim to find out more about him but in answer to your question, my dear young brother, I wish I'd never met him.'

But what I ended up saying to Orwell was 'For fuck's sake, brake!'

Chapter 5

Home to my stale life. I opened windows to freshen the air in the flat. If only I could open a window in my heart. I love the sanctuary of my own home. The chance to be completely at ease, the chance to be a cunt without anyone finding out. Time to have a chat with myself. I'm sure it is a pleasure to come home to loved ones but you can't really be yourself. It intrigues me that we can never fully be ourselves, that chance is lost at birth. There is a split second of realization of the pure self but from that moment we are influenced by others.

I wonder if my moment at the top of the mountain has come and gone and I haven't noticed it. It is terrible to think you might have missed the highlight of your own life. I guess that's why we busy ourselves with other people, so we don't have to give access to these thoughts.

I flicked through the diaries. I desperately wanted to dive straight in but couldn't. There was a knot in my stomach, there as if to remind me of something. Scanning the pages I came across the name 'Hazel'. I knew Hazel. I worked in her office for a month. It was Dad's idea. He wanted me to get into public relations. He said I had a gift for talking crap and set me up with this company called Hazel's PR. I was Hazel's PA. Hazel back then was an attractive, dyed-blonde forty but dressed ten years younger. She had great breasts and always wore light blouses and no bra. During a typical working day you would get a composite picture of them. She used her breasts to force her points across. Clients were putty in her hands. It was fascinating to watch her system in which I was a cog: the young pawn who led the prey into the siren's office. She would greet them with a smile, not a plastic one, a brilliant genuine smile. Then off came her glasses and manicured hands were shown as she shook theirs. Then, this was the classic, she didn't leave her desk: instead, she leaned across it. Bang! First sight of her charms. Then she'd straighten herself up, the breasts wobbling back into position, and the business would commence. Her winning formula also included hiding her arse, which she had a problem with. Me, I have no problem with big arses, but Hazel did. She practically sidled into the office every day.

I used to have Hazel's phone book at my desk. It was always chock-full with names of people she would always call but who would never call her back. She took great joy in flicking through the torrent of entries to impress me. One day, curiosity got to me and I had a good look through it, to find she had written in the likes of Pizza Express, ABC Cinema, Hertz Car Rental. I could hardly find any real people but still the charade went on as she boasted of her packed social life. There were six of us in the office and we all hated her but were too afraid to show it. The main problem with Hazel was her very severe mood swings. For instance, if she couldn't get through to her best mate Miss Selfridge's, somebody would cop it. Invariably she'd hand out an unnecessarily horrible dressing down. Being the only guy in the office, I was an easy target. She'd always finish her tirade of sexist abuse along the lines of 'We've got a boy doing a man's job' or 'Make me some coffee, needle-dick'. These days became known as bad-arse days.

I knew I wasn't cut out for the office and my opportunity to quit came on Hazel's birthday. She dropped heavy hints that she wanted presents. The girls amassed blouses and perfumes and the official office nutter gave her some balsamic vinegar. Mine was the last to be opened. I'd got the fanciest wrapping paper I could find. She ripped at it impatiently to find a copy of the Yellow Pages. She stared at me blankly. I looked her in the eye and said, 'I thought I'd save you the hassle of having to fill out next year's phone book.' The others laughed, she stormed out and I was sacked. What Dad ever saw in her I don't know. Dad used Hazel's company when the TV people started to razzamatazz the whole weather forecasting scene. He decided to change his image when a review said he was 'a little man who was a little staid'.

I read the diary for an hour, taking occasional notes. It was fairly run-of-the-mill stuff until I noticed a strange coded language recurring. At first I paid no attention, thinking it was lazily written, but certain entries started bugging me, like 'The rain was harmless tonight', 'I miss the wind' and 'The sun enjoyed my company'. It didn't make sense, a man who had written two books on climatological change and the environment being so playful with the elements. I tired of life as I pondered Dad's. As I started to nap on the couch, I suddenly twigged what Dad was doing in his diary. It was obvious really.

The rain, the wind, the sun, the clouds – they were all people. People I didn't know but whom he was obviously involved with. I decided to take one at a time, make a list of all their individual entries until I had all the information at hand. As I worked studiously, I was buzzing with the idea that I was creating my own Frankenstein.

I was going to get to the bare bones of my father and construct him from there. Strange memories of him which I thought I'd forgotten came flooding back. Now I wasn't just remembering them but analysing their meaning. The one time he hit me. Why did he do that? Why did he never apologize for it? It was my birthday, my difficult fifteenth. I'd never liked birthdays. I don't like people wishing me 'Happy Birthday', it's embarrassing and false. I'm not always a miserable fucker, honestly, I just like moments of spontaneity. If I have a really good day during the year, I'll gladly consider that my birthday. That's what it should be, just one of those days when you're glad to be alive. That's why I feel really sorry for the Queen – poor bitch has to enjoy two days of enforced fun. What's the rule when she dies – do they give her two deaths, actual and official? Anyway, my difficult fifteenth.

I had wanted a Chopper bike for six months, mainly because my pal James Fentelli had one and I pretty much wanted what he wanted, as I copied what he did. He was a mad fucker. His parents were wealthy and well-bred but he was a tearaway. I know now it was because he was an only child and they didn't pay him much attention but smothered him with gifts instead. James developed a fascination with fire. One night over at his house, out of sheer boredom he put his fist in the fire and kept it there for at least ten seconds. That smell has stayed with me and I've never been able to eat pork since. His hand went reddish-brown and blistered straight away. I, because I was a total idiot, followed suit. In went my hand for ten seconds also but James swore it was only two and from that moment his nickname for me was Underdone. The pain was excruciating, not while my hand was in the fire but the second it came out. Running it under cold water was the worst. Why did I do it? I guess I loved James or, at the very least, wanted to be him. Also my parents, who were beginning to notice my little fixation, would never be able to go down clichéville with 'If James put his hand in the fire, would you?' crap. After the incident, James was sent to a shrink. I had my pocket money stopped for a month. I never did anything like it again and James and his family left the area six months later, rather quickly too as James had burned their house to the ground.

Once he was gone, so was my obsession with the Chopper, but lo and behold there waiting for me on my birthday was the little beauty. At the breakfast table, Dad asked what I thought of the present. I was still really missing James and this was a sad reminder, so I said, 'It's all right, nothing special.' At this, he leapt at me, started throttling me and slapped me hard across the head which resulted in me flying across the kitchen floor and knocking myself out on the cupboard. He was livid and kept mumbling, 'Be grateful, be grateful.' Then he started crying and it was never mentioned again. But it always puzzled me because he'd never done anything like it before and you just don't do that on a kid's birthday. There must have been an ulterior motive and I wanted to find out what it was.

I continued reading the diary, writing down little snippets of notes, until I came across a sentence which stopped me in my tracks. It read, 'I fear that El Niño will be my undoing.'

Chapter 6

RH had demanded an emergency meeting. RH, as you might not have guessed, stands for Robin Hood, and LJ for Little John. Robin intimidates me. Reluctantly, I headed off to his place the next day.

On the way I popped into the local chemist with some negatives I had found belonging to Dad. The woman in the pharmacy is stunning looking, as in she looks stunned all the time. I think she is second-generation Greek, big brown lazy eyes, pout and white coat. On her left breast she has a name-tag – Paula. I don't know if this is the name of her left breast or her in total. We small-talk every time I go in. I try to come across as interesting and friendly but I'm afraid she probably sees me as an ongoing sufferer from flu viruses and piles. She comes across stunned. I see her sometimes walking with people I assume to be her mum and dad. Her mother looks post-traumatized while her father appears ready for a rumble. They walk her as if she were their prisoner. I saw her once in a pub. She asked me for a cigarette. I was that far gone that she might as well have asked me to marry her. I asked her what she was up to later on and she just looked well . . .

stunned. There lies one of the problems with alcohol. When I get drunk I think I'm eighteen, which is great fun for me but not so much for the eighteen-year-olds I meet.

I had some errands to do in town so I purchased the *Daily Angel* for the tube journey out of family loyalty and to avert the gaze of the huddled masses. Orwell had been credited on a piece demanding the resignation of a prominent Labour MP for illegal earnings. The politician, on his MP's wages, had amassed two houses, a holiday home in France, four Rolls-Royces and some pricey antiques and the maths simply didn't add up. In his defence, he'd offered it was nobody's business but his own. The front page put his country abode beside his parents' semi. It was an nice, sneering piece but totally ineffectual. Politicians had always used their Member of Parliament commitment as a part-time occupation, some as a hobby. But the annoying thing was that other people would read this and laugh and then forget all about it. The MP in question would probably frame it and keep it in his bathroom as a little trophy of arrogance. A tut-tut made me look at my fellow passengers; the row opposite consisted of two old ladies, an ageing goth, two gay men and a Japanese tourist. All had differing levels of sour-faced dissatisfaction about their person. I looked where they were frightened to, and saw a tramp pissing on a well-worn seat. He had a can of Red Stripe in one hand and used the other to balance himself on the dangling handle. His slightly erect penis wavered free, pouring out a stenchy yellow piss which was flowing in the direction of my companions. I don't think he was aware of what he was doing until the flash of light from the Japanese

38

tourist's camera had him turning in that direction. A panic ensued as the goth got it full in the face. He tried to block the piss with his copy of *Bonfire of the Vanities*. The down-and-out tried to apologize by continually repeating, 'Relax, relax,' and offering the goth some of his lager. The train came to a station and as it slowed he fell on the two old ladies. The whole row departed, leaving the tramp to sleep soundly, his todger still on display, ensuring he had plenty of space around him. I had a chance to study him.

He was wearing one sneaker and one shoe, no socks, black jeans, a 'Frankie Says Relax' T-shirt and a huge overcoat. His hands wouldn't have looked amiss on a mechanic and his face was covered in hair. His eyes, partially hidden, were striking, an impenetrable blue. I'd seen the eyes before and this freaked me a little. On quick inspection, you'd have him well into his fifties, but he was probably early forties . . . Jesus Christ, they were my dad's eyes. I knew they weren't really my dad's but the adrenalin that the realization had caused made thoughts harder to decipher. My mourning was obviously still on the go. I had often heard of seeing dead loved ones passing you on the street but here I was trapped with mine, in a slow-moving oversized coffin.

Did I say slow-moving? I meant stopped. My nervous system was ready to jump ship. The announcer, in my dad's voice, spoke of a delay and I dearly wanted to talk to my brother, have him by my side, calming me down, laughing at the ridiculousness of the situation. It went pitch-black and the ghost of my father started shouting, 'Relax, relax.' I was momentarily Hamlet: was this the start of my descent into paranoid hell? The lights went on. The tramp was beside himself and stumbling towards me.

'I've something very important to tell you, son,' he said in a Scottish accent. Son? SON!? This was freaking me out. I tried to breathe deep and wished to be anywhere else. But I also desperately wanted to know where this was taking me. He sat beside me and took my hand. I was powerless and tried not to look him in the the eyes. I tried to say, 'What's the message?' but the terror had me mute.

'Don't be afraid, child.' This actually calmed me and I wanted to hug this stranger for all the times I didn't show love to my father. His sweaty grip tightened and he looked me straight in the eye, even though he was probably just seeing a blurred mess. His pupils were tiny but intense. I was frightened again, there was anger in those eyes. He pushed his head upright to try and concentrate on his message. 'We all do bad things in our life, son, bad things . . . We are only human.' He had my complete being under his control. 'You can go two ways. I went the wrong way. Two ways. One, never forgive yourself.' He let go of my hand, now sweaty of its own accord, and thumped his chest hard while repeating softly, 'Me, me, me.' Then he took both of my hands in his: 'Or the other way, which is the right way . . .' Then silence, total and utter, no pausing for reflection. He pursed his lips.

'What way? What way?' I asked.

'He says, son, he says,' the man began to answer as he pointed upwards with his eyes.

'Who says?' Praying he wasn't a Godhead.

He let go of my hands again and stood up. The train jerked off to a start and he fell over. He got straight up again.

He paused for breath and said, 'Frankie says, that's who, Frankie says, "Relax."'

I was disappointed to say the least and my senses started to come back. I'm sure my mother once told me I should never talk to a stranger whose penis was free-swinging. I gave him a tenner and told him to buy himself a new T-shirt.

Robin Hood's house was above a Turkish social club on Green Lanes in leafy Turnpike Lane. This isn't a seasonal description of the place, I just think the bin-men in the area are lazy. Past the tube station the shop-infected road runs up to Wood Green Shopping City. It's the lower end of the market dressed up as something smarter. The shops upgrade the further in that direction you go. They start with hamburger joints, everything-for-£1 shops and the 'there's nothing worth nicking in this shop' shops, gradually building towards pizza parlours and everything-for-£2 shops. In the other direction are a shabby cinema and a few residential streets before you are hit by six thousand Turkish grocery stores. Directly opposite the tube station is a little park, to give you a false impression of peace. I decided to catch my breath there and steady my jangled nerves.

I did so until a six-foot-six black guy ran up to me and shouted 'JUNKIE', then he flinched, took three steps back, came forward and shouted 'JUNKIE' again. He was acting as if I was a vicious dog. God knows what he was on but I was in no mood for this so I walked off, leaving him to bark 'JUNKIE' at thin air. I was over an hour late for the meeing with Robin but decided to stop for a quick pint, hoping the day wouldn't become any stranger. It did.

The only other person in the bar having trouble coping with the day was my brother, Orwell. I touched his shoulder lightly and he pre-empted me by asking, 'What the fuck are you doing here?'

'Visiting a friend,' I lied.

He was even more cagey with his reason: 'Bit of business.'

I talked him through my day and was taken aback by his lack of sympathy. He looked worse than he had at the funeral. He put a stop to any concern I had for him with a 'Who are you? My mother?' After that, we just stared at each other. I left without ordering a drink.

It was starting to get dark and the world seemed tired. Even the Radio Rentals display of bright childish colours looked jaded. Maybe it was me projecting my own mood on to my surroundings. Maybe the shock of my brother's appearance was plying me with bad vibes. He's going through a bad patch and I can't help him. He's determined to play out some role which obviously doesn't include me. He went through a similar cycle aged fifteen. We didn't speak for four months and he refused to tell anyone what was bugging him. He tends to suffer in silence and came through that phase with an all-encompassing 'It was nothing.' He always had a tendency to allow lots of little problems to build. My own analysis of that period was it was down to a mixture of acne, loss of virginity and a particularly bad season for Tottenham Hotspur.

I tried to remember myself at twenty-five. Is that a particularly hard time? The final letting go of teenage-hood. Playing at being an adult, knowing you're past your physical best, responsibilities looming, taking stock of your life on top of your personal traumas. What has him so down? Maybe it's just Turnpike fucking Lane.

As I approached Robin's house twilight was kicking in, night light creeping over us, giving the brain no choice but to overload on the information that was churned at it. Four o'clock, people work slower, they talk slower, the grime of the day speckled over the body, irritable motorists beep their horns louder, lights flicker out shadows, children shout, the temperature goes down a notch, smiles are replaced by frowns and those afraid of the dark quicken their pace.

As I mentioned, Robin intimidates me. He's in his early sixties and it doesn't help that he's a dead ringer for Samuel Beckett and has the same slow, demanding speech delivery. He can make the most trivial task seem monumental. I've known him for four years. I first came across the organization at Mum and Dad's house. They were discussing an article in an underground magazine. Dad was so anti the organization that I decided to join them. I met up with Robin Hood and he explained his criteria but never his motives.

The organization combined propaganda and direct action. He had printed up a black book outlining the group's aims. All very worthy yet impossible. I was drawn to them because he had pushed all the right buttons for me. I wanted change, however small. We discussed his views over a two-week period during which

43

I considered where I stood. Robin was tired of people dismissing the old gods but simply replacing them with new ones. He believed that each and every one of us was god and the prime aim was to make people understand this. He stated from the off that we couldn't do this through preaching but had to plant tiny ideas. Initially this was done by letters to all sorts of officialdom while trying to affiliate with other direct action groups, whether it be Class War, Reclaim the Streets, Animal Liberation Front – you name them, we wrote to them. There must have been people with money who agreed with us because we were privately funded. I've never known how many were in the organization as Robin used army cells like the SAS. I worked autonomously in charge of gathering information.

I'd been growing tired of Robin. His autumn years were making him dogmatic and he kept moving the goalposts. I reckoned he realized he wasn't going to see real change in his own lifetime and his actions were becoming increasingly erratic. He had become obsessive about the media. I could see where he was coming from. The press barons in tandem with the government could slant the news whichever way they wanted. Unfortunately people never question this. His other main worry was that the media had become too saturated, so even an authentic voice was swamped amongst the small-minded sales-oriented journalism. Apparently, in the Seventies Robin had started a magazine but it was shot down in libel suits. This killed off the organization for six years but he had come back more aggressive. I had become frustrated with Nineties complacency. Everybody is too busy accepting their lot. They don't want to fight and lose the little they have. The smokescreen of New Labour has dampened all causes because people have entrusted them with the responsibility of real change and they feel they can sleep with a clear conscience now that they have moved their 'X' slightly to the left. At the meeting I was going to tell Robin that I was determined to quit but I knew he was capable of talking me around.

'You're late.' Robin charmed his way into my day.

He wasn't one for small-talk and got straight down to business. I noticed a box of Black Magic chocolates on the side table. My stomach turned as their significance overcame me. Whenever we'd finished a job, that is, destroyed somebody's life, we always left them a box of those chocolates as a goodbye gift. The victim always took them with good grace, which astounded me. They would often mutter a 'thank you'. I guess it was out of habit. Just seeing them there scared me, that somebody was about to receive them saddened me. I know these idiots deserved what was coming their way but I never enjoyed this rubbing-in ritual with the Black Magic. It was humiliating, not humbling, which was Robin's reasoning on the matter. And also, Black Magic are a particularly distasteful chocolate.

Robin didn't offer his condolences, which annoyed me to the extent that I stopped him mid-sentence by blurting, 'I've had enough.'

Very calmly, he said, 'You can't just quit.' He droned on about big upheavals. I only listened to the sound of his voice without taking much in. The gist of it was he now had a contact with the newspapers and I know he repeated the phrase 'about to make a very big noise'. Again, I stopped him in his tracks.

'What have we achieved?' I wasn't saying this for the sake of it, I'd been saying it to myself lately. All my hard work had amounted to a dozen highly placed scumbags getting their comeuppance. The reality of the situation was that I was just giving them enough rope and, in all honesty, they would have hung themselves eventually. This wasn't apathy rearing its ugly head. I wanted to know if we were really just being spiteful to those who had been given an easy ride. The system is in place, we can't change that system. These thoughts I should have kept to myself but they tumbled out.

Robin simply said, 'You can't leave.'

I had to be careful here because I was aware that some of my past activities were not strictly legal. Nothing major, just handling of illegal publications, blackmail, a bit of phone-tapping. I changed my tack: 'Why can't I leave?'

As I had feared, Robin countered with 'I'm sure the police would be delighted to find out what you've been up to.'

'The police? The fucking police? Excuse me for a moment but I thought we were against the fucking police.'

Robin, thinking he was Noël Coward, tenored, 'Oh but the fun of using your enemies as a means to an end is rather good-humoured, is it not?'

'Hold on a second. If I'm going down, I'm taking you with me, oh mighty one.'

'Think about it, messenger boy. I'm a delegator. I

46

consider myself a good citizen who stays within the law. I prey on young, disaffected, enthusiastic boys, eager to please but who put their actions before their thoughts. Now, if I tried to fuck any of you, that would be illegal.'

'You're quite an evil man, aren't you.'

'And you're a tiresome one. Look, we live in a capitalist society so I'll cut you a deal. You do one more job for me and you're free to walk.'

I grabbed the remote for his television. 'What's the point?' I turned the TV on and started to channel-hop. 'Look at all these inane people! We've made so many of these championed people retire and they just grow back, muttering the same old shit. Is that progress?'

Robin butted in. 'Think of all the hypocrites who have disappeared. I have made them suffer for their lack of art.'

'Robin, you've lost sight of the bigger picture. It's not about suffering. It's about change.'

'You said it, boy, change, that's the key word. For your final task I've got something very different in mind.'

'What?'

'You just wait for instruction. All will become clear.'

I left his flat hating that man but knowing that the fucker could still pull my strings. The wind accompanied him under my skin. Home to Crouch End.

I underestimated my mood and its magnetic pull towards depression. The harsh light of Dixy Fried Chicken had my hunger sensors on alert. Fast-food joints fill me with sorrow. The smell of disinfectant, the jolly piped music, the staff with no prospects, the childish uniforms, the solitary table, the uncomfortable plastic chairs designed to make your stay there as short as possible. At least McDonald's has given us a few drive-thru's, understanding our pain and showing their staff cars they'll never be able to afford. Just as I was about to enter Dixyland, I was stopped in my tracks by something that doesn't stop normal people in their tracks. But the sight of the middle-aged man sitting alone at the solitary table shot my appetite to bits. Every sad bite he took filled my belly with hollowness. Surely everybody has somewhere better to eat than here. I should've edged this intruder out of my mind but no, I built up his life story with my tormented imagination. Divorced, living in a bedsit, losing the will to live. Potless and alone, dragging us all down with him, getting by, just getting by. This allowable poverty moves me more than extreme poverty.

The homeless, the third world, refugees: they're the very visible bummers. But seeing the invisible, just-below-the-breadline types sucker-punches me every time. It was Dad's constant speeches on dragging himself out of the gutter that helped me to summon such strong feelings. He always banged on about how hard work was all you needed to get on in this world. He could never comprehend that he had been a jammy bastard and there was no winning formula in life, only luck. Some are given the other's amount and there's fuck all you can do about it. It's an odd one that, me despising poverty so much considering I'm in the depths of it myself.

What do I do for a living? As little as possible really. I was in marketing for a while, but found it the Devil's work. I did music journalism and found the bands tedious. For a little while I was a researcher for a daytime TV show. I stuck with that for as long as possible to gather information on the sly for Robin. Those people take themselves so seriously. Every morning I had to motivate the team by continually reminding them that it was just a fucking TV show.

What do I live on? You're not going to believe me but one night I came home and through my letterbox somebody had put twenty grand in cash with a little note that simply stated 'Sorry'. I've never found out who it was from or why it happened. I suspect it was Dad on some guilt trip. Hard work, Dad. Bollocks to that and bollocks to Dixy Fried Chicken. It was beans on toast for me that night.

Chapter 7

Do we ever fully awake during the course of our day? Is it the traumas people throw our way that startle our body into some sort of response? I'm shaking here with the fall-out of embarrassment. I'm with the secret love of my pharmacy life, collecting the photos belonging to my dad. A cursory look to check if they are the right ones leaves me in no doubt.

'Yes, they're the ones. That's a nice one of my dad being sucked off by Hazel the PR maestro, isn't it?' The pharmacist, as ever, looked stunned.

The council should designate holes into which we can disappear for these moments. Would I like a receipt? she asks. No, just enough painkillers to overdose with would be fine, thank you.

Back home, I put the photos on the table, frightened to look at them, frightened to be in the same room as them. The doorbell rang. Normally I would ignore it but surely an interruption was preferable to Dad's sexual endeavours. I opened the door and aged five years. There stood the randy hairdresser, whose name I'd again forgotten.

'Can I come in?' she kind of pleaded. I knew exactly what was about to be revealed. A defiant trepidation registered in her eyes. 'I would have rung you only I didn't have your number.'

I didn't know what to say. I braced myself for the shit that was about to follow.

'I want to keep it,' said the mother of my sperm. An hour of her plans, an occasional gulp from me and then I used the excuse of needing time to take it all in to get rid of her. I knew I wanted nothing to do with her and I thought she was incredibly understanding of my plight until her parting shot which was 'My parents are looking forward to meeting you.' I felt like reciprocating the offer with one of my own: 'Do you want to see some nudey pictures of my dead dad?'

I eased her out of the flat, arranging to meet her in a pub the following week, hoping stupidly that the problem would sort itself out. I was determined to buffer this one for as long as possible. I lay on my bed cursing my penis, wondering how much children's allowance the social gave these days. I never accounted for fatherhood. All the girls I knew were modern, pill-popping, abortion-seeking freewheelers. Maybe it was a sting. She'd got herself a boyfriend and they wanted a bit of extra cash. It probably wasn't even mine. Kinky sex can never result in a baby, it's just not morally right. I couldn't look a kid in the eye and say '. . . and then your mother asked me to piss on her'.

Maybe I should just give up, marry her and become part of the human chain, live the family life, get up every afternoon, pop a tranquillizer and smile wanly at the world and its stupidity. Jesus, I'd even get free haircuts and a place in a couple of South Londoners' hearts. I would be the house-husband, get a part-time job on a perfume counter, drink with my in-laws on Sunday afternoons, do the *Evening Standard* crossword, enjoy friendly racist banter with my neighbours, put tomato ketchup on everything and wear blue jeans that were a little bit too big for me, knowing my middle-age spread will be accommodated before its arrival. Or I could just remain the way I am, a pointless wanker running away from all responsibility, and live a life of regret, hanging around outside Mothercare, drunk, haranguing shoppers with shouts of 'That could have been me!' Where's the girl I was supposed to fall in love with? Rebecca had sucked the love from my body. I replaced it with integrity, which I now think was an almighty blunder. Having integrity means you miss out on a lot of fun.

I eyed my dad's photos – they seemed innocent now. Twenty pictures of various sexual positions. They were enjoying themselves and it struck me that I'd never seen my dad's penis before. Of course I thought of poor old Mum, eroding away in the New Forest, totally unaware of Dad's peccadilloes. It's hard to look at photos of your dad having sex. It's not something I'd ever pictured him doing. I didn't know what to think. I didn't hate him for it. I thought it strange that the sight of his hairy arse was what showed me his human side. He was always so prim and proper with me that it was nice to know he had, dare I say, a more interesting side to his personality. But what was even more curious was, who actually took the photos? Hazel would have some answering to do.

It was unsettling sitting at the reception of Hazel's office. Some of the staff I had worked with remained. They were curious to know what I had been up to. 'This and that' is the vague way of saying, 'Fuck all.' It always takes relative strangers to enable you to take stock of your life. Why do we feel this need to impress people we are not impressed by? But there I was accepting a cup of tea, stating quite strenuously that I didn't take sugar any more, as if I was hinting at big changes in my life. Hazel kept me waiting, wanting that upper hand which I was about to crush. She had no idea why I was here, which was the way I wanted it. This way I could get a true picture of her, start with her as queen of her own domain to remind me why I disliked her so intensely, then watch the bubble of confidence fall before the big pop. She appeared about five seconds after her perfume warned of her arrival.

That perfume, the same smell brought back that whole period but was now accompanied by the thought of my dad and his smelling the same scent and the different effect it would have had on him. Perfume is amazing, really. It is purely a memory aid. If you've had a night out with a woman, a subsequent whiff of her scent will immediately return you to your feelings of that night, good or bad. The slight fragrance left on your pillow the following day will have you either caressing the pillow or heading for the launderette. Long after the moment, you can find out more of your true feelings for that person than actual communication will offer. Lovers who are heartbroken should simply buy the perfume. It will help you deal with the heart's upheaval. Spray it on yourself or if there's no getting over your lover drown yourself in their preferred smell. Mind you, what kind of person uses perfume? One who hides their true feelings? One who is hiding from their self? Or am I being too kind and it's just really shallow people who think it smells nice?

'Sorry to hear about your father.' Hazel looked concerned and tired and it hit me that she too was in mourning and instantly all her bad points disappeared and I wanted to cuddle her. She took me out to lunch at a busy bistro where she ordered the house red followed by another bottle in quick succession. I don't know how much she thought I was wise to but she wanted to take the edge off the moment. We small-talked about Dad but her whole body was begging for an admission. I put her out of her misery.

'I know about you and Dad.' I looked her straight in the face and was determined to stare her out but her pain was too easy to see and had me looking anywhere but. I mumbled that I wasn't blaming her but I simply wanted to get to know my father better.

She shot back, 'It's between me and Terence.' She didn't say it in an 'It's none of your business' way, but more out of sympathy for my reaction. I could understand this. What they had had between them was obviously special and my line of questioning was dirtying those memories. I eased her into a confessional with the help of more booze and by by-passing her involvement with my dad towards a more general picture of the man. She was soon chatting and reminiscing, a little bit drunk. She decided we should continue the conversation at her flat. She lived in Little Venice.

Her flat had clothes flung about the place, mainly blouses, and the decor was cosy and modern, but overall it had an unlived-in look. She opened a bottle of wine and ventured me on to the sofa, where she flicked off her shoes and squatted with a cushion between her knees and belly. I took off my the jacket and felt the photos in my inside pocket. I sat at the other end of the sofa and asked her about Dad's chat-up technique. This brought a little smile to her face.

'Your dad was a bit of a rascal.' She stopped herself and squinted at me. 'Do you really want to hear all of this?' I nodded. 'You want the truth?'

'Absolutely.'

'I met him at an awards ceremony. He lost and became quite drunk. I tried to console him but he was getting ruder and ruder. There was a lot of press about and I thought it best I get him out of there so I brought him back here to sleep it off. I wasn't at my soberest myself, but when we got here he insisted we have a game of Scrabble. I agreed, only he had a new rule which amounted to any time anyone scored over twenty-five points with one word, the other had to take off an item of clothing. I reckoned it might be fun, not knowing your father was a bit of a whizz at the game. Within five minutes I was naked. It's not that I'm stupid. I was wearing an evening dress that night so there wasn't much to take off. Anyway, I'm soon naked and he scores over twenty-five points again and he demanded a kiss. This went on and – I don't know if I should be telling you this. Oh, to hell with it, suddenly he scored high again, with the word "blow-job" . . . do I have to spell it out for you?'

I missed her little joke and lost all interest in Dad. I'm sorry, her talk was turning me on and I just wanted to fuck her. She had been touchy-feely all evening so I decided to go for it. I gently kissed her on the mouth. She hesitantly kissed me back. Just a few quick kisses, her breath on mine, and I don't think I've ever been hornier. Soon we were kissing full on, hard-pressing kisses, wide-mouthed, trying to swallow our bodies whole. Soon my hands were swamping her breasts and before I knew it I was on the bus home, trying to hide the big red mark on my face where Hazel had slapped me hard.

The clarity of morning had me feeling even worse. All my good intentions are just intentions, the actual acts I do are repulsive. Shame was biting at me. Why was I chasing my dad's ghost? To follow him through every mistake he made? Was this the steadying course towards my own suicide? By delving into his past, was I trying to predict my own future? Were our genes that tightly locked? The headrush of self-doubt. Come on, was my life so hollow that I had become obsessed by another's?

The last time I was this low was after a street mugging. I had just come out of a newsagent's and watched two guys eyeing me up. I wasn't at my most attractive so I knew it wasn't sex they were looking for. I felt safe because it was a busy street and it was daylight. As I walked along at quite a pace, I could see them coming for me. I was already trembling in anticipation when they grabbed me either side, interlocking my arms as they pretended I was an old friend. One of them ruffled my hair in a friendly way while putting me in a headlock. It must have looked like any old mates' reunion as they frog-marched me down an alleyway. I was sapped of energy and the 'Help' I desperately wanted to shout was stuck in my gullet. They pushed me up against the wall and one of them punched me hard on my ear. This left a ringing and a hazy stinging about my head. The other one was going through my pockets which was a relief as I thought for a moment that he was knifing me. He found my wallet, which contained twenty pounds, a bank card and an unused scratch card. The one who had hit me turned to me and demanded to know my PIN number. He threatened to kill me. Under such strain I couldn't remember it but he kept asking me for the number while repeating, 'Don't be looking at me, boy.' But that's all I could do, stare at him in absolute terror. He punched me in both eyes. My hands were free but I didn't want to protect my face in case they had a knife. They started playing good mugger, bad mugger. All I could hear was 'Leave 'im', 'No, let's do 'im.' A punch to the stomach and they left me there, a wreck. I expected help to come but it never materialized and I didn't budge until they were well gone.

The strange thing was they didn't look like muggers, they were more like two out-of-work actors who were trying out the method way. The other strange memory of it was that they never once swore and that their accents were put down a peg or two from their natural middle-class origins. I can laugh about it now in company and exaggerate the tale of the polite luvvies, but in truth it shattered my life for at least a year. I became mistrustful of everybody. I'm still paranoid when out. I had to leave the area I was living in and became acutely hateful of myself as I started to blame myself for the incident, as if it was karma, a pay-back for some bad shit I had loaded on to somebody else. And, of course, it didn't help my relationship with Rebecca. I also realized that the police didn't really give a fuck about the likes of me. Friends who were unsympathetic to my plight I instantly dumped and I tended to bond more easily with other unfortunates. I'm still not fully over the incident and occasionally go to fringe theatre to see if I can ID them. I only hope they got some pleasure from my twenty pounds.

I spent the rest of the day going through Dad's diaries. It became clear that there were five people who had a big effect on Dad's secret life: the Sun, the Rain, the Clouds, the Wind and El Niño. El Niño I would have to ask Mum about. The Sun I realized was Hazel. The Wind and the Rain were somehow linked as they cropped up together a lot, and he gave the impression that they might have gone away together. The Clouds were baffling. They had by far the most entries and the least direct contact. I assumed it was a man because the Clouds weren't ever spoken about with any fondness but rather as a constant ego battle. I knew he held the key to my dad's state of mind. The writing became erratic when he was mentioned and he cropped up a lot towards the end. Entries like 'The clouds are out to get me, following my every move.' And 'A cloudy day full of regret now but unavoidable. I am waiting for them to off-load their heavy burden. I worry that it will saturate me. I sit here praying for clear skies.'

I decided to sleep on the information, wondering

where my appetite had gone. I manhandled the kitchen's cupboards to see if there was anything palatable. A tin of pears was all I could muster. The fridge offered an onion bhaji well past its sell-by date or carrot soup. Memories of the mugging made me reluctant to go shopping. I kidded myself that a thirty-six-hour period without food was good for the soul. Didn't Jesus do it for forty days and nights in the desert? Mind you, he did come back a bit of an arrogant cunt. I was surprised to see my answer-machine was blinking. Four messages. I pressed for a little communication.

Beeep . . .

'Shea, it's Rebecca, I need to talk, would you phone me back please?'

Beeep . . .

'Are you there, Shea? Are you there, Shea? Would you phone me ASAP. It's Ruth, by the way.'

I knew I shouldn't have given her my number.

Beeep . . .

Long silence. (That'll be Mum . . . Sure enough . . .)

'Shea, the will is being read tomorrow.' Long silence. Phone finally clicks down.

Beeep . . .

'I'll pick you up at ten a.m. tomorrow. Orwell.'

More interruptions into my reclusive existence.

Chapter 8

The doorbell persistently rang . . . a deep sleep broken into. My head weighed twice its size as if I hadn't exhaled the whole night. My brother's gaunt presence helped me get a focus on the day. Sunrise had happened. Its championing of a new day was being outdone by hailstones and gale-force winds. These winds positioned one black cloud after another. Nature was pissed off and bombarding us with its light artillery. Dad had always warned us about ozone depletion with its increased ultraviolet radiation, and he used to laugh at the many surprises the atmosphere was going to shoot down at us. But also it used to depress him that people's ignorance and complacency made light of a major problem that lay ahead. I never really listened when he went off into one of his doom-and-gloom prophecies but I can remember him saying Europe's weather upheaval was just around the corner. The only consolation I could take from this was that 'around the corner' in environmentalist-speak could mean a thousand years from now. There lies the problem. Even the most staunch family man doesn't really give a toss about their great-great-great-great-great-great-great-

great-grandchildren. I remember Dad's description of being caught in a hurricane: he likened it to being forcefully attacked by a thousand acupuncturists.

I was soon in my brother's car again. He was pumping out a drum 'n' bass tape which didn't suit the claustrophobic seating arrangments but I guess it gave the hailstones something to dance to. The windscreen wipers were giving it a bit of a remix. My brother was keeping the vow of silence from his imaginary monastic sect. My appetite approved of the 'Services 5m' sign. We pulled up, nodded at the RAC salesman and were welcomed in by the soothing piped music of James Galway. Obviously not James Galway himself – he was a bit too edgy so they'd got someone else in to bland it up. There was a trucker in the amusement arcade, forced into one of his regulation breaks, giving it some on a simulated motor-racing game. We plumped for the Little Chef. It was packed and we had to queue and sit with two priests.

Using this opportunity to try and humour my brother, I quipped, 'We'll be here all fucking morning now.'

'Why?'

'Well, it'll be grace before meals, after meals, and a little prayer to Saint Nicholas for the road.'

'Yeah,' he monotoned.

We ate in silence and were soon back on the motorway. My fry-up went straight through my system and I amused myself letting off those little silent, bubble farts. Orwell continued to reject my attempts at conversation. The least he could have done was fart back. I felt a need to blurt out, 'Dad was a tart, you know, I've got some dozy hairdresser pregnant and some illegal activities from the past are about to come out into the open.' Instead I asked questions to which I knew the answer would be 'Fine.'

'So how are you keeping?'

'Fine.'

'Work?'

'Fine.'

'Rebecca?'

'Well, it was just a matter of time, wasn't it? You always bring it back to Rebecca. Well, you'll be interested to know we're having problems, so why don't you get back in there, give her a ring. You deserve each other.'

'Great. Can I borrow your mobile?'

Continuing the farce, Orwell handed me his mobile.

'Don't be such a div, Orwell. The baby's due soon, what's wrong?'

He ignored me.

'Orwell, do you want to talk about it?'

'No, I don't want to talk about it.'

'Well, would you mind telling me exactly what I've done to you?'

He was still refusing to give me anything but I could sense he was fuming and about to explode. I continued baiting him.

'Because we got on fine until you stole my girlfriend.'

That did it.

'That's you all over. I'm sick of cleaning up your mess. You've always done exactly what you wanted to do. You've never cared for anyone but yourself. You treated

63

Rebecca like shit. You treated me like shit. Well, like attracts like. Is it any wonder we were drawn to each other?'

This had been a long time coming and I ran with it, letting him get it all off his chest, holding back the hurt I was feeling.

'You always came with this patronizing big-brother persona. I want to lead my own life. Oh we always had fun together, didn't we? Lovely, cosy memories for you, I'm sure. But they were always on your terms. You never once considered what I wanted to do. The Rebecca thing was a smokescreen. You were suffocating me. I was looking for an excuse to dump you from my life. So don't flatter yourself that little brother was following in your steps, having your woman after you discarded her because – I didn't ever want to have to tell you this, but remember the night you met Rebecca, the party? You were smitten. You went home early because you didn't want to get drunk and try and fuck her, because you thought she could well be the one. Well, she tried to get off with me that night but I wouldn't because you had your eye on her. She wasn't interested in you. She rang me every day of the following week to tell me it was me she wanted, but I wouldn't because you're my brother and that means something to me. Remember that week when you sat patiently by the phone waiting for a call? I put you on a pedestal for her and it worked. You started seeing each other and I was happy for you, and every time the three of us were together I persevered with the constant passes she made at me because she made you feel alive. I kept this to myself because I didn't want you to feel what you've made me feel, but you're the one who likes the truth. So there it is. Welcome to my world.'

Fuck, my throat had dried. This was a lot of information to take in. My personal history was being rewritten and this overwhelming realization that my whole past was being undermined had the panic rising. I said the only thing I could say.

'Yep, you're better off ditching the bitch, all right.'

'Typical' was his reply but surely he must have known I was grasping at straws: had we moved that far apart? This was a bigger shock than his admission.

Mum was dressed in a business suit which made her look like she was coping OK. The giveaway was her shrinkage, which conjured up the image of a clown. She settled us in the kitchen where sandwiches were presented formally. The three of us sat at the table made for six. Dad's chair was situated at the head of the table. Even though this was never the family home, I was transported into our old kitchen, Dad reading *The Times*, ignoring our pleas for teenage faddish things, Mum constantly buttering toast, Orwell and I larking about, Dad chastising us. It was a pleasant memory but a false one. We never shared breakfast. Dad was always up an hour before and gone before we rose. Turning to the empty chair, this was a fairer picture of how it actually was and that made it harder to deal with. I took in the scope of the kitchen in the hope of focusing on something less poignant. On the top of the fridge, I saw a box of chocolates. This had me out of my chair.

Already knowing the answer I asked, 'Mum, are they Black Magic?'

'They'll play havoc with your stomach. Eat your sandwiches, dear. '

'Where did you get them?'

'I don't know, they were a gift.'

Fuck this shit, this really was too much. I started to hyperventilate. The blood rushed to my head and I collapsed. I came to in bed, a second's relaxation before the stumbling blocks of my life appeared again. I was sure the chocolates were from Robin. Whether he had a sicker sense of humour than I thought or he had been somehow involved with my dad, I didn't know. I just knew the chocolates were from him. My brain was mush. I had always been intimidated by Robin Hood but now I was petrified. My life was a walking nightmare. My mistrust of the human race had been replaced with an overabundance of trust in a couple of wrong'uns. Fuck. Fuck. Fuck.

Mum came in with some Lucozade. I was scared to look her in the face in case I didn't recognize her. Who could I trust? She gently put her palm on my forehead and I flinched. She put this down to my illness but I was having trouble dealing with myself.

'Mum, have you any tranquillizers?'

The second I said this, the urgency to have them quickened.

'That's not the answer, dear.' This didn't comfort me.

'Look, Mum, I'm not dealing with any of this very well. I'm in pain here.'

'Very well.'

She left the room but I felt safe again. My mother was looking after me, all was well. The little boy in the man's body was all snug and I knew Mum was Mum, no complications. She understood me, I could talk to her, she knew who I was. We could read each other's minds. I came out of her very being; there is no closer relationship. She came back into the bedroom. A smile approached my face. She handed me two pills and a glass of water. She left a packet of six tranquillizers on the side table in case of emergencies. It was wonderful. She soothed me with mother-talk and everything was OK. She left me to get some rest and put a package beside the pills, mumbling, 'You and your sweet tooth'. I didn't have to look at the chocolates. I grabbed the six other tablets and wolfed them down, praying for a weak metabolism and short life. I pulled the duvet over my head, breathing my heavy load in and out, an exercise I hadn't done since I was seven.

The morning brought slight tinnitus as if my dream had consisted of attending a Motorhead concert. I'd read somewhere that humans change every seven years, maybe my time had come. This modern atheistic society left those in isolation nowhere to turn to. Dad's body would soon be a mere skeleton. The soul, like the *Starsky and Hutch* actor of the same name, left to struggle on, existing, but for what reason? Orwell came in with a cup of tea, no doubt thinking he'd started a cumulative rush towards blackout. He was chatty but I couldn't reimburse his good nature. I missed the reading of the will. Orwell and I were to receive fifty thousand each. My financial burden lifted, but spirit remaining unmoved.

Orwell left me with a slightly less parched mouth to rebuild my personality.

The friends I had led the bachelor life with had all succumbed to the fear of loneliness and had picked their life partners. I worry it's akin to those childhood football games where it's the wasters who were last to be chosen. I sometimes reason that if the population of the world was ten billion, nine hundred million, one hundred and sixty nine thousand, four hundred and eleven, I would be the one left out when everyone paired off. I've never asked a woman out. I wouldn't know how to go about it. I've only recently sussed that I've always let the lady make the first move. This has limited me to those who like their first impression of me. A mix of laziness, ineptitude and lack of confidence has left me dating forthright, confident, loud women. They are not my type. Those who shout have very little to say. I want someone similar to me but I'm never going to meet her, am I? It saddens me the amount of times I would have been in the same locale as someone who was right for me, and me for her, but we would have sat on opposite sides of the room, quietly sniggering at the ones who were obstructing the view of the other.

I have lived alone now on and off for eight years. I don't know any other way of life. I'm used to my own routine. The gentle push into the day, the radio for company an easy eavesdropping on the opinions of the moment without having to join in. This is bliss. Even as a child, the mornings brought to me an out-of-kilter peace, surrounded by my family who mingled and jostled for the right footing. I was accepted as invisible, joining in at will. Now I have a reputation for not being good in the morning. But I am. It's the people who say these things who are not good in the morning. A nap, I think, before the restart.

Mum and I took a walk towards the cemetery. It was more a stroll as I had to adjust my natural pace to stay by her side. Inanimate objects overtook us as we went back in time. Orwell didn't fancy the trip and I didn't force the matter as I wanted Mum alone. I looked at her innocent face and thought of the photos of Dad and Hazel and how he must have hated himself the following days when looking at the sweet face of his wife. I've never placed Mum in a sexual scenario but she must have been quite a dish in her youth. You could see it in her face. Age had blurred the beauty but if you wiped away the wrinkles, you could easily put her in her glory again. They must have loved each other, a love that faded into acceptance.

I'd never seen them really fight. I remember frosty conversations and occasional raised voices but never passion.

'Mum, how did you meet Dad?'

Her face lit up exactly as Hazel's had done when I asked her. I wonder if Dad was aware of this legacy he had left. In the newspapers it would list achievements and financial clout but wouldn't it read better as 'Terence Hickson, 1939–1998: people smile at his memory.' Mum rarely had a conversation these days so when she did she spoke as if delivering the Queen's Speech.

'We were at university. A gathering of lost left-field students. We thought we could change the world, put wrongs to right. But in fairness, myself and your father were part-time revolutionaries. The others questioned our beliefs and we were forced together. Out of habit we sat together, ate together, studied together. We became close without really being aware and slowly fell in love. I loved him from the moment I saw him. It wasn't love at first sight, but more a feeling that we were right for each other. Of course, he refused to make a move on me. One day, an afternoon wine-tasting became night and he stole a case of wine. He said it was for the revolution. He was so funny sometimes. We had a shared language, you know, a similar way of looking at situations. That night we got back to the hall of residence and the lightbulb in his room had blown. He always insisted this was the case but I still have my suspicions. We went back to my room. He started the revolution there by opening a bottle of wine, a lukewarm white. He suggested a game of Scrabble with a few new rules.'

Mum told me the same story as Hazel and it was hard to take in. We reached the grave and Mum burst into tears. I comforted her and was crying myself. Mum, with fond loving memories, me with the knowledge that those memories weren't as precious as she believed. Being the go-between for a secret was seeping the life out of me. I looked down at the gravel grave and headstone, wondering what other mysteries my dead father would let me unravel. It seemed it would have been more appropriate to bury his skeleton in a cupboard rather than in a coffin.

On the meandering walk back, I broached the subject of the man I knew as El Niño. Mum couldn't place him but she had pared him down to two candidates: Percy Fincham, a neighbour, and Anthony Bowlam, a TV producer. Anthony was definitely the man. The only thing Mum knew about him was that he was a confirmed bachelor who had lost most of his money on holiday homes in the States.

I persuaded my brother to stay one more night as my intestines were still kick-starting little balls of anxiety which I knew I had to deal with on my own. But I fancied company around me, regardless. I thought with the reading of the will that Dad's memory would be allowed to gently fade but Mum mentioned a memorial service to be held in London in a couple of weeks. This would be my opportunity to check out Dad's less savoury playmates who wouldn't dare show their faces at the family home.

I confronted the morning with a cold face and a mummified body. I managed to mangle the duvet tight to my skin. I dread to think what my dream had consisted of. The fragility of my mind was always exposed harshly in the intangible flicker between consciousness and sleep. In dreams, I was usually hassled by strangers but now I was dealing with them in my waking hours – Hazel, El Niño, Ruth the Hairdresser, new shades of my father, Robin Hood, Rebecca and my brother – and possibly I wasn't that aware of my own good self any more.

The two brothers were soon waving goodbye to Mum. This went on longer than we'd all have liked, as the freezing conditions meant we had to heat up the car for five minutes. Mum poured a kettle of hot water over the windscreen and Orwell put the heating up full. I love the

71

heat from a car, the way it heats in sections. You can feel it defrosting the feet, working its way up to the head. This took longer than it should have as Orwell had his window open. The air-conditioned heat did battle with the sharp breezes, making parts of the body contradict each other. Orwell insisted the opened window helped clear the condensation. We kissed Mum's icy cheeks and we were away.

I found it hard to relax as I was aware of Orwell's fidgeting. He would close the window a bit, turn down the heating, close the window completely, turn the heating up. My body temperature was crying out for some consistency. That and having to deal with the ten-second dismissal of radio stations was driving me crazy. It was as if he was trying to simulate my state of mind. I took out a copy of the will, to give me something to concentrate on. I wasn't really taking in all of the information because it was written in legalese. But I thought my eyes were deceiving me because I could see three separate fifty-thousand-pound beneficiaries. I put the paper closer to my eyes and squinted at it. Yes, it was there in black and white: fifty thousand each to me, Orwell and one Robert Townsend of Melbourne, Australia.

'Who the fuck is Robert Townsend?' I asked my brother.

'I don't know,' he muttered.

'Have you seen this?'

'Yes.'

'Are you not interested in who he is?'

'Not really.'

'But Dad obviously thought as much of this Robert guy as he did of us.'

'Come on, Shea, we were never that close to Dad, it doesn't mean much, does it?'

This was hard to take in, as Orwell had always been closer to Dad. He was always Dad's favourite and here he was as if he were talking about a distant uncle. I wanted to go into a huff but no, I was really losing Orwell here and I didn't like it. Even if we could salvage some semblance of a relationship, it was worth fighting for. All those years of fighting causes for the good of faceless people had blunted my heart but here beside me was someone I loved, someone I had disregarded since the Rebecca episode and I didn't know how to get through to him.

I remembered when he lived for me, when I was eighteen going on fifteen and Orwell was thirteen but physically bigger than me. His body was too big for his brain. He was a cumbersome bag of bones, banging into mischief, never aware of his build. Strangers assumed I was the younger brother and because of this he was seen as slightly idiotic. I took him under my wing with a mixture of piss-taking and protection. My mates would join me in taking the mickey out of him but I couldn't stand this, seeing other people laughing at my brother. It sometimes incensed me into violence. And there lies the rub. I'd protect him by hitting out at my mates, but I was rubbish at scrapping and would soon be taking a hiding. Usually at this point, Orwell would come to my rescue and, with sheer force, pummel the others. Soon the whole neighbourhood became frightened of him and he had the reputation of being the best fighter in the area. With this association always comes some tosser who wants to take on the best, so inevitably he fought regularly and mostly against more than one. When weapons started to come into the fray, Dad decided to unburden us of his working-class roots and we moved to Highgate.

I was twenty and ready to fly the nest but Orwell was only fifteen and having to start his life all over again. I stayed at home for another six months to help Orwell out. This is when we became very close. I think I pushed him into growing up too quickly but he was happy shadowing me at the time. I know he was keen to be an adult and, despite my daily remonstrations, he refused to shave off the full beard he had been sporting. At school, the other kids mistook him for a teacher, and were always stubbing out cigarettes when he came into sight. He persisted with that beard for three years and even when he shaved it off he kept the ridiculous-looking moustache. I looked at him and was surprised to see it wasn't there.

'When did you shave off the 'tache?'

'The other day.'

'Why?'

'No reason, just fancied a change.'

It was hard to get Orwell to talk. When we were close events would just occur and that would cement our bond. I guess you are never able to just sit down one on one and get things off your chest. It's always outside forces that bring about empathy. I thought Dad's death would have the required effect but Orwell was going the opposite way. It dawned on me that a fight which he could rescue me from might do the trick, but at thirty that wasn't going to happen. Was I wasting time getting to know my dead father rather than my living brother? I also wondered, was it worth telling him the new information I had unearthed about Dad? Would that bring us together? I tested the air.

'Orwell, if you were to describe Dad to a stranger, how would you describe him?'

'What's the point of that?'

'Just humour me, please.'

He exhaled loudly. 'You mean in relation to us or as a whole person?'

'Either.'

'Well, to us I guess he was always there without being physically there for us. He tried to clone us into what he thought would be ideal children. I suppose in that way we were a disappointment to him. He had us boxed off. You, he wanted you to study medicine and me, he wanted me to get a sports scholarship. I guess like most fathers, he wanted his sons to live out his dreams, then he became frustrated and . . . eventually, he let us get on with our own lives.'

It was beautiful to hear my brother speak like this. I joined in. 'Remember that time he enrolled you in all those summer classes – boxing, judo, karate, wrestling, basketball?'

Orwell laughed. 'I came home every day with bruises. He only let me quit after I broke my nose and lost my two front teeth.'

'Yeah, God, I remember that. How did that happen again?'

'That was the stupid thing. It was during basketball. I

could handle myself in all the combative sports but you know my co-ordination has always been shit. I got a basketball straight in the face. Bleeding friendly game as well.' We started laughing together. It was all coming back to me.

'God, that summer Dad really fancied himself as a bit of a carpenter, didn't he? He built that trophy cabinet for all your impending glories.'

'Yeah, Mum ended up using it for her spices.'

'Do you think that's why he could never stomach curries, because it reminded him of your failures?'

'You can talk! What about that Christmas when he bought you that set of videos of open-heart surgery and by-passes. He brought you into his study to watch them and you puked all over his desk.'

'Poor old Dad, it just didn't go his way.'

Orwell became serious. 'I think he was disappointed in himself. He wanted to be the top of his field. He wanted to make a difference. He was aware and annoyed that scientists were playing God with nature and it was going to end in disaster, but then he just gave up and took the money and ran. I don't think he ever forgave himself. He knew he was weak, and rather than fighting it he let it become his norm.'

It was strange listening to Orwell because that's what I would have said in the past about Dad, but now I knew things were much more complicated. I didn't say this to Orwell because he would have seen it as patronizing. I was content to hear him speak from his heart.

'We must go out for a pint some night' was all I could offer.

'Yeah, that would be nice,' Orwell replied without being too committal. 'Oh, by the way, there's a Christmas present for you in the boot.' I'd totally dismissed Christmas and suddenly felt bad.

'I didn't get you anything.'

'It's not from me, it's from Dad.'

I got home at the drizzling five o'clock hour protecting Dad's wrapped gift from the rain.

Chapter 9

I bought ten fags, hoping they might calm me. I trudged up the stairs to my flat on the first floor. The landing belonged to nobody, so it was your typical frayed grumpy carpet, hints of a cheap pattern. I pushed the timed light to see the various markings of previous tenants on the walls. There was one letter for me and a couple of organizations offering to push me into debt. I had only one neighbour. She was a teacher with a bit of a drink problem but we kept to ourselves mainly. Rather than turning on the lights in my flat I lit a couple of candles, which suited my mood better. I put Dad's present on the table, knowing I wasn't going to open it for a while. I cursed myself for not asking Orwell what Dad had got him. Dad hadn't bought us presents for years and I wanted to know, was this a goodbye gift or simply a Christmas present? There was no card with it.

I lit a cigarette and some unwanted nasal hair from one of the candles. I looked at the present again, its silver wrapping forewarning of bad news. The newly received letter beside it would also have to wait for daylight. The answer-machine promised four voices. A total of six people trying to communicate with me, but not me with them. I knew nobody was going to bear good news. I needed a little diversion, a way-out clause. I picked up my phone book to see who could offer me respite.

The As were an assortment of friends I'd neglected, people whose numbers I'd taken but never bothered to ring. The Bs were mostly old music contacts, journalists who would bitch about other journalists, and a couple of one-night stands I'd tried to form a relationship with. By the Cs I was becoming cynical and pondered that phone books were really just a litany of failed relationships. I was shocked by the small number of Es I knew and made a mental note to meet more people whose surnames started with E. At F, I came across James Fentelli's number. It was probably redundant by now. It was at least five years since I'd last spoken to him. That had been a coincidence in itself. I'd bumped into another old schoolfriend who had kept in touch with him but by the time I got round to ringing James he was embarking on a trip round America with a one-year visa. I put James as first reserve as I continued my directory hopping.

By L, James was looking clear favourite as L was full of friends who had coupled off and lacked spontaneity and if you wanted to meet them it usually meant arranging it a month in advance. By O I was getting depressed by my lack of real friends and the poor people whose surnames began with an S or a T I'd given such a rough deal to. There were some good people there, but by the time you got to them, your diary was usually full. I know for a fact that if Daisy Slater's surname was Butler, we would have been good friends by now. As for the Ws, they are the ones who end up kidnapping people and eating them out of sheer loneliness and hunger. I dreaded finding out what happened to my W friends. What the phone book threw up at me was that it consisted mainly of ex-shags.

There's plenty of people to kill time with and there's the occasional mate who you only realise after meeting up with them that you relish their company. Maybe it's a London thing where we're all ghettoized in the areas where we feel comfortable and we don't like to leave our safe havens. Crouch End is the in-between-relationships ghetto, an area to get your shit together in, some on the up, others coming down, all on nodding terms with each other, aware of each other's pain but not willing to share it. It isn't by chance that Crouch End has a lot of shops that sell candles.

I rang James. He surprised me by being in. We arranged to meet that night in the West End.

Spruced and showered I was still sweating a bit as I waited for James in a smelly pub in Soho called The Pillars of Hercules. A carpet thick with years of spillage made it like a country lane. The pub was half full with loud suits and media types. I took a good look at everyone as I wasn't sure I would recognize James. I had to check every bloke who walked in. I sat down at the far end of the pub, leaving James a good run-up for when he arrived, allowing me time to suss him out. Two young ladies sat to my right. They didn't say much and were dressed for a night out. The one with her back to me I assumed was black as she had long, black slightly ridged hair as if it had been straightened from an afro. I was surprised when she turned around to find she was white, and must have shown it, because she asked if I was OK. I nodded, knowing that if I tried to say anything it wouldn't come out right. I was uncomfortable and went up to the bar to fetch a Bailey's to accompany my watery bitter.

The premises were soon playing host to just the three of us as the businessmen went home or on to strip joints. James was over a half-hour late and I was beginning to think he was a no-show. I watched the door. I don't know how he did it but before I knew it he was behind me with his hands over my eyes, his lumpy, scabby hands which he obviously had no problem with. He hugged me and then shook hands in a double clasp. His hands were patchy red from his childhood burning episodes. His appearance hadn't altered much. He was still bright-eyed and clear-skinned and had kept his body in shape, but his mannerisms were all wide-boy and accent, fragmented cockney. It wasn't all luvva-duck, more stock-market floor-trader. He didn't really talk to me, it was more like he was chatting me up, giving me his spiel in a charming way. He handed me a fifty and told me to get a bottle of champagne and four glasses. I did it because he didn't do it like he was treating me as a lackey. I came back and he had his arms around the two ladies.

'Shea, this is Catrina and Alison and they have kindly invited us to the Therapy? gig at the Astoria. Apparently, the girls know the support act.'

We listened to James talk for ten minutes before we

departed. As we left, James took me aside and asked which one I wanted. I looked at him as if he was mad and he just said, 'Shea, I'm not guaranteeing a result, I'm offering you space for whichever one you want.'

To save an argument, I chose Catrina, and with that he sped up to Alison and put his arm around her. Catrina and I were a couple of paces behind. She was probably pissed off that James had gone off with her friend and she was stuck with me.

'Do you like Therapy??' she asked.

'Not really,' I replied, rusty at date-speak.

She was quiet after that. I'd obviously exhausted all avenues of conversation. I thought she looked beautiful, as I did a lot of women. But this night I just wanted to get drunk. I'm not sure whether it was because I was disappointed or because I wanted to avoid disappointment. I knew that was my agenda.

The bouncers at the Astoria don't like people. We were practically shoved into the venue. The support band had come off stage so the girls made their way to the backstage area. The upstairs bar was packed with long-haired, leather-clad metal-heads. Every third person had a Kiss T-shirt on. The serving area was five deep with people anxious to buy warm, overpriced canned lager. James slid me off to one of the bogs. We headed for the cubicle, avoiding the urine puddles. There was no lock on the door and James asked me to put my heel against it. I was glad to have a little distance from the actual toilet as it was overflowing with bad-diet turds and the last of the toilet paper. The stench was appalling and I remembered at that instant why I gave up reviewing music. It's hard to wax lyrical about gigs when you've been treated like animals. James chopped out two lines of what I presumed to be cocaine. I take it from the speed of the process and the assorted paraphernalia that this was a regular occurrence. I'm no Cliff Richard, but drugs don't figure in my life. Then again, I never refuse free gifts. I still get excited by free shampoo samples.

Back at the bar, it was quieter as Therapy? were on-stage – we didn't bother watching them, nor did another fifty or so people who obviously preferred the sound of their own voices to the primal boom of Andy Cairns's. The girls reappeared and James sorted them out with some coke. We were all soon too buzzy for the dead bar and the girls quick-talked us into going downstairs. We stood by the merchandising stall, necking down beers, talking enthusiastically about nothing. James kept dis-appearing and coming back with double tequilas. I was pissed but the edge the coke had given me I had mistaken for sobriety.

Suddenly there was a big cheer as the singer announced it was the merchandiser's birthday. He looked embar-rassed and turned to us and said, 'It's just part of the show, they do this every night.' They referred to him as 'Mary', probably because of his big girl's laugh. As the tequila kicked in, Catrina went from beautiful to girl I wanted to marry. Her smile warmed my heart and her dancing was giving me a hard- on or, should I say, made me aware of my hard-on. It was coming to the end of the gig and Therapy? started playing a few numbers I actually recognized. As soon as the band had left the stage the crowd began streaming out like meek sheep but with worse jumpers. The bouncers-as-farmhands weren't keen on the punters analysing the gig in their space and were aggressively asking them to exit.

James appeared once again with four more tequilas. One of the bouncers told him to leave. James just lost it, stating quite fairly that he had just bought a drink and he was within his rights to drink it. The bouncer offered him a ten-second reprieve. It probably would have been longer if he could have counted properly. Coming to the end of his evidently very short tether, he grabbed James by the lapels and shoved him out the door. James turned around quickly and splattered his plastic glass on the guy's nose. Before anyone had any time to react, there were four bouncers on him. They waded in with a couple of body punches and threw him out into the street, a limb each. The crowd, leaving peacefully, were knocked out of the way. As the girls and I followed James out, one of the other bouncers pointed at us and soon had my left arm tight behind my back and punched me on the back of the head as a way of getting me out. Alison was being dragged by the hair by a female bouncer. She was hysterical.

The four of us regrouped, the humiliation intensified by the gaping onlookers. James had a bloody nose and was deep-breathing purposefully. He kept pointing at the bouncer on the door, warning of pay-back time. The bouncer folded his arms and smirked at the very idea. Alison hooked up with the support band, deciding another party was what she needed. Catrina was still in shock and James suggested I take her home. He said he had a couple of things to deal with and would ring me tomorrow. I offered to get Catrina a taxi but she wanted to walk back to Camden Town.

We headed up Tottenham Court Road. Her teeth were chattering, a mix of after-shock and the cold. I was dealing with little body tremors and my legs felt like they might give way at any moment. I put my arm around her for comfort. She accepted but it made it hard to walk. There was hardly anyone on the streets and I was a little spooked as we walked through the no-man's-land between Warren Street tube station and Camden. To our left was a shadowy high-rise block of flats and I knew I couldn't deal with another confrontation. I quickened the pace until we reached the Camden Palace, the sight of late-night revellers appeasing my paranoia. Catrina rented just off Delancey Street and she invited me in for coffee.

Once there, we headed straight for her bedroom, where she left me. The room was a messy pit of clothes, CDs and a mattress. A poster of Brian from Placebo looked down on me, offering a more glamorous setting. She came back with a half-bottle of wine and a two-bar fire. She didn't apologize for the mess, which I thought unusual, and there was no more mention of coffee. We soon calmed down and very naturally she had her head on my bony shoulder. I asked all the questions and got the run-down on her life without finding out much about her personality. She was from the sticks, hadn't seen her folks for over three years, played guitar in a band but worked in a bar. She started touching my neck, working her way down to my pot-belly. I caressed the side of her bra, working up to a full clasp. We were soon kissing.

She had a small wet tongue and swished it around my mouth like wine. We went from lying side by side to intertwined legs, going through the motions of fucking – the term I think is 'dry-humping'. I think I prefer this to sex. There's no difficult moment of revelation as pants come off and equipment is positioned. She was grunting as I pressed her from behind more tightly against me; I soon came and subtly tried to slow the actions down. She must have known I'd come. Guys don't just stop in the middle of this scenario and decide enough is enough. I kissed her on to my side and crouched up beside her into a cosy sleep.

I awoke in the morning not having the foggiest idea where or who I was. I knew my feet were cold and the room had a musty smell and we were still intertwined. I started my morning cough, which was typically productive. I looked to see where I could put it. There wasn't any acceptable receptacle. I swallowed it back down, hoping it would re-attach itself to my lungs. I kidded myself that I hadn't succumbed to a squalid one-night stand. She would have no hold on my fading self respect. I could maybe get to know her at my own pace. I squeezed against her for her body heat but predictably it got me going again. I kissed her neck and nudged her arse towards me. I gently grabbed her breasts, pushing her upper body towards me. She turned around and we started kissing. Her breath was boozy, as I suppose mine was. Her eyes were still closed. I put my hand down her knickers, caressing until she was wet. She unbuttoned my flies and began jerking me off. My boxer shorts were still a bit crusty from the night before. We both started moving faster. I asked her to suck me off as romantically as I could. She rubbed me harder, saying she only sucked her boyfriend.

Boyfriend? I have odd morals but I don't like doing the dirty on others. My two rules are: I would never knowingly go out with another man's girlfriend or fuck a dead person because I wouldn't like it done to me. Luckily this dilemma didn't come into play, because I came before I had a chance to question it. The sperm which ended up in her hand she rubbed into my upper pubic hair. At that moment my hangover kicked in big-time. The coke after-effect added a layer of depression on to it. I didn't have many clothes to put on and I was out of the flat within minutes. I could see some bloke in the kitchen and I dreaded to think who he was. The cold sunlight probed my headache. All I wanted in the world was a couple of painkillers, tea and toast, a long warm bath and a brand new personality.

I struggled down the road, trying to get my bearings. People were rushing to work and I felt like a complete waste of space. I had no right to be among these people. I waited for a mini-cab. The controller was reluctant even to have me in his office, never mind a car, with my unkempt breath, panda eyes and slept in hair. I got into a clapped-out Ford which suited my state. The driver asked for directions which I had to concentrate hard on and then pumped up his radio full. The speakers at the front were broken so I was blasted home to the tune of some black American homeboy who wasn't gonna take no messin' from his bitch no more, full volume. I got out at the end of my road and gave him my last fiver. I had that tiny panic for my keys until I touched the outline of my trouser pocket. My liver was hurting and my head was knackered and bowing down. It was an effort to lift it back up as I reached my flat. But I awoke fully on seeing a squad car parked in front of my flat and two cops at the door.

'Excuse me, sir, are you Shea Hickson?'

Every crime I'd ever committed, every wrongdoing I'd considered, all those documentaries about miscarriages of justice spun around my spongy brain. They tallied up to reach just one conclusion: Robin Hood had stitched me up.

'Yes,' sounding guilty as hell.

'Would you mind accompanying us to the police station.'

'What for?'

'We would like you to help us with our enquiries.'

'And what is it I am supposed to have done?'

'Nothing, sir. We would just like to ask you a few questions.'

I got into the back of the cop car. Hunger, panic, hangover and sticky pants being my strongest personality traits. The two bobbies started to talk to each other about West Ham Football Club and what time their shift finished. I was expecting torture at the very least. At the station, I had to wait around for an hour. They gave me a cup of tea and a cigarette which made me feel a lot worse. They brought me into a room where it became apparent I was taking part in an ID parade. I eyed the rest of the line-up and was disappointed with the motley crew I was a part of. It doesn't do your confidence any good when you know that they see you as from the same stock as this bunch of ugly gits. Lined up we looked like a German World Cup team. Each and every one of this lot had done time, and the possibility of going to prison was superseded by my vanity. I made a note to try and look a bit more civilized in future.

The rest had your usual tough-nut expressions on their faces. Me, I couldn't do a stern face if the kids next door burnt my flat down. Now put me in a line-up with a bunch of understated jazz pianists and I might fit in, but this was ridiculous. We were shuffled out and the two policemen took me into another room, where I was introduced to DC Borrow. He sat me down and put a tape recorder on. The gallows humour of the situation made me think we were going to cut a demo-tape together. I felt the kickback from last night's cocaine. I sniffed it back into my system. I was determined to say nothing. I thought of a novel way for the cops to make criminals confess. All they have to do is give the suspect a line of coke and they'll talk all night. I kept the little idea to myself.

'OK.' Borrow sat down. He was wearing a pleasant cheap suit. 'Mr Hickson, you were at the Astoria at Charing Cross Road last night. That is right, isn't it?'

I was stumped. I wasn't expecting that. 'Yeah, that's right.'

'And I believe you got into a skirmish with some of the crowd liaison officers.'

'The what?' I started to laugh. 'Those thugs in the black jackets? Those wankers who kicked us out?'

'I am sure they were just doing their job, sir.'

'They're just scum who resent the fact that they

90

couldn't get decent jobs so they take it out on us.'

'So would you say, Mr Hickson, that they did you wrong?'

'Too bleeding right I would.'

'And what did you do when you left the venue?'

'What's all this about?'

'Just answer the question, please.'

'I went home.'

'Did you get lost, Mr Hickson? Because' – he checked his notes – 'according to officers Pearson and Brown, when they went to your address this morning, you were only then just getting home.'

'When I say I went home . . . one of the girls we'd met was pretty shaken, so I took her home and stayed the night.'

He shot me a slight grimace.

'Hey we didn't have sex, if that's what you're thinking.'

'Sex is not a crime, Mr Hickson, so it doesn't concern me.'

'What crime are you talking about?'

'This lady you were with, have you got her address?'

'I can't remember it.' Again, paranoia surged through me. Shit, shit, shit – some bad shit's going down. Somebody has been killed and Catrina will deny being with me, to save face with her boyfriend. I could feel the dried sperm mingling with little droplets of involuntary piss and new outbursts of sweat.

'I could probably show you her place. Look, has one of those bloody thugs accused me of something?'

'Mr Hickson,' raising his voice, 'you seem to be getting a little hot under the collar.'

The next thing I said, which I'd thought I never would, came from watching too many cop shows.

'Look, either you charge me or you let me go.'

'Don't be impatient . . . What do you know about James Fentelli?'

'He's just an old schoolmate. I haven't seen him for ages. Why? What's he done?'

'Did you know he's on probation at the moment?'

'No.'

'And he's broken that probation.'

'What was he in for?'

'Mr Fentelli has been in and out of prison since he was seventeen, each time for arson.'

'For fuck's sake. We used to play with fire all the time when we were kids.'

'That's my problem, Mr Hickson. You and Mr Fentelli meet up at the Astoria last night and this morning the place is still smouldering.'

'There was a fire?'

'Quite a big one. You can understand why we want to talk to Mr Fentelli.'

'Sure, yeah.'

'Have you any idea where he is?'

'Have you checked his house?'

'Yes, the police force is wise to such procedures.' Funny man.

'No, as I said, I haven't seen him for years.'

'And did he tell of any intentions of burning the said building?'

'No. He was really pissed off, but he just said he had to deal with some business and left.'

'OK, Mr Hickson, we'll have to check out your alibi.'

He turned off the tape recorder and the two officers explained that they would take me to Catrina's house. I was to point at the door and then to have no contact with her. I was more relaxed now and said, 'Whatever.'

I found her house more easily than I thought I would and of course her boyfriend opened the door. He called for her and the police went in. All I could do was shrug at her. After fifteen minutes, the cop said I was free to go for now but they might be back in touch. Yeah, like I haven't heard that one before. I had no money on me and had to walk home with one more niggling problem to contend with.

Chapter 10

One more letter had arrived. One more message was on my machine and Dad's Christmas present remained on the table. I wasn't in a state to tackle any of them. I was aware that my life was hurtling along out of control. I know control is a matter of luck but everybody I was coming into contact with lately was taking me places I didn't want to go. I didn't have the ego to believe that all of this was predestined, that a higher force was pulling my strings. And if there was, it insisted that I run a bath. I amused myself with the bathos of some metaphysical influence monitoring my life and signalling bathtime.

Self-control interests me more. As a child, I would insist on not walking on the cracks in the pavement. I would walk down a road thinking I could touch that lamppost if I wanted to, but I didn't want to. Further down the road, the idea that I had had a choice was more acute. I *could have* touched it if I'd wanted to. Now I was regretting not touching that lamppost. If I had touched it, would my life be five seconds behind now? How might those five seconds have affected my life? Is there an inner voice which we have no control over, guiding us to certain points? Call it what you will – schizophrenia, guardian angel, instinct – at least it's company. As adults we hide from these voices and go out of our way to walk under ladders. The cynic's belief in nothing is maybe God calling. Early settlers mistook this voice for God. Vulnerable souls who are blind or, to be more exact, those who see nothing are chosen. Nothing sticks, their lives become purely cosmetic. They stop believing in themselves. Of course, they turn to God and cling on for dear life. This doesn't make God all-conquering, He is simply the last resort. The person you go out for a drink with when none of your friends are around. What the Christians won't tolerate is the fact that all the murderers, rapists and child-molesters went down the very same route as them but picked the Devil instead. We are all but one step away from this surrender. Cleanliness is next to Godliness so a bath was the right option.

The water was too hot and my foot started to throb. I ran the cold tap to lower the temperature. It is impossible to think we can have harmony in the world when hot and cold water don't even automatically mix. I love bathing, even in this tiny tub which fits three-quarters of my body. I have to see-saw myself clean. I like the bath to be a little too hot, to rid myself of the toxins which people have been breathing on to me. In the bath it's just me, no voices or pregnant hairdressers, dead dads, evil manipulators or pyromaniac friends. I once had sex in this bath. I pretended it was erotic as we sponged each other into arousal, but to be honest it was just plain awkward. My bathing partner was much more turned on. Well, I suppose it helps that your bits look bigger under water.

Hence you never see men shafting their girlfriends in rear-view mirrors.

I've gone off sex since Rebecca left me. I got to keep the CDs, she got the sex drive. I think I used to like it. There was one year when I couldn't get enough sex. I think my look was 'in' that year, as was my luck. I was young, hair short and spiked, the malnourished look was in. I believe it was the year of Live Aid. I was agile and full of life, cool with the hint of a smile. I was obsessed with having sex with strangers. I was addicted to the newness of the encounter. I didn't even have a preferable type. I loved the moment before sex. I guess it was the ego-boost of knowing someone wanted me inside them. The second I was in, it became boring. That's why we love queueing so much in this country. Once you're there, then it is a matter of going through the motions, making stupid grunting noises. On occasion I would come across the perfect fit where it was purely physical. But the weirdest thing that year was, practically everybody I had sex with kind of fell in love with me.

This I hated, and yet I adored giving them that beautiful moment of self-deluding pleasure, because even if love doesn't work out it is a fantastic interlude of grandeur which we all need from time to time. What I would give to feel love once more, but I can't see it happening for the foreseeable. I feed on the soundbites of love, the falling in love with a stranger's face and the imagined life we would share but I do not miss the full stomach-churning love. I suppose I'm not over Rebecca.

The cooling water brought me to my senses. I will have to sort myself out. I had a toasted-cheese sandwich just before bed to make sure I would have nightmares. That way the crazy days I was having wouldn't feel so isolated.

The morning brought chirping birds and irate binmen. I was calm but aware this preceded the storm. I felt within myself enough to open the letters, both from the hairdresser, concerned at my lack of concern for our baby as well as giving me a progress report on developments, as in: there've been no developments. Three of the messages were from her as well, all slightly the wrong side of hysterical. The last one mentioned an older brother who might make me see sense. There was also a curious call from Hazel asking for another meeting, and the final one was from James, telling me he had sorted out the bouncers, he was going away for a while and that he would get in touch soon. I rang Mum and arranged for her to put some cash in my account, in lieu of my inheritance.

She had company which I found odd but I was also pleased she was getting on with her life. She had a habit of whispering on the phone when other people were in the room. She surprised me when she told me she was going away for a little holiday. Dad had loathed holidays so they hardly ever went, and when they did it was to severe weather-spots so he could get first-hand experience for his research. I was even more taken aback when she said she was going to the Canaries.

'Mum, you've always hated the sun.'

'No, love, that was your father. I haven't really given it a try.'

I said goodbye and hung up, but something was niggling at me. I expected her to slowly fade away but here she was with a new lease of life. I should have been ecstatic but it was as if Dad's jealous gene had been reincarnated in me. I also knew I had no rights over my mother but at that moment I couldn't help butting into other people's lives. The phone rang again. My machine clicked on and the hairdresser shouted down the line. 'I know you're there! Pick up the phone!' I'm sure everybody along the radiowaves between her house and mine could hear her. I picked up the phone.

'Look, I don't know if you are aware, but I'm dealing with my father's death, so I will get in touch when I'm ready. Now, I can do without these threats, it's not really helping matters, OK?'

There was a silence and a hushed 'I'm sorry, I didn't know', and then more silence.

I eased my anger. 'I'll be in touch, OK?'

'Don't forget our date.'

'Yeah, yeah, no worries.'

You give an inch – she went into a spiel. I interrupted her.

'Not now, OK? I'll be in touch.'

'OK.'

'Bye.'

She behaved like an obedient child, loud meaning bad, soft meaning playful. Her reaction made me feel strong and, I suppose, arrogant because the next thing I did was ring British Telecom and ask for a new telephone number. I then arranged to meet Rebecca that evening. She lives in Hounslow but insists on calling it West

Richmond. I had no choice but to go all the way out there, considering her heavy pregnancy. My next task was to confront Robin Hood about the box of Black Magic. I still didn't know if I was just being stupid on that score. I guess they are a popular brand of chocolates. I was also curious to know what my final task was to be. I rang his number, something I was only supposed to do in emergencies. Whenever he wanted to contact me he always did so through the pager. An unknown voice answered the phone.

'Is Robin Hood there?'

'Who is this?'

'Little John.'

'What are you doing ringing this number?'

'Is he there?'

'That's restricted information.' Jesus, he's trained this one well.

'Just cut the shit. Is he there?'

There was a pause. 'Is this important?'

'Your life could depend on it.'

This one was easily scared. 'He's away at the moment. I can get a message to him.'

'Just tell him to get in touch as soon as he can. Oh and tell him I've sussed him out.'

I'd see if Robin would take my bait. I considered this the best way to deal with it: to see if he might offer information he thought I already knew. Regarding my own business up to scratch, I delved back into Dad's diaries to try to find who Robert Townsend was.

Chapter 11

Like many men before me, I went West; to Hounslow. The diaries weren't throwing any hard facts at me, but my gut instinct told me that Robert Townsend was one of the five elements. I pondered this on the tube journey. Most of the other passengers were heading for Heathrow. I'd always loved the idea of going to the airport and boarding a mystery plane and simply starting a new life. But I wasn't much of a flyer and I was still getting to grips with my own culture, never mind learning a whole new set of customs. I suppose the dream is to fall for a foreigner and the bonding of that love becomes so strong that you want to change, but it very seldom works out unless you're an eccentric pop star with a pot of money and a drug habit. I had done my fair share of travelling, mainly in Europe, and always ended up in the English bar trying to cop off with uninhibited compatriots (the locals never really went for my Johnny Foreigner persona).

I got off at Hounslow, which is ideally placed near the airport. Holidaymakers take one look at this place and then look forward to their break even more. Hounslow is a shit-hole and they should fly a banner which says as much. The residents mill around, embarrassed by their locale. It's full of video and hardware shops. The nightlife is miasmic pubs and plane-spotting and it is home to every mini-cab driver in London. The council must get bulk discount on grey paint and disinfectant. The buses are allowed to break speed limits and its centre has a one-way system taking you away from the area.

I arrived at Rebecca's house. It was situated in a cul-de-sac where identical cars sat in their identical drives. Nearly all the houses had extensions which would continue to be built until they reached Richmond. I rang the bell, which let out a dull non-musical sound. Rebecca was visibly more pregnant than I thought. The baby was only two weeks away. I was curious to see how they'd done out the house. It looked like they hadn't bothered. The minimal fuss of furniture was catalogue standard. The walls, grubby white, and the carpet obviously belonged to the previous owners.

'How long have you been here now? Is it two years?'

'Nearly three,' Rebecca corrected me.

The extension was allowing an almighty draught free rein in the house. I asked where Orwell was and she came straight to the point.

'You don't know?'

I said nothing.

'He's left me.'

I don't know where my paternal concern came from but I asked, 'Is he going to take care of the baby?'

She sat down, close to tears. 'I don't know, I simply don't know. I haven't heard from him in three days. I don't know where he is and work hasn't heard from him either. I thought you might have heard.'

I cut her short. 'I haven't heard from him.'

She started to bite her nails. Her face was puffed up and drained. I wanted to harangue her about our false history but didn't have the heart. She suggested places where he might be and it dawned on me that I knew nothing of his new life.

'So what happened?'

She shook her head. 'It was after your father's death. Everything was fine until then. He just . . . just changed, became withdrawn, he wouldn't let me near him. He kind of lost interest in everything. Me, the baby, work. He never came back from your mother's that time. Did he say anything?'

'No, he dropped me home. I assumed he was coming here. If anything, he seemed to be getting back to his old self. He was quite chatty.'

'When you say "his old self", do you mean his old self when he was with you or with me?'

'I wasn't aware there was a difference.' I felt slighted.

'I'm just worried he's going back to his old ways.'

'Has he disappeared before?'

'No, never. Did he mention another woman?'

'No, he said you, as in the two of you, were having problems.'

'I'm really worried.'

I didn't know whether to divulge our brotherly chat, but looking back on it, it was as if he was clearing his conscience before the big heave-ho. I came clean and told Rebecca what Orwell had said to me. She took it the wrong way.

'This is no time to be bringing up our past. It's Orwell I'm worried about.'

'I just thought it might be important.'

'Shea, you're so selfish. It's always about you isn't it?' That was rich. This was the second ear-bashing I was getting from my deceivers.

She continued, 'Big deal. I never wanted you. So now you know I've always loved Orwell.'

I couldn't help myself. 'The two years we were together meant nothing to you?'

'Frankly, no.'

All the precious memories of shared experiences were destroyed and the fact that I still had strong feelings towards her made me feel like a proper patsy. I didn't know what to say, where to look. I was troubled about Orwell and wanted to help, but this woman was making it difficult.

'OK. Let's drop this. Let's just say you used me for two years, probably what I still consider were the best two years of my life.'

'I stayed with you. Wasn't that enough?'

I wanted to say, 'Don't flatter yourself,' but that wouldn't have been true. She certainly wasn't concerned for my feelings now.

'Well, what do you want me to do?'

'Find him, bring him back home.'

'Even if I do find him, I can't force him to come back.'

'Oh come on, he's always done what you told him to. He looks up to you so much. He's never loved me as much as he loved you. Do you know, if you had told him not to see me he would have done that? That was always part of the deal. That's why I invited you tonight. You didn't tell him to leave me, did you?'

'No, no I didn't. I was always hurt but the way I dealt with it was to ignore it. I lost my brother because of you. We were never the same again. Maybe it's your turn to lose him now, then you might come near to feeling the pain I felt. Maybe the karma patrol caught up with you at last.'

'Will you please get over the fact that I didn't love you. It's as simple as that. Your brother is a sweet, caring, sensitive man. You, you're a shit, full of stupid dreams. A spoilsport who just gets in the way.'

'Can I book you for my best man speech?'

'Who's going to have you? A pattern is developing. You fool people into thinking you're interesting, but after a time they get to know the real you and then they always go. I don't know how you can bear to be in your own company twenty-four hours a day.'

She rose quickly, winced sharply in pain and then sat down again. 'Oh Christ, my waters have broken. I think I'm having the baby.'

I stood up, not knowing what to do. I went to her. She asked me to phone an ambulance. As we waited she was having quicker contractions. She asked me to drive her to the hospital.

'I can't drive,' I kept on telling her.

'You're a waste of space.'

It was nice to know she could insult me even during labour.

The ambulance arrived and this soothed her somewhat. They put breathing apparatus on her and sped us to the hospital. Rebecca grabbed my arm and dug in. The driver hit every pot-hole in the road, while the ambulance man in the back with us kept on repeating that everything was going to be all right and that she was doing fine. The sirens heightened the excitement and, for a moment, I wished it was I who was the father.

As we rattled down the hospital corridor, I asked if she wanted me to stay with her. She nodded, digging in harder. I figured having someone she hated would make it easier to claw into them. My adrenalin was going haywire as they pumped her full of drugs. The sweat was pouring out of her as she pushed and panted. I had never seen her look so beautiful. I kept on rubbing her brow with a towel, whispering shit I thought might help. I looked at my watch and was amazed that two and a half hours had passed. The midwife shouted, 'It's coming, I can see the head.' The junior midwife was soothing Rebecca, keeping her anxiety at bay. I could see the baby's head. I thought of my own mother's pain.

The midwife pressed a buzzer above the bed. I watched her and asked if there was a problem. Before she answered, the paediatrician was in the room. As if by magic there was a fully formed baby girl. The midwife looked to the exhausted mother, then said it was traditional for the father to cut the cord. I didn't contemplate the matter and said I was feeling queasy. Rebecca was smiling but eerily the baby was making no noise. The paediatrician had taken her to the resuscitator. There was an unspeakable tension in the room. 'Sophia,' Rebecca shouted. 'Sophia, that's her name.' Rebecca asked me what she looked like. 'Beautiful, just beautiful, she's definitely got your nose.' She still held on to me. 'When can I see her?' she asked the midwife. The junior midwife started crying. I knew Sophia was dead. I tried to comfort Rebecca, whose body heaved with silent sobs.

We remained still as the midwife wrapped the baby up. She asked if Rebecca wanted to see the baby. Rebecca held her hands up and took Sophia to her bosom and held her for the next four hours. It was gut-wrenching yet somehow noble. Sophia looked at peace while Rebecca eased the fatality into her psyche. I was the reluctant onlooker but felt part of the trinity. Looking at Sophia, you would sometimes think she was only sleeping. The junior midwife came back and asked in a broken voice if we wanted to take any photos, which I thought odd. Rebecca said that would be nice and the midwife took a roll of Polaroids. She then asked Rebecca if she needed any bereavement counselling. Rebecca declined the offer. The midwife, whose sturdy yet sympathetic professionalism had me humbled, returned to ask permission for the hospital to do a post-mortem of Sophia. She explained that Rebecca was under no pressure but it really helped them research deaths of new babies. Rebecca handed her baby over to her and I swear, this was the saddest moment of my life. Rebecca didn't know what to do with her hands. I cuddled up to her but it was awkward. I stayed with her that night in the hospital. Neither of us slept. We passed the night looking at the photos.

In the morning, we took a taxi to her place. Not a word was exchanged. I hugged her softly, as it felt like her bones might snap. I had no idea what she had gone through. There is no male equivalent. She leaned against me as I took her out of the cab and into the house. I stayed with her for the day. The midwife visited and the two of them started to bond. I guess they were the closest to Sophia. Her parents turned up that day as well. There was still no sign of Orwell – this would surely send him further over the edge. It was going to take Rebecca a long time to recover her normal self, that's if she ever could. A crisis like this kills a bit of you which you never get back. You can do nothing but accept it. I was having trouble getting on with my own day-to-day existence. That's two dead people I've had to see at first hand and I am sure they have scarred my mind. It's as if the positive section of my brain has been blown asunder, giving the negative an upper hand. And I can tell you now that cliché about an event like this making you cherish your own life more is total bullshit: it makes you regretful of having a life. I went up to say goodbye to Rebecca. She took my hand in hers and muttered, 'Sorry for all the things I said.' I burst into tears. This was the most heartfelt apology I've ever experienced and I knew I would always love Rebecca. She called me back once more and it was then that she handed me one of the photos of Sophia. Nothing more needed to be said.

Chapter 12

Back in Crouch End I felt I didn't have the energy to continue my existence. I was gripped by that horrible combination: listlessness accompanied by an urgent need to do something. I hadn't been to the toilet for two days, my body retaining all the shit, and it was making its way up to my brain. It was as if I was coming down from a trip, which I suppose I was. I had assumed that when getting over a tragedy, you would gently become normal again. The hiatus of looking after Rebecca had had me forgetting all else. Now again I was sleepily aware and I didn't want to be aware. I wanted ignorance thrust upon me. I would happily have swapped a life of continual bus-stop conversation for what I had now. Leaving Rebecca's house had been a reminder of how I'd been shut out of her life, a life I knew I wanted to share. She's at home, coping on her own; I'm here, willing and alone, and my dear brother has disappeared, struggling with his own demons, and yet to hear of the death of more of his own flesh and bone.

I took the picture of Sophia out of my pocket and thought of the one-hour photo places and how they always show the big smiling happy family. That family photo is a big lie and it gives normal folk false hope and unrealistic goals to aim for. Wouldn't it be more appropriate to have Sophia's photo on display with a little sign saying, 'Capture those moments in life that suck'? Or even put one of the photos of Dad and Hazel there, with the caption 'Marriage doesn't always work' beside it.

I looked at the photos of my father again. I studied the expressions on his face as he was being sucked off. I'd seen that expression before. It took me a while to place it, but it reminded me of when he used to do his crossword on a Sunday. I wondered what went through his mind when having sex with Hazel. Was he able to let himself go or did he play a role of sorts, pretending to be the great lover? Hazel certainly looked satisfied and keen on her own breasts, as she held them while sitting on my father's lap. I remember sitting proudly on my father's lap as a child while we pretended to be winning the Grand National. Was he playing the same game with Hazel? Before I knew it, I had my penis out and was giving it a good seeing-to.

I say "before I knew it" because there wasn't a moment when I decided to have a wank over my dead dad's photos. My penis had become aroused and it seemed the natural thing to do. Written down, it probably sounds disgusting but there I was, imagining shagging Hazel. As I got a steady motion going, I discarded the pictures, closed my eyes and thought of Hazel and her little sexy mutterings in my ear as I sucked her breasts and fucked her. I was coming in no time and the spontaneity of it all

110

meant that there was nowhere for my sperm to land. I tucked my penis inside my T-shirt and relieved myself. After a respectful passage of time, I checked to see which T-shirt I was wearing. It was a fading 'Cool as Fuck' Inspiral Carpets one and I decided it was probably time I chucked it. This T-shirt had lasted longer than any of the relationships I'd had, so it was apt that we'd sort of had sex before parting.

The weird thing I've found about masturbation is that once I do it I feel like doing it again straight away. There was many a night when I was feeling horny and, rather than going to the effort of a night out with a lady and the cumbersome post-sex atmosphere, I would have a wank instead. Satisfied, my penis would suddenly become greedy and have me on the phone arranging a date. Often, after blow-jobs, my intention would be to satisfy my partner but I never had the stamina. It's always a bit awkward when in the middle of a blow-job the lady puts you inside thinking that was just the 'getting-you-hard' section. They barely get two thrusts out of me before I'm apologizing. It's even worse when the condom comes into play and they always think I'm just copping out by saying, 'Really, it's not worth it.'

All this thinking of sex had me horny again. I don't know how those authors of porn books get through the day. It must take them ages to finish their books. It must be even harder for porn-film directors. You can't become so inured that you can be a neutral, immune onlooker. I'm sure when the director shouts 'Cut' the whole crew just jerk off. My dirty mind was interrupted by a persistent ringing on the doorbell.

I pulled my pants up and answered it and there, fuming visibly, was my moody hairdresser, Ruth. She was crying and calling me a bastard. We were supposed to have met in Camden last night and I'd plain forgotten. I didn't tell her about Sophia because I thought it might freak her out. I invited her in and tried to calm her down. Once she was relaxed, I suggested the pub. She was reluctant but I talked her into it. We went to the All Bar One because no one I knew drank there and the young, trendy crowd gave me the impression that all was right in the world. I ordered a beer for myself and an orange juice for the baby-carrier. I don't know whether I was lifeless or resigned to a life of hassle but I wasn't at all edgy about the situation. We did the small-talk on small sips.

I plunged in with 'What's the plan then?' She got defensive, saying she wanted to have it, that her family were very supportive and that they'd all talked the whole thing through. I looked at her and there was no doubt she was very pretty but already she was boring me and I knew I couldn't get a relationship going with her. And yet I was incredibly horny and toyed with buttering her up in the hope of a shag, but concluded that really wouldn't be wise. I tried to be adult about it.

'Look, Ruth, I'm sure you're a lovely person and will be a great mother but we barely know each other, so I have to say I will help out as much as I can financially but I can't commit to any form of a relationship.'

She'd obviously pre-planned every possible reply to every position I could take and I could imagine her mother hating me already. Without pausing for breath, Ruth came out with 'You don't want to see your own child?'

'Well, I don't really see it as a child at the moment. It's more a one-night stand that's gone wrong.'

'Thanks. Thanks a lot.' She turned her head away.

'You know what I mean. I'm not having a go but I have enough problems bringing up myself, let alone two others.'

'As long as you know that once you've made the decision, there's no going back on it. You can't appear in the child's life, a few years down the line. If you don't commit to the child, that means for life.'

I thought this was a little strong, and legally I was sure she didn't have a leg to stand on so I just nodded.

'Financially, I will have to give up work . . .'

I stopped listening, throwing in the odd 'mm-hmm'. I'd wait and see what figure she came up with and if it wasn't too steep, I'd pay. Otherwise, I'd see what the law deemed necessary. All in all, it was going to be a very expensive shag. I was always stupidly under the illusion that my sperm didn't work. The rest of me is feeble, so why should my sperm be so strong? When I get home there'll probably be a little baby Inspiral Carpets T-shirt waiting for me, demanding commitment.

We chatted on, which was a bit pointless, and soon I was a little tipsy. She talked on and on about always wanting a family and that she planned to have at least three kids. Thinking we were more relaxed about the situation, I joked, 'Feel free to give me a call when you want the next one.'

Ruth somehow didn't find this as funny as I did and slapped me hard across the face. Then, with the whole pub watching, she threw her orange juice in my face and stormed out. The couple sitting near us, who'd never, obviously, had a row in their life, stared at me.

'No, you see there was a wasp about to sting me and the wasp was on fire so she had to put it out. She probably saved my life.'

They lowered their heads and the pub slowly went back to its conversations. I stood my ground by buying another beer. The barman asked if everything was OK.

'Sure,' I said, my voice shakier than I would have liked.

The after-shock kicked in once my adrenalin went back to normal. My hands were trembling a little and my eyes were still stinging from the orange juice. She had strong hands for a hairdresser and it dawned on me what she would tell our child about me. Someone I had helped to create would be roaming the world with hatred for their old man. At least I know for certain in eighteen years I can expect another slap from a relative stranger. I was just calming down when my pager vibrated.

. . . LJ – ring me ASAP – RH . . .

Chapter 13

I awoke a second before my body, my left hand numb from lying on it. My belly was home to caterpillars who decided butterflies they were not and instead evolved into bats, pissed-off bats, determined not to be trapped. When the mornings began like this they rarely got better. The very idea of meeting up with Robin Hood had me nervous. This had a knock-on effect so that everything bugged me. The fact that the mattress was a fraction too small for the bed, leaving a crevice for the pillow to wedge itself into, was really annoying me; that I had to get out from under the duvet for a piss was a hassle. The longer I remained, the more my bladder would protest and the more indignant I'd get. The shouted conversation the binmen were having outside my flat seemed like a personal affront. It was 5.50 a.m. for fuck's sake. Dark outside but London was at work: soon, buses and lorries would be rattling my windows, kids would argue with their parents outside as if there was a plaque on my wall stating that this was the designated area.

Sometimes I don't know why I live in London. Maybe it has the greatest array of cultural entertainment in the world, but I don't make use of any of all that. I'm London through and through, in that I'm part of London's overall picture, on view for the tourists to gawp at. And what do I get in return? Its dirt under my fingernails, neighbours who don't talk to me and an above-average chance of becoming a crime statistic. If there was a slogan for London, it should read, 'It's Near Watford'. Watford's no great shakes but at least it doesn't have an attitude. I do like Crouch End, though. It feels safe, even though police sirens are an hourly occurrence (that's probably because of near-by areas like Finsbury Park and Turnpike Lane getting uppity). Turnpike Lane: I would be there again in an hour, getting answers from Robin Hood.

The bus journey was a blur because all I could think of was the Black Magic in Mum's house. I couldn't just bring it up. It would sound ridiculous. Was it a simple coincidence, a phenomenon I no longer believed in? I was edging towards predestination, cause and effect; simple coincidences didn't shape up. OK, say the chocolates were a condolence gift, they were still there for me to see and then question – a warning about Robin Hood, a sign telling me I was no longer one of his not-so-merry men. If they were from him, it would mean he was somewhat involved in my father's death. Was Dad one of the organization's hits? Maybe they found out about Hazel? But that wouldn't make sense. Dad had pretty much retired. He did the odd after-dinner speech. All our organization would have done was force him to retire. It was not part of our process to mess up private lives. As long as they disappeared from the media, we let them lead their lie. Dad couldn't possibly have been a hit. It must be my untrusting nature getting the better of me. Robin had always said other organisations would soon follow in our path. More extreme people who would simply kill celebrities for the sake of it. I rang Robin's doorbell. He wasn't his usual stern self and he had a bit of colour in his face. He smiled at me and shook hands as well as patting my shoulder. I hadn't seen him in such a good mood for a long time. He ushered me in and offered me a seat. As he sat behind his desk and put on his reading glasses he kept repeating, 'Very exciting times.'

'Shea, my good man, we've had a breakthrough.'

I was taken in by his enthusiasm but remained silent.

'What would you say is the most important way forward for the organization, Shea?'

I didn't hesitate. 'To get our message across to as many people as possible.'

'You remember well. So, given that is so important, how should we go about it?'

I joked, 'Get a newspaper to publish our manifesto.'

'You got it!'

'But that's impossible. We've tried before. The newspapers think we're a bit of a joke. And, as you keep pointing out, the papers themselves are part of the problem.'

'What would you say if I told you that the *Daily Angel* was going to publish our message and, in doing so, was going to destroy itself?'

'I would say that was ideal.'

'Well, that's what's going to happen.'

'How did you manage that?'

'Come, come, Shea, that's classified. But I want you involved. Don't plan anything for the end of March, beginning of April. But in the meantime, I want you to draft a message. Now, we can't bore the people with vague generalities. Let's hit them where it hurts. I think we should concentrate on the newspapers themselves, how they are part of the problem and not to be trusted, some inside information on the owners of the papers. In essence, let's tell the truth about them.'

As I left, all negative thoughts about Robin were vanishing and I was excited once more about the organization. This felt like proper work. It helped convince me that Robin's heart was in the right place. He wasn't out just to get individuals, he was biding his time waiting for the bigger fish. Bringing down a newspaper would really put the organization on a proper level. We would be taken more seriously. The blanket coverage afforded us after the event would help spread our message further. We would at last be in the big league. This could really make a difference. The organization would go down in history as one that changed history. How had he managed it? I know I'm jumping the gun a bit but the one thing you could say about Robin Hood was that he wasn't a bullshitter. If he said something was going to get done, it would. My appetite was coming back. My bowels were moving again and I hadn't even noticed that it was raining.

I got home soaked but for the first time in ages I didn't need a bath. I had forgotten how good news can spring-clean your mind; I was in a good mood for the first time since Dad's death. Remembering I hadn't played any music in the flat this year – it had been a mute household – I put on a CD of movie soundtracks. I wanted big sweeping strings, big important chords to scare the pants off the dust, to blow away cobwebs, to battle against draughts, to poltergeist all into its rightful place. I made a cup of tea and danced with it; I didn't need any company when I was on such sparkling form. If only they could bottle this feeling, there would be no need for the chemicals we usually turn to on bad days. I tell you, I even smelt brilliant. My pores were flowing over with all my favourite smells, my eyes saw deeper colours and the shit songs on the compilation were being reappraised.

I knew the time was right to open Dad's Christmas present. I soon wished I hadn't. Inside the wrapping was a book. This book let me know that Dad knew more about me than I thought and if the search for his true life was waning, this gave me a much needed kick up the arse. In fact it meant I had no choice but to get to the bottom of what had made him tick. How the fuck did he know? But I couldn't believe what I had in my hands. It was a first edition of *Robin of Sherwood*. This presented me with two clear facts. He knew I was in the organization and his suicide was not a spur-of-the-moment decision. It was clearly planned. The overwhelming feeling was that he was letting me know from the grave that I'd let him down. But this was at odds with the suicide note. *Don't let this shade your life*. Surely this gift was doing just that. I went to bed to stare at the wall and the responsibility I now held for his death.

*

Tomorrow came as punctual as ever. I'd always lived for my tomorrows but lately they were bringing nothing but grief. I've never been a yesterday person living off past glories, but always wished I was a now person. But to be a now person is an impossibility. To be one you have to be unaware of the self, which I have difficulty with. The now is really a mix of anticipation and afterthought – they are the good points of the now.

Dad's memorial was tonight. Mum had asked if I wanted to speak but I said no, I would be too confused. She was having trouble getting in touch with Orwell but I was sure he would turn up. I'd had my one black suit dry-cleaned and made an attempt at ironing my one white shirt. I noticed a dirt line on the neck but it was too late to do anything about it. I know I have a tie somewhere but I also know that on it it says, 'Ian Dury and the Blockheads'. It was a freebie from my journalist days and I don't think it would have been appropriate. Anyway, at thirty years of age I still don't know how to tie the fucker. I felt a little guilty about not getting up to do a turn at the service. Maybe I could do a slide-show of his photos.

All dressed up, I was uncomfortable and dreading the tube journey. I was also starving. I didn't want to chance eating with this clobber on. I looked out the window to see if I needed an overcoat and there outside, sitting on the bonnet of his car, was Orwell, talking to someone on his mobile. Fuck, I wondered if he knew about Sophia yet. I hoped I wasn't going to have to play the messenger again. I rang Rebecca quickly, under the guise of concern for her welfare. She was still finding it hard to cope and was apologetic about not turning up for the memorial and no, she hadn't heard from Orwell. I put the phone down and tried to make a sensible judgement . . . I'd play it by ear.

I put the picture of Sophia in my pocket as the doorbell went. Orwell looked like he had lost weight, and had a general fazed aura about him. There were so many questions. I didn't know where to start. He threw me off kilter when he looked at my table and remarked, 'I see Dad got you one of those poxy books as well.' All I could think was, why would he give Orwell a copy as well? Maybe there was no significance to it at all. But more pressing was the fact that Dad's nude photos were also on the table. Orwell was about to check them out when I out-manoeuvred him. I pretended I was tidying up the table but he eyed me suspiciously. To put him off the scent I asked, 'So why do you think Dad got us those books?'

'He used to read us that story when we were kids.'

I had no recollection of it. Continuing my investigation: 'And was that your favourite story?'

'No, is your memory shot or something? It was Mum's favourite story.' Picking up on my blank expression, he continued, 'Dad used to call her his Maid Marion. Remember that Christmas they lived out the fantasy?' He eyed me again. 'You're serious, you don't remember?' He sat down. 'What did Robin Hood do?'

'I know all that. He stole from the rich and gave to the poor.'

'Yeah, remember Christmas Day? We unwrapped our presents. I got a mountain bike and I think you got a CD player.'

'Dad never got me a CD player, I'd remember that.'

'That's the whole point. Once we unwrapped them, he made us give the presents to that poor family, the O'Connells or something, who lived across the road.'

'Fucking hell.' It was all coming back. 'I must have totally blanked that from my mind. No wonder I don't like Christmas. What a bastard.'

'He said that it was a socialist experiment.'

'Yeah, one that went wrong. What is it Dad used to say? *Socialism is about bringing about harmony and equality*. We didn't speak to him for a month.'

'Jesus, we gave him a hard time about that, didn't we? Every time he wanted us to do anything, you would always say, "Ask the O'Connells" which you kept up for the whole year.'

'Yeah, but I wasn't the one who stole that poor fucker's bike back.'

'That wasn't me.'

'Oh, come on. You might as well get this one off your chest.'

'I didn't steal it. I just followed Dad's Utopian dream and gave it to a poorer child.'

'That was a cruel thing to do.'

'I wouldn't have done it if the fucker hadn't cycled past the house every day ringing his fucking bell.'

'Actually, thinking back, the funniest thing that made it all worth while was their dad accusing ours of currying favour with his kids.'

'I don't think those were his actual words. If I remember correctly, he grabbed him by the lapels and shouted, "If you mess with my fucking kids I'll cunt you and

122

throw you in the fucking cell myself. Oh, and we're keeping the presents, you ponce." Do you think I should mention it in my speech tonight?'

'You're doing one?'

'Yeah, you not?'

'No, I wouldn't know what to say.'

'Listen, we better get going.'

In the car I tried to casually drop general enquiries about Rebecca but he obviously didn't want to tell me anything – he lied that everything was fine. I decided that I was going to have to take him aside after the service. He also lied about his job, saying he was working on the biggest story the *Independent* had ever been involved in. It sounded very unlike Orwell: he was never one to boast and was always picking up on others when they did so. The service was held in a rehearsal room in Soho which some of his old work cronies had booked. It was to be a non-religious memorial, even though the building used to be a synagogue. Soho was alive with fashion-conscious media types who weren't mingling with the homeless. When we arrived, Mum was the only one in the room. She had laid out about forty plastic chairs and a make-shift rostrum was placed at the front of the room. To the side was a table with a tea urn and buffet. The room had a high ceiling and was cold and smelt of disinfectant. The floor was like that of an old school gym and your shoes squeaked when moving. Mum was dolled up and her newly acquired tan made her look younger. I was about to hug her when Orwell interrupted.

'Have you not got any booze laid on?'

Mum replied, 'Do you think it will be necessary?'

Orwell, in humorous mood, said, 'Mum, it's not an AA meeting, people will want to drink to his memory. I'll pop out to an offie.' Which he promptly did.

I put my arms around Mum, complimented her on her look and was surprised that she had a hint of perfume about her.

Her face turned serious as she said, 'He seems to be dealing with Sophia's death really well.' I told her straight that he didn't know.

'Oh God.' She began to get flustered and calming her I said that I would deal with it.

Quickly changing the subject, I asked how the Canaries had been.

'Oh, we ended up going to Libya instead.'

'Libya? What were you doing, a bit of gun-running?'

'It's a beautiful place, it just gets a bad press. Anyway, we had a lovely time there.'

'Who did you go with?'

'Oh, just an old friend who figured I could do with a break. And it did me the power of good. Oh, Shea, you're not looking too perky yourself. Maybe you should have a little holiday.'

'Yeah, Iraq is supposed to be very nice at this time of year.'

She smiled and tickled my side with her finger. Her mourning was over and I don't think mine had begun. I wouldn't say she looked happy, more bubbling under. I asked her if she had brought a condolence book. She had. I told her I would look after it. I wanted everyone who attended to sign it, along with their full addresses. This would be vital in the search for the truth about Dad's past.

The first of our guests arrived en masse. They were his TV buddies and, of course, heading the pack was El Niño. On seeing him, it felt like someone had walked on my grave. I approached them with the book and made sure they all signed in. They were, to say the least, a little bit tipsy. The cold room fogged up their boozy breath. Orwell came back with two bottles of whisky and one bottle of vodka. I slugged a whisky from a plastic cup which made it taste even less palatable. Soon there were about thirty people gathered in several distinct groups. The more people who arrived, the quieter the room became, nobody willing to raise their voice in front of strangers. The atmosphere was one of a crowded dentist's waiting room.

Mum tried to get the service started by asking people to take their seats, with those willing to speak taking front-row positions. I headed for the back as Mum got up to speak. She thanked everybody for coming and I could tell by her manner that she didn't recognize many of them. I could see in her face that, even though she'd spent a lifetime with Dad, it is in the event of death that you realize you never fully know someone. She gave a potted history of their time at Nottingham. The struggle of the early days of marriage. The relative wealth Dad had trouble enjoying because of his working-class roots, ending with how they fell into a pattern of domesticity. She confessed to Terence being no angel but they'd always been truthful to each other and they were always able to work through their problems. She said the suicide wasn't preceded by any tell-tale signs and this left her saddened. Terence was an overwhelming man, who took risks. He dismissed his Catholicism at an early age, replacing it with scientific facts, but unfortunately the early guilt had gripped him and he had never been able to shake it off. She highlighted this with a story of how Terence had fallen out with his parents over their marriage. His parents had wanted a big church wedding but Terence had insisted on a registry affair. She didn't mind either way and liked the grandeur of churches. But Terence would never compromise and his parents ended up not attending. She told how Terence had booked a secret honeymoon and simply refused to tell her where they were going. She was more than a bit surprised to find them holidaying in Rome, where they visited churches daily. Terence pretended he was interested in the architecture but it was his way of dealing with his past. They even waited in the square to catch a glimpse of the minuscule Pope addressing the people. Terence's cop-out line was 'When in Rome'.

She finished by saying, 'That was the point with Terence, he was always going against the grain. He might well have done as the Romans did but never while in Rome. Terence was never, as I said, one for compromise, and I think as he accepted that life was a series of them, it wore him down. Now I know Terence's brother, Marcus, wants to say a few words.'

Mum sat down and Uncle Marcus took to the rostrum. He was a plumber by trade and fond of a drink. He looked nothing like Dad. He was two years older than him but it looked more like ten. His bald spot was bowl-sized and the little hair he had at the sides and the back was ridiculously long. His cheeks were those of a trumpeter and his nose was red and veiny. He was clearly nervous and had made notes. His voice was monotone and impossible to follow but the gist was of their parents being so proud of Terence and that he himself had video-taped much of his brother's TV weather reports. This was a sad admission and a certain amount of pity circulated around the room. He talked about their posh names and how, when they were kids, in the company of friends they were called Terry and Mark but their parents were always correcting them. He finished with a not very witty anecdote about them being asked at school what career they wanted. Marcus said a plumber, while Terence said he wanted to be a plumber's mate. They'd joked about how it would be great to have his little brother working beside him, but Dad apparently replied, 'Working? No, I just want to be a plumber's mate so he can buy all the drinks.' A gentle laugh went around the room.

But what made it so pathetic for me was that on the ten or so occasions I had met Marcus he had always told me this story. It was the only link he had with Dad's life and he was determined to hold on to it. Marcus went on to recount the basic nice attributes of a man who had more or less shut him out of his life. He shuffled back to his seat, proud of himself. Next up was somebody I didn't recognize. He introduced himself as Maurice Edwards and his opening gambit was 'I really don't know what I'm doing here.'

I smelt perfume by my side. It had to be Hazel. We quickly smiled at each other and then continued to listen to the stranger.

'I knew Terence in Nottingham. We were best friends for a year. We connected, being from similar backgrounds. We both had a curiosity for life and because we were students we tended to share everything. We were full of cloth-eared liberal ideas. This, and the arrogance that youth proudly bears, was a potent cocktail. It was an intense time and I wasn't aware that I didn't have the constitution for it. One minute I had everything going for me, I thought I was indestructible. Then Terence abused my trust and did a very bad thing. I wasn't old or wise enough to cope with this and I guess I had what can only be termed a nervous breakdown. I'm not here to badmouth Terence because I know some of it was my own fault and I forgave him a long time ago. I'm here, like the rest of you, to pay my respects and thank him for that wonderful year that opened my eyes to a new world.'

He had tears in his eyes. He apologized quickly to Mum and sped out of the room. I found his speech moving and it was immediately apparent that this Maurice Edwards knew something of Dad's secret life. El Niño waltzed up next to tell of the many showbiz tales that he and Dad had been entangled in. They all involved getting blotto and becoming involved in scrapes. I'm sure he was annoyed that Mum's presence acted as a censoring device. His chums thought he was hilarious but I found him utterly tedious. He had an annoying habit of pressing his tongue against his cheek when he said something risqué. This reminded me of his blow-job, which made me queasy. The audience's favourite story was when El Niño spiked Dad's morning coffee with farting powder and then doctored his weather graphics from 'Sunny with occasional showers' to 'Unexpected high gusts of wind'. His testimony consisted of Dad being game for a laugh, but he had no insightfulness to spark off any real interest.

Last up was Orwell. He launched into his speech without preamble: 'I stand here tonight, not as a friend or brother or wife of the deceased but as his son, as part of his gene pool. He plotted out our lives without taking into consideration how we felt. He wanted us to blossom the family tree one step up the success ladder to continue where he left off. See, we all know that he had good intentions but never the fight to carry them off. His failings he pushed on to us. I always looked up to my father. I wanted to be him. He could do no wrong in my eyes. I followed him into the media, thinking I too might have a hand in changing the world, but like all the other self-serving arseholes in media, he was only interested in power.'

What this would do to Mum didn't allow me to consider how it was affecting me. She looked on the verge of passing out.

'We all know he tried to manipulate every situation and he was bright enough to do that. Some great men give up on strangers and rightly concentrate on their family's welfare. But Dad wanted both without caring for either. All families have their secrets and they have to remain sealed within the bloodline. I would have had more respect for him if he'd walked out on us but that wouldn't have helped his public image. He lived a lie and the guilt that he carried around with him was there for a good reason. I could, like Maurice, offer forgiveness but

129

I don't think he wanted it. It frightens me that I'm from the same stock. Taking the tiny flicker of hope that comes from all bad experiences, I'm determined not to make the same mistakes and, in fact, I've learned that I'm not even prepared to risk them. I have recently walked out on my own heavily pregnant fiancée for that very reason. I can no longer play at roles. I am heavy with sadness, but the virtues that Dad instilled in me were only words to him. I'm sorry, Mum and Shea, but I would rather live in the gutter, and let people know it, than constantly perfume it.'

He collected himself and casually left the room. Mum tried to stop him but it was as if he was in a trance. I ran after him, grabbing the condolence book en route. I spotted him easily enough and I shouted after him. He stopped and I could see he was trembling. I looked him straight in the eye as I held his arm.

'What the fuck was all that about?'

'You don't need to know, Shea. He's dead now. Just keep whatever memories you have.'

'Come on, Orwell, that's patronizing.'

'It isn't, Shea, it's for your own good.'

'I think you'll find I know more than you think about Dad.'

'Shea, you're not going to get it out of me that way.'

'No, I'm serious. I've been going through his diaries. Is this all about Hazel?'

'Who's Hazel?'

'The woman he was having an affair with.'

'This isn't about a dalliance.'

'Well, what is it then?' raising my voice.

130

'Look, Shea, if you're doing some snooping around, I'd concentrate on Nottingham. That's all I'm going to say. And if you do find out, let it be on your own head.'

'Where did you find out all this stuff?'

'I work in the media, Shea. People talk. That's all those people do. I have to go.'

'Where are you going?'

'I'm going to try and rectify our good name.'

'Listen, Orwell, I think you should get in touch with Rebecca.'

'That's over. She's better off without me.'

'But there've been complications.'

'What complications?'

'It's really not my place.'

'Look, Shea, I know you're trying to patch things up but it isn't going to happen.'

'She needs you.'

'She doesn't.'

'Orwell, your baby's dead.'

There wasn't a hint of emotion in his eyes and all he said was 'Shit happens.'

'I've got a picture on me, if you want to see her.'

'No, I don't want to see it. I've really got to go.'

'Orwell, promise me you'll keep in touch.'

'We'll see.' And he vanished.

I wasn't sure I'd ever see him again. A sneeze came out of nowhere, as if the words Orwell had spoken were viral. I went back to the hall, my body now seemed immune to all that was being thrown at it. Mentally I'd gone beyond the pain threshold. The participants in the room clearly had not.

The showbiz crowd had gone. Hazel was still there, talking to a couple I did not know. Mum was busying herself offering finger-food. I took her aside. It was then I noticed she was wearing the same perfume as Hazel. This caused three quick sneezes, which meant I didn't have time to think about it.

'Mum, what was all that about?'

'I've no idea, son.'

'Mum, come on, stop fucking me about, I want some answers.'

She sighed and simply replied, 'That's where we differ, Shea. I don't want any more answers.'

'What about his will? Who was the other beneficiary, Robert Townsend? What do you know about him?'

'Again, son, I'm not being flippant but me and your father shared a life together. We weren't joined at the hip. We had our separate ways. That was always made clear from the start.'

'Are you not the least bit curious?'

'Yes, of course I am but what good would it do? It won't alter what myself and your father had. Is it not enough to know that your father loved you very dearly?'

'Well, it's obviously not enough for Orwell.'

She touched my shoulder. 'He'll come round. There's something about the Hickson males ... In your early twenties, you all want to take on the world.'

Mother somehow soothed me, but it felt like I was being treated as a child who was frightened of the dark, which didn't help when the only thing I'd been accustomed to was seeing the dark.

'Mum, your perfume, what is it?'

'It was your Dad's favourite.'

I noticed Hazel looking over. I approached her, not wanting the two perfumes to connect, and asked if she wanted to go for a drink: 'We could all do with one.'

She smiled. A low nagging throb at my temple made me aware that my body had taken enough. I thought for a moment that the weather was giving me a migraine but I was sweating with hot flushes, my neck being the meeting point. I took off the light scarf I was wearing and stuffed it into my trouser pocket. Another sneeze had me noticing I had a bit of a cough and aching bones and I only now realized I'd felt like this for a couple of days. I'd been so preoccupied with new information I'd forgotten to take a body check. As myself and Hazel went into the pub, I tried to ignore it further but as I offered to get the beers in, my act of chivalry, I could barely keep my balance. Hazel sat down in a corner and the barman was reluctant to serve me, thinking I was already pissed.

I ordered two hot toddies and a red wine for Hazel. I drank one toddy at the bar and made my way over to Hazel. The toddy did the trick for all of two minutes, then my body went into shivery spasms. Hazel was already a little the worse for wear and was talking like a coke fiend. I couldn't get whatever part of my brain that was still working around this. I just couldn't log on. My occasional nods became a steady rocking. A sharp pain to the right of my head had me clutching at her. Hazel at last noticed everything was not all right. She asked if I was OK – I didn't have the strength to pretend otherwise.

'No, no I'm not.'

Mucus was blocking all orifices.

'I think I'm going down with something.'

'That's no way to talk about a lady.'

Normally a comment like that would have been a kick-start to a wonderful night but I was no longer even there. I spoke in tongues for a while longer. The pub noise, although full-on, had moved to an adjacent room, but noises like coins being put into slot machines were somehow amplified and echoing. The freakiest sensation was in the palm of my left hand, which felt like a nail had been put through it. I became totally out of sync with my surroundings until finally it engulfed me.

I came to with a warm face-cloth on my forehead. I'm not sure if I was able to move but I didn't chance it. I saw strange feet in front of me. They were mine. I was on a sofa with a duvet over me. I was sweating all over and wanted to fall asleep again. In the other room I could hear a gang of cheap hoods arguing. Later I found out it was Hazel playing a Fun Lovin' Criminals CD. Hazel eventually appeared with some chicken soup but I couldn't get it down me. It dawned on me that I was back in her flat. She rubbed my forehead and tried a gentle conversation. I couldn't manage that but still needed the safety of her attendance.

'Do you want me to go?'

I shook my head a fraction and it really hurt. After that I ignored all her questions and closed my eyes and thought of when I was ill as a child. Mum would always get into the bed with me and gently rub her fingers up and down my legs and arms, belly and back. I suppose social workers would deem this odd but I loved it. Our bodies contoured beautifully, we were a life-force jigsaw. In my fever, I reasoned that was to blame for all my other failed relationships. The one brilliant thing about being sick is that you can have the most disturbing thoughts and none of them will bother you. Your body needs all the attention, the head finds it impossible to freak out. Maybe the police, when having to inform the next of kin about the death of their loved one, should give them a severe flu jab first. Oh, and the dreams – totally out there, making you want eternal sleep. The disappointment of consciousness is a major blow. Let me live back there in my dreams. It's weird and wonderful and I fit in. Jesus, I wish I could be sick more often.

Chapter 14

I awoke with my T-shirt sticking to me. I was totally dry. My gums were sticking to my teeth, which had collected a film of scum. I craved water. I tried to sit up. My head thumped with the foreboding of an enthusiastic drummer. I got up and my balance hadn't quite got me banging into furniture but holding on to it for guides. I came to a door and opened it. I couldn't find the light switch. I proceeded to feel my way around the room. I didn't see the bed and my shins were the first to have contact with it as I fell crashing on to Hazel. She was up like a shot to turn on the light. I dread to think of the sight she saw: me in my boxer shorts, head down, gasping for water. She must have known I was no threat, because there was no scream. I was flat out sideways and she had a lot of trouble trying to get me into a proper position. It reminded me of a game we played as children when you pretended you had no strength. This made me smile.

It was then I noticed Hazel was naked and acting uninhibited in my presence. There was something nice about a woman allowing you to share her nakedness. She brought me in a litre bottle of water which I downed in two gulps ignoring the pain it was causing my teeth. She went out and got another two which she put on the side dresser. I was soon nodding off again, the smell of her perfume on the pillow taking me new places. I heard her mutter something about sleeping on the couch. I asked her to stay in that slightly overemphasized way which you do when you're just about to fall asleep.

A ten-minute period of total dehydration left no focus as I sucked from the bottle as if it was Mother Nature's nipple. I fell asleep quickly and woke quickly, changed positions and started again. Sometime near morning I must have snuggled up to Hazel because that's how I awoke. I had her in a bit of a grip. She struggled free and asked about my welfare. I wasn't really sure at that moment. I wished the last couple of months were but a dream and that I was starting my life anew, in bed with Hazel. No history. Just a feeling of well-being and comfort. No future, even; just as is, forever. Hazel knocked my new lifestyle back with 'Do you think you'd be able to get home today?'

I was jolted back into reason, awake and feeling shit. 'Maybe.'

'Oh, you poor thing.' She cuddled up to me again. 'Stay as long as you want.' She started to run her fingers up and down my body and she became my mother. I was elated but somehow thought I was being unfaithful to Mother. I dozed off and was soon playing crazy golf with Bob Dylan.

I awoke as the day was becoming bored with itself. Hungry for the first time in ages, I was down to blocked head, runny nose and tickly cough. Not enough to keep the brain occupied so I sat up in a bad mood again, trying to figure out my dad's life. I wanted to snoop around Hazel's den but resisted. I was beginning to realize that Hazel was a bit-player in Dad's story, just his favoured source of sexual gratification, but I suppose we could all be boxed off like that. I was there for his parental gratification. Every time I coughed it was like a boxer was jabbing hard at the side of my head. So Nottingham held all the answers. Mum was either very forgiving or completely in the dark. Dad did something Orwell found unspeakable to Maurice Edwards, who didn't seem to think it was such a big deal. And then there was Robert Townsend, who now lived in Australia.

Papa Walton's life was never this complicated and they had a drama every week. Could one youthful incident control the rest of your life? Rather than every event being somehow connected, maybe there are major points in our lives that without our knowing act as the big deciding factors. There are times when your instinct totally takes the lead, when you won't listen to common sense. If this is the truth it's an awful shame, as most participants in this late millennium's gut instinct think they are suffering from a mild form of schizophrenia.

Sticking two fingers up at conformity, I popped two Night Nurse in my mouth even though it was still day. I turned on the television and took some of the burden off Ironside's shoulder, egging him on to another moral victory. The actor who played him, Raymond Burr, has beautiful intelligent eyes. His eyes slowly register as he susses out who the killer is. He is so hypnotic and as he closed in, my eyes did too. I slept for three hours. I'm sure

139

as you hit your thirties these naps are to make up for those couple of hours extra in your twenties you spent in clubs chasing glad-ragged drunken dreams. Both states are dreamlike, a couple of hours of pure fantasy. The difference being that with naps you wake up alone and your friends don't come up to you the next day and tell you what an arse you made of yourself in your dream.

The telephone rang and the answer-machine turned on. Hazel's outgoing message voice was slightly more inviting than normal. Some geezer left a message to the effect that he couldn't make dinner tonight. He had been called back to Bangkok at a minute's notice. 'Yeah, probably for his court-case.' Hazel still liked to hang out with the high-flyers. No doubt she would snare one eventually. I've learned to like Hazel recently. She has a lot of genuine love to give. I hope she finds somebody but it's unlikely. Some of us just aren't meant to couple up.

At a certain age, you are out of the picture and you have to rely on your own social circle. All Hazel has now is that preposterous wait for the perfect man to come through her office door. But she's such a pain in that office that she's going to attract the wrong man. It's only a matter of time before she bails out, gives up and decides anybody will do. Me, that's a different story. I have no social circle to speak of so how am I to find my perfect person? I am limited to pizza delivery boys and chancers peddling dodgy gear. I've become used to the idea over time and now it doesn't trouble me. I haven't given up hope because to do so would be to make a mockery of my life thus far. But I guess what keeps me sane is that I don't project too far into the future.

I was lost in bunged-up thought and didn't hear Hazel coming in. Her greeting was a work-weary 'Still here, then.'

Feeling unwelcome, I said, 'I'll be out of your way in a minute.'

She sat beside me. I'd never considered how big her thighs were before. Not fat, just big. She checked my forehead.

'You're looking much better now.'

'Yeah, I know. I'll be going soon.'

'I have to go out tonight, so I wouldn't be able to look after you anyhow. I'm sure you'll be much more comfortable in your own place.'

She was in for a bit of a surprise. I didn't want to tell her outright but figured she should know about the cancellation before she started readying herself.

'There's a message for you.'

She acted like she'd never had a message before and got a little excited. The disappointment registered on her face and she erased the message straight away. The poor thing didn't know where to look. I played ill and sniffled a little. I know from experience that last-minute cancellations leave you feeling more than just alone.

I couldn't help myself. 'Was that your boyfriend?'

She sat beside me again and sighed. 'He had potential.'

'You're too good for him, Hazel.'

She stroked my knee and said nothing. She'd probably been looking forward to this date for weeks and it was another rejection for her to handle.

'I'll tell you what, Hazel. I've got most of my strength back now. Why don't I cook you something?'

'No, don't worry about it.'

'I insist.'

I was feeling better having a task. I stood up, felt a little unsteady and conscious that I was topless.

'Hazel, can I borrow a T-shirt? Mine is still soaked through.'

She was getting into the idea of having company. 'T-shirt? I haven't worn a T-shirt since I was fourteen. Will a blouse do?'

'Why not? I've been toying with cross-dressing since jeans went out of fashion.'

I placed myself in the kitchen, having forgotten momentarily that I'm a crap cook. The mini-rack of wine I spotted first – that was the way to nip Hazel's tastebuds. I opened a bottle of red, handed her a glass and she told me to go through her wardrobe. When I came back she giggled and pointed: we had the same tops on.

Back in the kitchen I opened every drawer and closet. I spotted some scented red candles. I lit them and put them on the table and had a quick gander at her CD collection. A motley selection of soft rock, love ballads and hits from the Eighties, the perfect collection for the non-music fan. The Radiohead CD was the least offensive so on it went. Hazel, playing along, said she was going to have a bath and get relaxed. Was she aware of what was in her kitchen? The candles were the most edible item.

The fridge contained cheese, tomatoes, a clove of garlic, a jar of pesto and some out-of-date salami slices. I was determined to give her three courses. There was a French stick poking out of the bread bin. I heated that and layered the pesto over it as a starter. I'm probably on my own here but every time I get my hands on a french stick, I always want to smash it across somebody's head. There was pasta in one of the cupboards and I knew I could do a reasonable olive oil, garlic and chilli sauce if only I had some chilli. Bingo: there was a jar of crushed, dried ones in the spice cupboard. The deep freeze had ice cream and, for some unknown reason, condoms. It struck me how comfortable I felt in her flat, being part of a couple.

Was it because it wasn't for real, it was my pretend time? Is that how bigamists work it out? They love doing the washing-up with one woman and cuddling up with another. They deal with individual difficulties by knowing they have an escape route. They have different troubles with different women. Surely all divorcees who remarry are simply bigamists with a bad sense of timing.

Hazel reappeared, perfumed of course, and wearing an evening dress which was holding on for dear life. Her earrings almost blinded me and she had her hair up, which gave her a regal quality. Less queen, more queen bee. I served the hot French bread and complimented her dress. She enjoyed this, which made me feel less of a prat for stating it. I tried to ease my way into a conversation after my first bite but the bread burnt the roof of my mouth. This caused discomfort for half an hour and made me want to dive straight into the ice cream. I watched Hazel eat and a lot of crumbs fell down the inside of her dress. My minimal pasta was spot on and did my battle against flu the power of good. As we drank, we quizzed each other on our sex lives. I confessed that I

143

still had feelings towards Rebecca and how upset I was with Orwell's version of history. She suggested I give her one more try. I knew this would be futile and the comment had me eyeing the remains of the French bread and wondering if it would hurt her cheek. She, as I had suspected, had never had a love of her life. But she astounded me with her aside – 'except sometimes I regret maybe the man I left at the altar'. It transpired that she'd had a boyfriend throughout her teenage years and they were supposed to marry at twenty-one, but on the day the compulsion to experience a little more of the world overcame her and she dumped him. She was the talk of the village, to the extent that she had to leave soon after and move to London. She had never been back. No wonder she wants to go off with a high-flyer.

Inevitably, we got on to talk of my father, which was what I wanted. But I also thought it was a pity because we were getting on so well on our own terms. I asked, did Dad ever confide in her? She mused that Terence didn't really confide in anyone, that he had a tendency to bottle everything up and let the odd fact slip while drunk. She told of the time that he broke down in tears for no apparent reason in the middle of the night. The only thing he'd say was he didn't even know why he was crying. But the discovery I took from this was that if he was able to cry in front of her, then surely he must have felt trustful of her company. I wondered, did she really not know anything or was she another in his circle who was trying to protect him? I asked about his Nottingham days but that drew a blank. I eventually came clean and told her about the diaries.

She was flattered that she was coded as the Sun and told me he used to refer to her as his little ray of sunshine. I knew who El Niño was and I pleaded with her for any information about the Wind, the Rain and the Clouds. All she could say was that she also thought all the answers would stem from Nottingham. I couldn't hold it in any longer and admitted that I had pictures of her and Dad. She just looked at me, waiting for me to make the next move. There was no look of surprise, which meant she had been aware of the pictures' existence. I waited for her to speak next.

'What about them?'

'Who took them?'

Rather than give me a straight answer, she wanted to put them in context.

'Your father was doing some filming up in Liverpool one weekend and he asked me to join him. He hated being away from home so I thought I'd keep him company. One night at the hotel bar there was a big media party and we were talked into doing some cocaine. I knew it was stupid, especially at our age, but we sort of got carried away and before we knew it the party was continuing in our suite. The next thing I knew, the men were popping pills which I later found out were Viagra. Soon there were only five of us left in the room and the other couple started making out while the one single person started to take photos. I've got a conservative view on sex and have never even seen a porno flick. But what can I say? I was incredibly turned on and without quite realizing it, we started having sex for the photographer ourselves. We were naive and totally out of it. It was really stupid.'

She was shaking her head at the memory and I was pissed off that Dad's sex life was more eventful than my own. I piped up, 'But who took the photos?'

'It was El Niño, but he said he'd never get them developed.'

'He never kept his word. I found the negatives. Was there a possibility that he was blackmailing Dad?'

'I wouldn't think so. That was his way. El Niño just cares about having a good time. He wouldn't have done anything to hurt your father. He adored the man.'

'Could they have fallen into the wrong hands.'

'Well they obviously did.'

I decided I was going to visit El Niño tomorrow. I was suddenly overcome with tiredness and as a way of shutting the book on Hazel asked her when she last saw Dad.

'It was about six months ago. He called out of the blue very late one night. He was in a right state.'

'What, drunk?'

'No, I don't think he was capable of getting drunk that night. He was deeply troubled and all he would say was that we couldn't do this any more. I didn't pay much attention because he'd said that before. He always went a bit doolally around November. He would start to assess his year and pangs of guilt would start to torment him. So he tried to get rid of any thing or body associated with it. Then he'd ring around February when his resolve had gone. To be honest, we stopped having sex after a while and just became cuddling friends. Of course, looking back at it, that last time, I should've known he was at the end of his tether.' She started to cry. 'But you don't look out for signs like that. Now it's obvious, he was saying goodbye to me.'

The cries turned to sobs and I took her to my chest and thought hard about the last time I'd seen Dad. It would have been September and our occasional visit to the theatre, which always kept chat to a minimum. Orwell was supposed to come with us but flaked out at the last minute. Dad didn't like West End theatre or 'any of that nonsense', as he termed it. We always went to the Old Red Lion in Islington, regardless of what was on. This was a pub theatre with a down-at-heel sixty-seater upstairs. Depending on the piece, it could be very disorientating being that close up to the actors. That night it was a shouty piece but thankfully not too long. Dad enthused about the play, stating that that's what theatre is all about. We always had a beer in the bar afterwards and then an Indian in the restaurant a couple of doors up. Here we would touch on the surface of many subjects, moving on before there was any time to dig deep.

He'd behaved no different to any other time – at these rendezvous we'd sort of given up trying with each other. There was certainly no semblance of another life, which makes me think he was too embarrassed about what he had done to confront me with it. But the Robin Hood book he had left me . . . I didn't buy into the story that Orwell gave me, that he was somehow looking for forgiveness for that shitty Christmas. That might well be a little bit of it but I think he knew I was involved with the organization and with that association came implications which made me to some extent culpable in his death.

I still wasn't thinking straight, the flu draining my resources. I asked Hazel, could I stay the night? She agreed and surprised me by offering to share her bed with me. That was a nice treat as we re-acquainted ourselves with the child/mother position of yesterday. I slept fast and furiously but only for three hours. Waking, I couldn't find my bearings but Hazel's perfume acted as smelling salts and I pressed in nearer for her body heat. I touched her breasts by mistake and she let out a little sigh. I stroked her nipples and felt them getting hard. I started to nibble her ear, breathing hot breath in. She turned and started to kiss me as our legs connected. I knew this was wrong and that's why I went about it with more passion than normal. Keeping the momentum going, I started to suck her nipples while my hand went down to stroke her vagina. She was very wet so I decided to oblige her. I went down head first, hinting at a blow-job. She went about it in manic fashion. I was soon hard and we slipped into the missionary position. She was bigger-framed than me and I wasn't making much of an impression. I took her from behind, hard thrusts. She buried her head in the pillow and moaned. I steadied up the pace holding her cheeks as I fucked her. I let her know I was nearly ready to come. She told me to come inside her, she wasn't able to have children. There was no time for clarification.

I don't know if it was that word, but I was put into a mindset where I was fucking my own mother. This was the nearest thing to it. As I came, she came. I collapsed on to the side of my hell, out of breath and a little scared of where my brain was taking me. You have helped kill your own father and now you have fucked your mother. I was playing frightening games with myself. Oh dear. But you must ponder that moral question. Wouldn't every man like the opportunity to fuck his own mother? Is that what I just did? Did the idea repulse or excite me? Is there a difference? Hazel cuddled up to me. I was wideafuckingwake.

In the morning I learned that I was a pathetic man first and a thinker second as we had sex again. And even then I repeated the exact same moves. Hazel went to work and I went to freshen up. It was ridiculous but I wouldn't use her toothbrush for hygiene reasons, even though some of her pubic hair was still stuck between my teeth.

Chapter 15

The journey home was one of extreme self-loathing. I seemed determined to give myself a hard time. Even the dandruff in my hair wants away. I wondered, was this the point where drunkards have had enough and just give up and become fully paid-up members of the Tennants Super Club? Was this Dad's state, where he couldn't stand himself any longer and quit life? The bus's jittery movements were doing my head in. The other passengers and their tired contentedness were doing my head in. The old ladies with their bags of shopping and pointless gossip; the schoolkids trying to force their personalities on to their peers, the student reading Irvine Welsh's latest drugged-up morality tale; the two office girls flicking through their holiday brochures, picturing themselves on sandy beaches; all of them existing but unaware, none of them hating themselves, even though they probably had plenty of reason. I don't know why I keep thinking like this; I've never done anything really bad. All these people had tiny purposes, they were all going somewhere. Me, I wished a terrorist would hijack the bus, take us somewhere new, but no, this one was going to Finsbury Park.

It was only eleven o'clock and too early to go back to bed.

My flat smelt of old air. Heavy sighs from the last six months meandered round the rooms, looking for an open window to escape into brighter atmospheres. My post consisted of red bills, a free sample of porridge and a letter from Robin Hood. Well, more of a fact sheet, on Sir Mark Rumininger, the proprietor of the *Daily Angel*. Our man went to Cambridge but didn't do too well. His father handed down his newspaper business to him. The family, old-fashioned Conservatives, had fingers in Australian TV, Eastern European radio stations and some regional newspapers in middle America. Our Mark is pretty much hands-off when it comes to the business. He has two children, and his missus is seventy-ninth in line to the throne, which makes him one below the corgis. He has homes in all the major cities in the world, collects art and is trying to buy a football team. I got the distinct impression that Mark doesn't hate himself, but probably employs somebody to do that for him.

Robin had very kindly slipped in a sheet of hearsay information which would never stand up in court. His father allegedly came into his money by insider trading. Of German origin, he did very well out of the two world wars. Mark is a womanizer and his marriage is one of convenience. He has a lot of chums in Parliament who were renowned for doing little favours for him until the rules were tightened up, and they have since all lost their seats. The family is sticking with the Conservatives but is believed to be holding information on one or two Labour MPs in the event that the government bring in any new bills which might hamper the family's business interests. There was certainly enough information there to write a piece for his wholesome newspaper. I was again overcome by a quick succession of sneezes which blew the old negative air back into all the rooms. If it was possible, I'd take my whole flat out for a walk just to air the fucker out or maybe get a bunch of pleasant American tourists to stay for a week.

I spent the rest of the day looking at the text of a novel without having the concentration to read it. The sentences were filtering in and out of my brain. I'd go back, re-read and not take it in again. This started to agitate me; my tired body couldn't fight it any more and I simply gave up. I'd always prided myself on not possessing a television. Three years ago I found myself watching a daytime soap, addicted to the characters. It wasn't a matter of caring for them, but I did want to know what they were getting up to. I knew them better than my own family and I found this a little disturbing. Even more disturbing was the lady from the TV rental shop who couldn't understand why I was giving the television back. She persisted in trying to sell me a bigger set with surround sound. My plan was to read more but when I came back from the bookshop with a handful of classics I'd been promising to read all my life, it dawned on me that I didn't like reading. It was a chore and the sad thing was that the soaps used all the classic plots in a more accessible format. I persevered, kidding myself I was in a rut and that, eventually, the joy of reading would overcome me and I would meet fellow travellers on park benches and we would have profound discussions of great works of literature.

It was also around this time I promised myself I would visit art galleries and museums and catch the occasional play. It was obviously one of those fragile moments when you pretend to yourself that you're a better person than you actually are, to get through a rough time. I went as far as doing all of these cultural exercises but found myself bored senseless, which, in turn, made me feel stupid. I then began to question what it was I actually liked about life and couldn't quite put my finger on it, there being no gun handy. I guess in truth my life really just amounts to moments of spontaneity but they were happening less frequently now. I rarely left the house. I think I missed my soap opera friends. I wanted to know what they'd been up to. In my heart I know that this is my level of culture.

If I could only admit to it rather than persist with this pretence, my life might be more fulfilling. Oh, but no, I was blessed with intelligence and it has been foisted on to me that it is a sin to waste it. To me, intelligence is the ability to know that life is crap and memory is never forgetting it. That's what keeps my brain ticking over. It's like having a permanent hangover without the joy of a night of overindulgence. This is the annoying thing: alcoholics can give up the booze and get their shit together. What is it I have to give up? Thought? There's no meetings for that. If only I could start asking different questions.

I read on and it had the desired effect. I nodded off.

I woke up in a sweat not remembering my dream. I had some toast and on the third bite noticed the bread was slightly mouldy. I finished it regardless, had a cold shower and got ready to meet El Niño. I'd arranged to meet him in a pub in Soho. He'd invited me to his house but I didn't trust him after our first little encounter.

El Niño was fashionably late. I'm sure he did this on purpose, because the second I arrived at his choice of establishment I knew it was a gay pub. It wasn't outwardly gay but the mix of hi-NRG music, slacker service and the fact that the punters eyed everybody who came in were give-aways. I was a little disappointed I didn't warrant a second look. The barman who served me did so with disdain, sussing I wasn't one of his number. There were no seats available and I had to stay at the bar, eavesdropping on the barman and his friend making plans for after closing time. They were bitching about a friend who used other men and I couldn't help but laugh when both of them kept referring to this person as a 'cock-cosy'.

I can never relax when on my own in public. I always admire those punters who cuddled their beer, shutting out the rest of the world, deep in their own pain. I have to keep my body moving, fiddling with beermats, continually gulping because when I have nothing to do my brain puts thoughts into my head which I'm usually not able to cope with. It's not that I dislike my own company, I just don't like it in public places. Right now I felt like an exhibit, there to be looked at and talked about. Taking in my surroundings again, I could see how drably I dressed. Sensible shoes, black trousers with various stains which in this light were magnified, dark grey pullover and black denim jacket, collar frayed and curling inward. I've always worn dark clothes, not as a statement but because I like to mingle in.

When I was sixteen, a personality change swooped upon me and I came out of a middle-range clothes shop with a white suit. In the shop, I'd looked in the full-length mirror and thought, 'Yes, this will do me. This will help me be more outgoing.' On the way home, I carried it with pride in its carefully folded way, building up scenarios in my head for when I would be King Pin of the Saturday Night. Getting home, I went straight to my bedroom, determined to start my new way of living and adopt my new look. I put some records on and with hairbrush in hand, sang along, with the white suit giving credence to my role as lead singer. As I did the more extreme stadium posing, I realized the arms were way too short and the material was starting to itch. I didn't mind because I was fashionable and I was looking good. I took it off with care and put it in my wardrobe and it never came out again.

I still think I got value for money, as it served as a useful reminder to somebody I could never be. I refused to throw it out because it became my bubbly friend who never got invited to discos, functions and all those other occasions one gets dressed up for. As the years wore on and I physically outgrew the suit, it looked like it belonged to that little guy on the TV show *Fantasy Island*. It became my imaginary friend who brought back tales from the society world. After that purchase, I have always stuck to black, at a push plumping for dark red. I have always felt scruffy on the inside so I might as well let it show. I just feel comfortable in shitty clothes. But this also means I can never remain stationary in the Soho area because when I do passers-by tend to give me their spare change.

My arse was pinched and I quickly turned to see El Niño's smiling false teeth. The crow's feet around his eyes made them bigger. He had an arm on my shoulder which I wanted off straight away but he kept it there even as I moved slightly away. I offered to buy him a drink but he insisted that he bought the drinks. He also disregarded my choice of drink and ordered me a Purple Hooter, a vodka-based cocktail. Miraculously a little table appeared to be empty and he motioned me towards it.

'Well, young Mr Hickson, to what do we owe the pleasure?'

I was in no mood for small-talk and blurted out, 'I want to know why my father killed himself.'

A nano-second of thought and his hand was on my shoulder again. 'My dear boy, there can never be an answer to a question like that. He'd simply reached that part of his life. An accumulation of life and thought amounted to that terrible decision Terence made. What can I tell you?' That was a sensible answer but also a cop-out.

'Did my father have an affair with you?'

He was amused. 'An affair? Lord, no. What we had amounted to hanky-panky. He loved your mother. She was the only one he ever loved. He would never do anything to harm her. He lived for her. Look, you're a man. We all have needs. Strong men resist and hate themselves for it. Normal men juggle their morals and learn to live with their misdemeanours.'

'But surely that's the point. Dad couldn't live with them.'

As I said this my tears welled up as if for the first time I could understand my dad's pain. The mess he was in to go through with that solution, throwing away the opportunity to spend any more time with the woman he loved.

'Shea, I'm an old man and I wouldn't say I have learned much but the only wisdom, if I can call it that, is to stop fighting life. Your dad never forgave himself that his way of living was better than his parents'. He was bitter with success, which meant he never enjoyed what he should have cherished, whether it be his wife, his family, his fame, the trappings of his wealth. There's enough bad shit to bring us down – with your father the perks of life brought him down as well. I see a lot of your father in you. It would be an awful shame if you let life destroy you too.'

He read that right and I thought of Orwell, who was going through a severe bout of exhaling Hickson air into the poisoned atmosphere. At least I had no success to battle against. It was time to count my blessings. Where would my head be if I was smelling that sweet, sickly success? I was taken in by El Niño's charm, as I'm sure all those who came into contact with him were. But what did Dad mean in his diaries by 'El Niño will be my undoing'? I looked at him closely. I could see his charm was fragile. He was easily cracked. It was then I also

158

noticed his flamboyant clothes were shabby and he smelt a little of cheap living. The dotted cravat was a throwback to his heyday and all I could see was a broken man full of anecdotes who had died a long time ago. But the pact he had made was allowing him to continue to exist as if as a punishment. I didn't want to bring this to his attention so I asked him where he got his name. He lit up as one who is only interested in oneself does.

'Your father gave it to me. He always said I was trouble. Did you know that weather disasters are twice as frequent during a year of an El Niño event?'

He was pleased with himself. Excusing my ignorance, I asked him what exactly did El Niño mean?

'Oh, the El Niño southern oscillation is a large irregular, unstable ocean system which produces short-term climate changes over the Pacific region.'

'Do you think it's a fair nickname?'

'Well, I don't change the weather but Terence always saw me as danger in a fun way. I am what you would term a bad influence. I used to entice him into situations which he really wanted to get into but was too frightened to do so.'

'Like what?'

'As I told you, hanky-panky.'

'Like with Hazel?'

'Exactly.' Forgetting momentarily who I was. 'How did you know about that?'

'I've seen the photos.'

His whole posture changed. He shrivelled up in defence.

159

'See, like all good Hicksons I've been fighting life, not just accepting my lot. So help me here and tell me what you did with those pictures.'

'I gave them to your father.'

'What about the originals? I have the negatives, which means there's at least one other set out there somewhere.'

He was stifled into silence.

'Come on, El Niño. You said that you adored my father. What did you do with the photos?'

His upper lip was sweating now and he refused to look me in the face. 'I told you, I gave them to your father. Do you want another drink?'

'No I don't. I know you're not telling the truth. I don't want to drink with you and I'll find out what you did with them. Shame on you and the sham your life is. At least Dad had the dignity to bow out but you . . . ah, what's the point?'

I walked out and I must say I hadn't felt that good in a while. There is something about overpowering another man. This is the buzz fighting men must get. I didn't feel any sympathy for El Niño. I felt pride that I was able to do something for my father. I'd never done anything before for him. It was always a take relationship, taking him for granted, knowing I was his responsibility but now I was able to avenge some of the wrong that was done to him. The only niggle snapping at my euphoria was the expression on El Niño's face. I could see the agony but there was also a look of trepidation and I don't think it was strictly for him. It was a forewarning to me.

Chapter 16

I read the diaries once again. More protective towards Dad this time, trying to see it from his point of view. For a moment, I yearned for an afterlife where I could feel his presence, a spiritual connection, an ecclesiastical pat on the head, a small ghostly nod of contentment, but I knew it wasn't going to happen. Reading through the diaries, I could sense his anguish. The idea came that he was a fugitive from an imaginary prison and it was only a matter of time before he got caught or caught up in himself.

September 12th
No sign of the sun today. The clouds and the rain made it impossible to relax and I just wait for the wind to blow me over.

I'd thought all the coded people who had affected him were isolated, but in fact it was starting to look as if they might be connected. Hazel, being the Sun, and El Niño were, so why not the Clouds, the Rain and the Wind? In any given entry, these three combined to agitate his state of mind. Dad had used the code on purpose – he was aware that between them they could cause untold damage. He knew that the climate was changing and that we had all played a small part in making nature angry but the victims of weather disasters were affected randomly. A tornado doesn't go seeking one person out. Why should London's over-use of fridges wipe out a village in South Korea? I let out a little snort of laughter. This could be modern warfare. Saddam Hussein should buy a load of old fridges and aerosol cans and then bide his time; the UN weapons inspectors would easily be fooled. I dozed off on the sofa and woke at around four a.m., cramped.

The lamp that had mellowed the room earlier was now harsh and I knew I wouldn't be able to get back to sleep. The only time I'm frightened for no reason is when I awake in the middle of the night. It's total confirmation that you're out of kilter with the rest of the race. Just you and the bogeyman for company; you can't think straight because your head's in a vice; the tiredness is given free rein and determined to fuck up the rest of your body, toying with your nervous system; your gaggle of niggling worries is transformed into a devouring host. I pray for a companion but know that it would feel alien. I become mistrustful of touch. The soothing image of a mother's gentle rub on my arm is the swab softening the skin for a lethal injection.

My biggest dread is that I will settle down with a woman I love and have responsibility for a couple of children and then one night I will awake before day and have to leave, knowing I've been kidding myself, and become yet another missing person and have to go to that place that exists for us. The suffering of those close to us is superseded by our right to sanity. In this place we meditate late into the night and sleep all day. The unmentionable is never mentioned. We are all born again without worshipping the geezer with the facial hair. It's New Year's Day every day. We forgive ourselves every time until we all get bored sinning. These are the thoughts of the sleepy ones. I stared at the inside of my eyeballs until natural light gave me permission to get up.

I went out for a long walk and watched the newspapers being delivered, single men with big dogs dodging the poor unfortunates heading to the unmentionable place. The early birds were preparing London, making it presentable for the nine-to-fivers. And again I was mis-placed. What was I doing? What part of the equation was I? Strolling by the bottle bank, I wanted to squeeze myself into the hole so I too could be recycled, repackaged, reused. Mothers were soon dropping their kids off at school and they were always me and Rebecca, always just out of arm's reach or harm's way. Clothes were left outside charity shops, from the midnight good-deeders, the bereaved throwing away their memories, the murderers hiding their evidence. Freshly baked bread scented the air and businesswomen straightened their skirts on the walk to the bus stop. Old people bolted for the Post Office; the head-bowed-low masses went about their business, side-stepping me along their way. I was the double-decker bus on the motorway. I pretended to be normal too and had a coffee and a croissant in a café at my own pace. People-watching was my full-time job now and although it's enjoyable I was still waiting for a passer-by to tap me on the shoulder and take me with them.

When I got back to the flat I rang a few old girlfriends in the hope of some company. I got a result with Jenny. I knew her from my music journalism days. We liked similar music but I didn't see this as a reason for a proper relationship. She did. She fell for my lost look and I played this up. It didn't last long and I can't remember what snapped first, the fact that she couldn't change me or my uninterest in her. It was mean of me to give the impression that I was going to give it a go but her total love towards me was hypnotizing. I know how beautiful that love can be. If I was being altruistic, I would say I continued the pretence so that she could enjoy that rare feeling of all-encompassing love, the exploration of body and mind, but I really just enjoyed having sex with her.

In my relationships, there is seldom a bust-up, more a filtering-out, and that way we remain friends. I stopped trying to build on relationships once a pattern was evolving. After a time, the mornings would bring an emotional hangover, a pathetic gathering of thoughts and a constant muttering beside me. I don't know if this is what they mean when they say all men want to marry their mothers, but I couldn't hack it. Most relationships falter over a big decision like having children, rather than being childish. I never loved Jenny so it was wrong to continue but I did love her presence. My problem was, when we were doing nothing she would insist on talking about nothing. This drove me crazy until I plain ignored her. But when we did things, it was magical. Of course, it was a weekend away that drove the nail in. Forty-eight hours together. I'm sorry, I just can't do that.

When I see people living together I bow down to them. Those people you see walking the streets with their heads hanging low are actually bowing down to co-habiting couples. Maybe it's that initial forty-eight-hour period that is the pain threshold, then the rest is a piece of piss. Imagining the old-fashioned way, where the first time you live together is the honeymoon period, a bad head in the morning from the wedding night and your cut-in-half personal space, chills my bones. It's strange that in bed in the morning I don't mind the chat but something happens when I'm vertical that makes it intolerable. Maybe I'd get on better with the race if I was horizontal more. A stranger bores me on the street – Excuse me one moment, I'll answer your questions about the weather the second I lie down. I could levitate my way through life with the personality of Mary Poppins.

I was anxious to see what had become of Jenny. I had heard she had moved on to radio and was courting the bass player in some drab indie band. She was always ambitious and I was slightly disappointed that she wasn't dating at least the guitarist. We arranged to meet at one of our old haunts, the Dublin Castle in Camden.

I arrived promptly and saw a few old hacks I was still on nodding terms with. The pub was packed with the great unwashed. Tattered clothes and expensive haircuts, indie girls doing strange things with eye make-up, a smattering of Japanese kids and four old men refusing to believe that Camden had changed in the last twenty years. A racket was blasting out from the back room where four unsigned bands went for it in the hope that in the audience of forty there might be a big cheese from a record company. This had been my social life for six months a couple of years ago. I got bored of beer in plastic glasses and my hearing's gradual disintegration. There was no sign of Jenny as I opted for my second pint. I always give dates two pints' leeway before I give up on them. I never look at my watch because that is too much of a giveaway for the pools of punters surrounding me that I am being stood up. No matter where I stand in a pub, I'm always in the middle with a sign above my head which flashes 'Loser'.

I drank Fosters to appease my discontent and to relax me. I only had one gulp left, which I saved like a kid waiting on a friend and deciding to count to ten, a ten that could last anything up to half an hour, the blasted waiting game. How much of our lives is wasted on the waiting game? Jenny now owed me forty-five minutes which I knew I would never regain. I hate lateness. I simply don't believe people lose track of time. If they are half an hour late, I reckon they better have a good excuse. An hour better involve a serious injury, and anything more better involve a funeral. I finished my pint, determined to Tipp-Ex Jenny out of my life. The beer went down surprisingly well and I didn't want to go home. With a deep breath, I pretended I didn't need company and went in to see the bands. I waltzed in as if it had always been my intention.

As I opened the door the sweaty air clung to me for dear life. The band on stage were shit. Every song was a similar drone, the singer had no voice or endearing character-istics. But I couldn't take my eye off the drummer, who looked vaguely familiar. I stopped listening and con-centrated my energies on trying to place him. That he was in a band I had seen previously was the most likely answer. But he made my memory itch and it was bugging me as they limped into their last song. Their families and friends at the front demanded an encore as the rest of us herded out. I glanced around the bar, expecting to see Jenny in all her glory and full of apologies, but I guess she'd lost that loving feeling. Used to being on my tod now, I had one more pint. The band came into the bar and I got a closer look at the drummer. Fucking hell! I recognized him all right. He was one of the bastards who mugged me.

My head flipped, the body went on alert. Here he was standing five feet away, smiling with his mates. I didn't know what to do but I was ninety per cent sure it was him, and the other ten per cent was me being scared of him again. I knew I had to confront him regardless of what good it would do. If he said yes it was him, what would I do? Ask for my money back? No, I wanted him to know that he'd ruined a year of my life, to be able to put a name to that person, to find out if they had pur-posely picked on me or it was random. He noticed me staring at him. I stupidly looked away too quickly, giving us no middle ground. I gazed everywhere else but my eyes refused to not look back and, when I did, he was still looking. This was obviously confirmation for him and he started manfully coming towards me. I relived the mugging the nearer he came and wanted there to be a glass partition between us.

'Have you got a problem with me?' His voice was softer than before.

'Yes. Yes, I have.'

This surprised him. At least his stance wasn't aggressive. This gave me a bit of confidence. I stuttered a little.

'Y-you and your mate m-mugged me years ago.'

He inspected me closer. I knew he recognized me, which gave me the jitters. He turned to his mates and then gestured that we go to a quieter corner. When we started to talk, he was a little too near my face for my liking.

'Look, man, I'm really sorry. I was in a bad way back then. I was on the shit, I didn't know what I was doing. I'm really glad I've met you because I felt so bad about it. But you know, it worked out OK for us in the end.'

I thought this last sentiment was incredibly cheeky. 'What, the fact that we're both here tonight, that we both survived? I could get you arrested.'

'I know, man, but I've done that time in my head and my mate Charlie is dead. We'd never mugged anyone before, or since.'

'Is that supposed to make me feel special?' He frowned.

I continued 'Did you follow me or was it random?'

'It was totally random. We were trying to score but our dealer didn't turn up. We thought you were him. And then, in a mad head-rush, we decided to take your money. We actually thought you were a user yourself and that you might be carrying. That's why Charlie was so rough on you. He needed a fix. It was unfortunate, wrong time, wrong place. But as I said, it worked out OK for us.'

'What the fuck are you talking about?'

'The money.'

'What money?'

'The twenty grand.'

It took me a moment to connect. 'That was from you?'

'Yeah.'

'The shame got to you that much?'

'You don't remember what was in the wallet?'

'Twenty quid.'

'And a scratch-card . . . it came up, forty grand. Your address was also in the wallet and, I know, strictly speaking, I owed you forty grand, but I decided to split it with you.'

I was gobsmacked. I'd always assumed Dad gave me that money. The mugger was no doubt a cunt, but what a nice one.

He extended his hand. 'No hard feelings?'

I shook it.

'I tell you what, when the band make that first million, I'll give you that other twenty. OK?'

'Yeah, very funny, mate, I've heard the band.'

He smiled and was off. I felt weightless.

A mystery cleared. I got home cheered for the second night running. I went to the answer-machine to hear what excuse Jenny offered. There were no messages. A moment of quiet indignation quickly distilled into hoping nothing was wrong with her. I rang her number. There was a party going on. I asked for her and the person on the phone shouted her name. Jenny was drunk. I asked what happened and she said a party just developed. I hung up and wondered, was there any virtue in digging up the past? I slept alone, knowing that people just aren't any good.

My dream conscience is a moral fucker. In the land of nod the doorbell rang and a courier asked me to sign for a big box. Inside the box, carefully bubble-wrapped, was a new-born baby. The paper I'd signed was from Ruth the hairdresser giving me full responsibility for our child. I don't like to analyse dreams and I don't like it when they pull out stuff I thought was safely tucked away. You're on the verge of madness, then sleep brings no rest but a set of new problems.

This morning I had one of those 'I've got to get out of the city' moments. The polluted air was destroying me. I've always lived in London and have never pined for the countryside. Any time I have spent there has always been a battle. When one is used to a late-night police siren and its implications, the night creatures' wailings are a far more daunting prospect. The city streetlights' laying of shadow is preferable to pitch black. Squashed-in neighbours' offers of assistance, rather than a scream which is heard by nobody. And yet I still see the countryside as a refuge.

I kid myself that long walks and brisk air are what I want, that mountains are for beauty and streams, relaxation. The birds sing the Top Ten hits, foxes show you a natural order, the food gives you health, people show you the uncomplicated way, the isolation helps clear your head, the stars are your feature film, the valleys are a warning and the forests your amusement arcade. So that's the first five minutes in the countryside, but what the fuck are you supposed to do after that? It bores me. I know I'd end up sitting in a rickety old chair twiddling my numb thumbs with the same shit in my head. The City vs. Countryside debate is a pointless one because neither way works. People thought they could mix it up to find the middle ground and they came up with suburbia. The caged suburbia where city and country folk come to laugh at the strange people who volunteered for an experiment that went badly wrong. Suburbia is the place that took on the misery of the city and the boredom of the countryside, and how were they rewarded for this nightmare? With a pleasant driveway outside their abode.

In short, fuck open spaces. The city offers a place to hide, a place to bleed to death, a place to feel out of place.

Orwell rang out of the blue. He wouldn't tell me where he was or what he was up to. He wanted to express his love for me. He was on the verge of tears and simply said, 'I love you, Shea,' and hung up. Nobody had said that in such a long time and meant it. Mum finished all our conversations with it and because of this it had lost any emphasis. It would be kind of helpful if on occasion she said, 'I'm just about tolerating you at the moment.' Orwell didn't give me the chance to reciprocate his love and his call made me worry that I might never see him again. What prompted this gesture? Did a memory of me fly back at him? Or was he really saying goodbye? Was he about to do something stupid? I loved Orwell with all my feeble strength. If he died, most of me would be dead. Why was I so useless? He was crying for help and I didn't know how to.

Another day in London loomed large. I stared out the window and watched a pigeon fly at will and change direction mid-flight. On impulse, I booked a flight to Melbourne, Australia. It was time to meet the other beneficiary, Robert Townsend. Maybe it wasn't the countryside I was longing for but a different country. I rang Mum to tell her where I was going. She asked, could she use my flat when I was away? Mum was freeing herself from the shackles of her old life and was really going for it. I'd never heard her so fresh and vital.

Chapter 17

At the airport I had second thoughts. The buzz of my fellow passengers was lost on me. Again I was lacking that sense of purpose. I was going to a place I had never been before where I knew nobody. I wasn't keen on being buckled up in a can for twenty-four hours either. The plane was a jumbo and watching the first-class passengers embarking really put me in my place. What was up those stylish stairs? Why were their hostesses prettier? We were left with the plain pleasant ones with plastic smiles dishing out plastic meals. I was placed in a middle seat, a businessman on one side and a young family on the other. I put on my complimentary headphones and listened to bland music rather than conversing. I thought of the criminals who were shipped to Australia as a punishment and wondered whether was I being forced to this destination.

I was trying to make the most of my space, wishing I could numb my legs for the trip. A couple of deep breaths appeased my aura when the fat guy directly in front reclined his seat, leaving me snared and angry. Long-haul flights are like staying at your aunt's: shit conversations, a couple of family entertainment movies and tasteless food; free booze was the redeeming factor, sleep the cure; turbulence is equal to the disagreements. We refuelled at Bangkok, which left us two hours to suck in hot air. I looked out the big windows at the sunshine baking the building. All the airport staff appeared to be carrying guns, including the toilet attendants. My head was fogged up as I zombied about the duty-free shops looking at products you could get anywhere in the world. The second leg of the flight was worse, longer and no chance of surprises.

I strained to look out of the window at the distant thunder and lightning and couldn't have cared less if there was a direct hit. Australia beckoned and what did I know about it? My education was from those soaps I still dearly missed where people with white teeth managed to overcome all their problems in twenty-minute slots. My head was screwed tight as my nose tapped out snot and germs at a worrying rate. My body was refusing to adjust to the time difference, the brain emitting signals that this was the longest day ever. Eventually I was at passport control and there wasn't enough room on the form for my 'Purpose of Visit'. I just put 'Holiday' rather than having the guy go, 'So, your old man killed himself, and he gave some money to someone here and you wanted to find out why. Haven't you heard of the telephone?'

'Yes, but London is getting me down because my brother's gone insane, I've got a hairdresser pregnant and the culture deems pop groups as role models.'

It was a relief to breathe in some proper air. It was six a.m. there and everyone did have white teeth and no worries. I decided to treat myself to a taxi and a fancy hotel, from which I could search for a bed and breakfast, which was more suited to my temperament and bank balance. The taxi driver helped me with my bags and asked me, 'Where to?'

'The hotel district, please.'

This amused the driver. 'What, the place where all the hotels live?'

'Just the centre of town. If we see a hotel there, just drop me off.'

'Right, I'll keep my eyes peeled for one.'

I would have enjoyed his banter normally but I was beyond tiredness at this point. The highways were very American but with English names. The speed and the open windows perked me up a little. At last, it felt like an adventure. I even got a thrill as the city came into sight with its futuristic skyscape. The pavements bore a mass of smiling people commuting to work. Melbourne was an intriguing mix of Victorian wooden structures and metal-and-glass towers, of a tram service and Japanese cars. The pace was less frantic than London's as if the bigwigs didn't mind their staff being a little late. These people were just getting on with their lives, proud to have little history to compare itself to. I was surprised by the number of Asian Australians and stunning women. I could see myself not fitting in here very nicely. The cab braked to a halt.

'I've spotted one, mate.'

I stood outside Rothman's Regency Hotel as the electric doors welcomed me in. The concierge took my bags, which I thought was a little presumptuous. The receptionist greeted me with her long brown hair and wholesome bumpy face. Yes, they had a room at the inn. They asked for my credit card as I looked like a convicted criminal. I booked in for two nights. and went straight up to my room and flopped on the bed. Sleep proved elusive so I checked out the facilities. When I say 'checked out' I mean read about them. They had a pool, spa, sauna, solarium and mini-gym. I did a little bit of exercise by opening the mini-bar. I sipped a miniature Bailey's, hoping it might bring sleepiness, I ran the bath and flicked through the TV stations. The fact that the pro-grammes were the same as the ones we got in England was heartening and sad in equal measure.

The bath oozed away all the toxins from the middle of my body, the rest of it not being able to fit into the tub. Melbourne was obviously a shower culture. I put on a pair of shorts and T-shirt. The last time I'd worn shorts was when I was forced to bring Jesus into my life during my first holy communion. Back then I had nice white golf-club legs. Now I have knobbly knees with hair and enough pimples to give kids hours of pleasure playing join the dots. Maybe I should try it myself: it might unravel the code which is the core to my very being. I wasn't embarrassed by my legs because I was a stranger here. And in the confines of my hotel room. But I was even able to walk the streets with no fear of the past creeping up and punching my psyche, and walk the streets I did.

Directly across from the hotel was a theatre with an Andrew Lloyd Webber musical on. Well, they didn't think they'd get away with palming off those soaps, did they? Melbourne didn't have a big centre but lots of outlying epicentres, little oases of civilization amongst the sprawl. There was Fitzroy, full of veggie cafés, colourful clothes shops, New-Agers and lazy revolutionaries. Camden without the tourists and the goths. The other side of the city had St Kilda: Melbourne's beach culture, swimmers and roller-bladers mixing with old Jewish money. A run-down fairground still took centre-stage over the new theatre.

Melbourne didn't rebuild itself area by area but more building by building. Each step would throw you thirty years backwards and forwards. The only constant was the café bars which were all humming with the young folk. Basking in the sun was their full-time job and it seemed to really tire them out. I hunted out the shade and sat in a café, flicking through the free street-press, sipping decaf, waiting for my Caesar salad to join me. I people-watched, not used to such skimpily dressed bodies. To me, the whole population of the city was catwalking before me. It was a thing of beauty to the eye rather than the loins. It didn't bother me that they would have partners equally as beautiful to go home and make love to. I knew I could never be part of this equation and it would have been stupid to try and place myself there. If these pleasurable creatures came from the union of criminals, I suggest we change our own penal system straight away.

The walk in the sun whacked me out and back at the hotel I slept for fourteen hours. In the morning I was feeling relatively normal and decided to concentrate on the area in which Robert Townsend lived: Swanley. It was a fair distance from the centre. On the way there I passed little patches of communal living which wouldn't look out of place in a Western. I found Chamber Street and walked up and down, passing No. 8 a few times, seeing no sign of life. The house was a lovely old-style detached with another nine similar houses alongside it. Melbourne, keeping to its weird asymmetry, had the equivalent of council blocks across the street. After my third trip around the block, I felt I was snooping and if anyone was watching they would know I was casing the joint. On occasions like these you should be able to hire dogs to give the impression you're just ambling along.

I headed back towards the centre and noticed a pub that had vacancies for rooms. It was called the Paradise Motel. It was dirt cheap but when the old man showed me my room, I could tell it wasn't a bargain. The rooms were directly above the pub, a long corridor of one-roomed bedsits. The room contained a single bed, whose previous occupant I tried to clear from my mind, a table with two chairs, in case I wanted to bring a lucky lady back with me for a meal, a portable black-and-white television and a wardrobe, no doubt to hide in. I took the room, knowing this was the standard of living my resources amounted to, and left the old man a hundred-dollar deposit, half hoping he would deny all knowledge of me the next day.

One more night of luxury then. I ordered room service back at the Rothman's, as I still think eating out alone is taboo and I don't do it out of respect for normal diners – no matter what anyone says, it is depressing watching a lone diner. For company during my meal I watched the queues form outside the theatre. There stood Melbourne's society people waiting to see a show that the Western world had gone to in their droves. So why should they be any different? I wanted to shout the ending at them but I was feeling at peace with this race of people. They had gone to a lot of effort dressing for the occasion. I reckoned if you donned a tuxedo you should be guaranteed a good night whether it was one or not. I spent the rest of the night making full use of my hotel room.

I shaved and bathed, using all the toiletries. I wore the white robe around the room and pocketed the toilet roll. Who was I to care if the maid thought I had the runs? I also took all the tea-bags and coffee sachets, every bit of stationery I could find, and the two business magazines. I trouser-pressed every item of clothing I had, put my traveller's cheques in the hotel safe and even flicked through the Bible. I went to bed with the television still on and used every inch of the bed.

Check-out time was twelve o'clock and I walked to my new residence as slowly as possible, stopping at every shop front. As I neared the pub I could clearly see the standard of living drop. When I got there it was about three o'clock and a few out-of-work types were sipping beer and playing pool. The old man was at the counter reading a newspaper, bored with his life. I stood him a beer as a way of getting our relationship off to a good start. As I sat the other side of him drinking mine, he didn't offer a glint of a conversation.

I tried to get the ball rolling. 'Are you busy upstairs?'

'There's a couple of working girls, a dosser and the other two rooms are for drifters like yourself.'

He didn't even bother to look up from his paper, which gave me enough time to contemplate being a drifter for the first time in my life. I quickly finished my beer, crossing him off as a possible soulmate and went up to my room. I had stupidly assumed it would have been tidied but no, this is how it came. A light drizzle tapped on the window as I lay on the bed trying to formulate a plan and ignore the smell from the sheets. I ended up returning to Chamber Street and trying not to look suspicious.

I knew I couldn't just knock on the door and say who I was. If there was only some way of gauging a reaction. It didn't feel right snooping but what else could I do? And anyway, this was preferable to hanging out at the Paradise Motel. After a couple of hours, a man left the house. I had no option but to follow him. I'd never done this before and the only clues on how to go about it came from old black-and-white movies. I pulled down my imaginary trilby. He was a very fast walker, which meant any time he took a corner I would semi-jog towards it. Oh joy of joys when he stopped in a pub. Tonight I would be drinking in the Chesterfield Hotel.

The pub was relatively empty. The man, who I assumed to be Robert, sat at a table with a bunch of cronies. They were playing cards, which was going to make an intrusion difficult. There was a couple of poker machines near their table. I bought a beer and got some change for the machine in the hope of earwigging. Robert was in his fifties. His hair was thinning out but he had a full grey moustache. His eyes were dark brown and the overall picture was of friendliness but someone you didn't mess with. His mates referred to him as Pom Thumb but he didn't have much in the way of banter himself. I'd worked out a daily allowance for myself and the poker machine had already taken a day's worth. I went back to the bar to get more change and listened in again. He was a builder and they were on a big job out at the docks but there was a big dispute on there and the dockers' unions were asking them to down tools in support. Robert, apolitical, just wanted to get on with his work and claim his wages. Most of his mates agreed with him except one who argued for the power of the union.

A loud noise had me concentrating on the machine. Four of a kind had lit up the front and coins were piling out. Everybody looked at me, which was embarrassing, and the men at the table started whooping. In the mayhem, I learned something important when one of his mates turned to him and said, 'Hey, is that your Rob?'

'Nah, he's working at Little Momma's tonight.'

To get a little closer, I offered the table a drink. They graciously accepted a jug of beer and were intrigued by my accent. They all gave their names – the man I'd followed here was actually called Andy. This confused me. I knew he wasn't my man. I asked Andy after a time where he'd got the nickname Pom Thumb. One of the others answered.

''Cos he's married to a Pom and she's got him right under her thumb.' They all laughed, having a stranger share a joke which had now become a ritual for them.

Another one of them wouldn't let up on the fact that Andy's stepson was a ringer for me. It was clear that this Robert was the beneficiary. I said my goodbyes and tried to figure out the whole sorry state.

I hadn't brought Dad's diaries over with me but I did have my notes. The Wind and the Rain were my concerns here. They had disappeared from Dad's life very early on. The Rain dropped out at Nottingham and was never seen in person again. Dad had written letters but never got any reply. The Wind Dad had never met but he evidently longed to. There were lots of entries concerned for his or her welfare. Then I saw what was so blatantly staring me in the face. The Wind was actually his son, my half-brother, Robert Townsend. No wonder he looked like me. And the Rain was Robert's mother. Dad must have had an affair with her at university and got her pregnant and because Dad ran away from his responsibilities, she ran away to a new life. I wondered, had Dad had feelings for her? Had it been a choice between her and my mum? From the diaries there is no feeling of lost love for her. I can only guess what Dad went through but he must have tried so hard to blank it from his ongoing life. Because it's only natural the fondness would have grown over the years; it's so easy to love a memory, especially a fading one. But his son: not a day must have gone by without a hammer-blow reminder. The times he would have looked at me or Orwell and ached. The fucking lottery of life: Sophia's still-birth and my own responsibility towards my unborn baby. Big deal that it was a mistake. That's not fair on the child, and how will I feel in years to come when I know I've let down my own flesh and blood? I must try and work something out. If not to be a good father, at least to be a father. My wholesome thoughts were interrupted by a rap on the door.

I was a little scared and wondered who it could possibly be. A second knock frightened me more. I called out, asking who was there. I heard giggling and a drunken 'It's your welcoming committee.' I opened my door to find my neighbours, the two working girls, standing there with a couple of bottles of wine. One was sexy in a trashy way and the other was barely hiding absolute beauty. I invited them in and once they heard the English accent they started to flirt in a patronizing way. The news that British males are sexually hung up had obviously travelled. I had never been with prostitutes before and I didn't know how to approach the situation. They introduced themselves as Gabriella and Bejam and welcomed me to the Paradise Motel. They said the name of the place like it was magical. Bejam, the obvious one, opened one of the bottles. They were both dressed in jeans and sweaters and explained that Tuesday was their day off because the punters weren't horny on a Tuesday.

Getting into the spirit, I offered, 'I would have thought Monday night would be your quietest.'

Bejam was straight in. 'Think about it, honey. Most of our clients are in sexless marriages or closet homosexuals. They don't get any at the weekend. They're fit to burst by Monday.'

Gabriella added, 'And it's a scientific fact that they

183

come quicker on a Monday. We can usually get a couple more tricks in. So we celebrate on a Tuesday.'

Bejam enquired, 'What do you do for a living yourself, Seamus?'

'It's Shea and I dig up corpses.' I replied, deadpan.

In unison, 'That's gross.'

Then Gabriella flirted, 'You must have strong arms, though.' She tested them and was satisfied there was little strength there. 'Because we're all in this together, you know, we're neighbours. Who should be for one another, that's when neighbours become good friends.' They laughed and only then did I twig it was the *Neighbours* theme-tune. Gabriella continued, 'If you hear one of us is in trouble,' putting her arm around me, 'you'll come to our rescue with your shovel-lifting arms.'

Playing along, I said, 'Yeah, I'll be glad to.'

Bejam patted my head and said, 'Good boy.'

This was comical, as they couldn't have been more than twenty-two each.

'Have you not got a pimp?'

They giggled again. 'Yeah, Huggy Bear does the rounds every hour. He clocks us in and out.'

Bejam found this hysterical but Gabriella put me straight. 'This is a small operation. We're trying to put some money behind us so we can go travelling. We're not in this for the long haul.'

Bejam took over. 'We want to see Europe and maybe marry a priest.' She burst out laughing again. 'Oh my God, did I say priest? I meant prince. What must you think?'

We chatted into the night, me asking most of the questions. I knew we were running out of steam when

184

Gabriella asked what my star sign was. Until that moment, I had completely forgotten that my birthday was in two days' time. I waited until I was fairly drunk before I asked them, would they ever be able to enjoy sex again?

Bejam got defensive. 'Of course we will. It's about separating the head from the heart. This is a money-making venture.'

Gabriella turned the conversation round to me. 'Do you enjoy sex, Shea?'

'I suppose I do.'

She continued, ' You see, the men we encounter don't. It's just a release which they hate themselves for and they pay good money for the privilege.'

Bejam, who was beginning to annoy me, joined in, 'So who's the fool there?'

Gabriella gave me proper eye contact for the first time all night. 'The point is, Shea, we don't make love to these men, we have sex with them. That's worlds apart.'

'Yeah, but Gabriella, next time you want to make love, will you able to without the constant reminder of all those sexual encounters?'

'I don't know. I guess that's the price we pay.'

Bejam was drifting off and lay on my bed. I continued to talk with Gabriella.

'But do you not think that's a heavy price to pay?'

'I don't know.'

There was a long silence. I have a deep love for people who pepper their chat with 'don't knows'. This is always preferable to others who continue to spout their strung-together sentiments so they can have an opinion. It's not right to have a point of view on everything.

Gabriella broke the silence. 'Shea, the sad thing is I don't think I am capable or ever was capable of making love. I lost my virginity to a sweet boy when I was sixteen. We'd been seeing each other for over a year and we wanted it to be special and of course I pretended it was. But I felt nothing. There wasn't a connection. There was nothing. Just a mess. I thought I would want to embrace him for eternity thereafter but I wanted to be on my own, alone with my disappointment, my own inadequacy and for him it was special and that made me feel worse and he couldn't understand why I was pushing him away. Shea, do you think maybe he wasn't the special one and that one day I will meet the right one and I'll have those feelings of love?'

I caressed Gabriella's neck and wished I could tell her what she wanted to hear, but my silence answered her question. I thought of my own experiences. I'd assumed I'd had those feelings with Rebecca but the very fact that she hadn't meant that they were meaningless. Since then I'd tried but it was nearly always the case that where my penis went, my head refused to follow. Yet here I was with a woman who I hardly knew but I already had feelings for. There was a connection but I didn't feel the need to consummate it. Was this the nearest I could come to real love now? We fell asleep in each other's arms. The Paradise Motel was living up to its magical name.

Chapter 18

I awoke with all my clothes on, alone and cold, wondering for a moment, was last night's visit a dream? But somebody must have taken off my shoes and there were two empty bottles on the table. I wanted to have breakfast with Gabriella. I figured we had much in common but I'm sure she also had a sore head and had forgotten our chat. It wasn't how I'd imagined a conversation with a prostitute to be and the last thing I'd have expected was her to put me straight on sex, even to a degree put me off it. The thought of all the times I'd had sex with a woman who meant nothing to me was reproachful. Even if it's a given that that's what the deal is, two consenting adults agreeing to have bad sex, it's still not right. Ever since Dad's death, it's as if a cleaning process has come into effect where I want to do the right thing, running parallel to finding out more and more shit about my father. Mind you, it was hard to feel clean in this place when the shower area was so utterly horrible. The girls told me the punters sometimes used them before they went home. I braced myself with my little bag of stolen hotel toiletries for the trip down the corridor.

I noticed for the first time that the carpet was shitty brown and became shittier the nearer I came to the toilet. Tonight I was going to check out this Little Momma's place to see if I could get a glimpse of my *doppelgänger*. I had a healthy appetite this morning but wanted company. There were a few other doors in the corridor. I knocked on the first two and there was no answer. I was yet to come across the bloke the old man described as 'the dosser'. When I knocked on the next one, Bejam opened it sheepishly and bluntly asked what I wanted. I told her I was looking for Gabriella. She told me to leave her alone, that it would do her no good to fuck with her head. This must have been what she meant last night about separating the head from the heart. I bowed to her better judgement but knew that Gabriella was from better stock.

Gabriella had an aura which so few people had, an ability to get on with what she was given and make the most of it. If love is about wanting to get to know someone, I was falling for her. This is all love can really be, that glorious beginning. I might as well enjoy it, because if experience had taught me anything, it was that we were already past our peak.

The sun was out in force again and I had a dance in my step. And even in this down-at-heel suburb the people swept past me as if framed in a perfect picture. It was on days like these that the great waltz occurred. Where you picked a stranger and danced into their lives. You danced together until you saw fit to stop and then you simply

188

danced into somebody else's life. It was basically real life speeded up, leaving no room for wretched emotions. Maybe that's why I've always hated musicals, because I've secretly always wanted to be in one. Obviously, one without the crap songs and dances but one with that impish energy. On impulse I bought a disposable camera or, as the display stated, 'fun camera'. I spent the day pretending to take pictures of monuments but secretly focusing on people who tickled my fancy. I was casting the bit-players in my movie. I walked all morning with a sense of purpose which didn't really exist, feeling right for the first time in ages. A spring of goodwill I couldn't tap into normally was surging out of me, a grin was tattooed on to my face, using muscles I never knew I had. Before long, I had no idea where I was and stopped off in a pub for a beer and a sandwich.

The only other customers there were two businessmen and a grizzly middle-aged man who had the most beautiful dog I had ever seen. She was some sort of pit-bull. All her emotion was in her eyes and her eyes alluded to far weightier concerns than protecting her master. It was as if she resented the aggression which occasionally she had to revert to. The man had his head stuck in a paperback but she kept darting looks at him to see if he was OK. I couldn't resist and took a snap of her. I gave her a moment to pose as I framed my photo. Before I knew it, the camera was out of my hands and I was shoved to the floor. Grizzly was all over me, blaming me for all his failings while using the excuse that Shelly didn't like to have her picture taken. I didn't get up immediately, feeling a mixture of humiliation, fear and need for revenge. The bar-girl talked him into giving me the camera back. If Orwell had been with me he would have flattened him. I wanted to know what pain his beard was hiding. The dog didn't budge during these shenanigans, probably used to such flare-ups by now. My nerve-endings were raw and adrenalin was coursing through my body but I didn't feel like leaving. I wasn't standing my ground as he was already back into his book, fantasizing about being someone else.

In the corner, they had a couple of motorbike games, the ones where you sat on the make-believe bike, the computer screen simulating a racing track. All the excitement without any of the danger. I lost myself on the machine for an hour until I became half-decent at it. When I finished, I expected the crowd to give me champagne and flowers but there was nobody there to celebrate my victories. I walked back to the Paradise Motel, wondering if all my victories would be celebrated alone.

I thought of Rebecca. She still wouldn't budge from my head. But I thought of sharing my life with her and then wondered who would want to live with my thoughts. They're OK to visit once in a while but nobody should be expected to live with them. I often wonder, do people have similar thoughts to me but somehow manage to escape them? Is everybody on the verge of tears, just waiting for a trauma to put them to use? It was getting dark as I got back to the Paradise. The second 'A' was missing from the name as if out of respect for my encounter. I lay on the bed, coaxing a little nap upon me, which turned into deep sleep. I can remember thinking it was exceptionally relaxing and woke to find I had wet myself. My visit to Little Momma's was put off as I went in search of a late-night launderette. The big fear was whether those ancient sheets could withstand another wash. They looked like they were ready to evaporate. I asked the old man for directions and his name. It was Regan.

In the launderette, I sat with two old Greek women, watching the dirt fly off our garments. I love the smell of clean clothes, that added fragrance given to it by the hot air. As the two women chatted and giggled in Greek, I was soothed and became hypnotized by the spinning, wondering where the dirt was going. If the machine had been a little bigger, I'd have been tempted to get in myself. Back at my bachelor pad, I could hear Bejam fucking a customer. He made no noise as she played her part. My timing was pretty shit – as I walked past Gabriella's room she was seeing a customer out. I tried to give her a friendly nod but she looked straight through me. Her eyes were heavily made-up, hiding her beauty further, and her clothes were overtly suggestive but I suppose handy for her occupation. What I wasn't expecting was the heavy waft of perfume. The same as Mum's and Hazel's. I was beginning to wonder whether the manufacturer was fucking with my head.

It was a restless night punctuated by the grunting coming from the other rooms and the revelry from downstairs. Both were noisy but you could tell there was no fun being had. People go to the pub as they would the emergency ward, searching for something to ease the pain. From my lofty position above them, I wasn't looking down on them but I knew that booze wouldn't work for me. I can never casually get drunk. My metabolism tends to miss out the fun factor, going from pleasant to can't stand up. There is never a body warning that I'm over my limit. I could really have done with a pint just now but I'd missed the start of the show and there could be no catching up. Again, typical of me being out of sync with everybody else. Apparently I was a late birth and I've never caught up with the rest.

My initial fascination with Australia was waning as it became clear that Western society was grabbing hold of everybody else's culture and replacing it with their neon lights. We are all buying into the media lifestyle, living in half-hour soundbite society. Newspapers tell us what to think, the magazines what to aspire to, the radio what to listen to, television reminds us of our stupidity and pubs give us somewhere to blank it all out. As I battled for sleep, I realized that we are manipulated from day one. If only the education system would let us start with a blank page rather than a full one which we are supposed to memorize. I think things would be different. The bar below was now swinging from joy to frustration as the drinkers realized that the medicine wasn't working and the morning would bring them back to square one, that they would start another game of hopscotch with a sore head. Glasses were broken by some and cleared by others and this was deemed civilized. Next door the girls were banging away, their waste-paper baskets brimming with condoms filled with sperm but soiled with regret.

And here I lay, the result of a winning union, celebrating alone again, looking for a meaning which wasn't there, wishing wishes would come true, dreaming about having nice dreams, refusing to pretend that everything was going to be all right. The heart pleaded with the brain to stop this nonsense but they had entered a pact, both fucking up each other at every turn like childish infants, not minding missing out as long as the other missed out too. I eventually went into a half-sleep, my ears distorting sounds, orchestrating them into a pleasing rhythm which I could get my head down to. It occurred to me just before I fell into the dark that the overall effect was a plea for approval.

Chapter 19

Happy Birthday, Shea. I'd survived another day, another year. The sun was blistering, streaming through my window, showing me the quarter-inch of dirt which was filtering my view. The fresh sheets were a welcoming smell and I felt OK. Being here alone there was no pressure to have a good birthday, no disappointment with gifts or wan thank you's to those wishing me a happy one. I decided to treat myself to presents today. Fuck the budget. Today I was reaching out to myself. I tip-toed past the girls' rooms into proper daylight. A clear cobalt sky hinted at infinity, leaving me slightly unbalanced, but a light wind offered assistance. A café beckoned me with its shaded seating out front, a waitress blossomed before me with a menu. She had a pretty teen-age face, spots probably being her biggest concern. The local newspaper, the *Age*, was left on the table. I ordered an omelette and read the paper. There was very little in the way of news and they filled the pages with features on fashion and a profile of Kenny Rogers. Through boredom I read it. The only information I gleaned from the feature was that Kenny was delighted to be back in

Melbourne as it was one of his favourite cities. Why do celebrities lie about such things? Is there a moron reading the article thinking, I'm not mad about Kenny but he's mad about us. We should show him some respect and return the compliment by paying sixty dollars to see him go through his repertoire. After my omelette I thought I might as well try and chance my arm.

'Excuse me, miss. The Melbourne omelette is one of my favourites.'

'Why thank you, sir, have it on us.'

I caught a tram into the city. They were like commuter dodgem cars, the electrics sparking every time they came to a halt. More by luck than judgement I came across Little Momma's. It was a restaurant-cum-cabaret. By the look of its advertising pictures, the cabaret acts were old-time crooners who still favoured the tuxedo. Everyone looks smart in a tux. I'd worn one only once at a friend of the family's wedding. It was a loose fit and I was mistaken for a waiter all night. I guess my glum face gave me an air of authority but I didn't mind and I did OK with tips. According to the poster, tonight's cabaret was booked for a private function. I poked my head round the door. A tall Momma asked me what I wanted. I booked a table in the restaurant for that evening, saying it was for two, to avoid the embarrassment. I decided later on I would put it down to a no-show.

Back in the sun it was time for some serious shopping. What to buy for someone who wasn't into materials? In new towns, you assume there are going to be new and exciting shops but there never are. I came across the usual mix of shoe shops and hairdressers. The little markets were full of knick-knack stalls but once you've been to one market you know that all they sell is over-priced crap. The only people who are fooled into a purchase are the kind who want to impress friends with things they don't have. Who was I trying to impress? I thought of getting something for Gabriella and Bejam, but what? A 'Honk If You're Horny' sticker? I could get a big 'A' for old man Regan's sign, or an alarm clock for the dosser who has never got up. A whole day of window shopping tired me and I was eventually laden down with imaginary gifts to give to my imaginary friends. I ended up buying a bunch of thirty-one flowers to freshen up my room.

I couldn't find anywhere to put them so I laid them separately round the room. They gave the room a lived-in look. Well it did if you were a florist with a nervous disorder. The effect was very satisfying, as if a colorful carpet had been laid before me. I was lost in my new career as interior designer when somebody knocked at the door. It was Gabriella in civvies and she had her civvies personality on. She made no reference to last night's meet and her face was heavy.

'What's the matter?'

She sat down on the bed. 'I'm a little under the weather.' She sniffed in air and sounded bunged up. 'I've got some infection.'

'Shouldn't you see a doctor?'

'Nah, it's one of the drawbacks of the trade.'

I wasn't fully following her and this must have shown on my face.

'My tools sometimes need to be rested up.'

She had lost me and I stared at her until she bluntly said, 'My cunt's sore.'

Can't wait to bring this one home to meet Mum, I thought, but I chose to say, 'Right.'

There was a silence.

'So why the flowers, Shea?'

'It's my birthday.'

'Why didn't you say so? Who sent them to you?'

'I bought them for myself, didn't I.'

'What a smart idea. Nobody ever buys flowers for themselves. They really brighten up the room. Mind you, if someone was to guess which room the prostitutes live in, you'd win hands down.'

'Are they a bit too much?'

'No, not at all. What's your plan for the rest of the day?'

'Nothing special, a bite to eat.'

'Lie on the bed.'

'What?'

'Take off your clothes, keep your undies on and lie on your stomach.'

'No, no, you're all right, I'm not into clinical . . .'

'I'm going to give you a body massage. I'm half-way through a course.'

'Are you sure?'

'Yeah. I know enough not to do you any serious damage.'

She went to get some oils while I took off my kit. hoping my body didn't smell too bad. She came back wearing what amounted to a see-through nightie. She saw me eyeing her up.

198

'More fluid movement' as she did a little dance. She was soon straddling my lower back without putting her full weight on me. I'd had a few massages in my time but this was a new approach. She started with the back of my head and kept complaining that I wasn't totally relaxed. She moved down to my shoulders and rubbed them as if she was having trouble finding them. It hurt a little but I didn't say anything. She went for a few karate chops on my back before she eased into a much more tender touch. This put me into a state of warm relaxation and there was no more talk until she asked me to turn over. This was when she tried to make my arms twice their normal size. My limbs were barely hanging on to their sockets as the brain registered fear of amputation. Then relaxation again, until I felt fingers on my genitals. She sensed me tense up.

'They're very full. Do you want me to lessen their load?'

I'd never heard it put that way before. She moved to the base of my penis, which was obeying her command. Her hand was still oily and it slid up and down very easily but it didn't feel right. My brain didn't have long to come up with an answer.

'Only under one condition,' I said.

'Oh yeah?'

'You let me take you out for dinner tonight.'

'Deal.'

She started rubbing my penis against her belly and her facial expressions went into work mode. Not at any point did I expect penetration. I was too chilled to want to move position. She slid down and put me between her tits. They were small but her nipples were erect. I wanted to tweak them but resisted. I came on her chest and she rubbed it over her stomach.

Not knowing what else to say I blurted out, 'Thanks for the present.'

She was studying my semen. 'You know, you'd be surprised how little of this I actually touch. It feels nice on my belly. I thought it would be stickier.'

'No, no, the sticky stuff comes out on a Wednesday.'

We continued in this vein for a while as if it was the most natural thing in the world. It didn't feel like sex. It was the nicest present I'd ever been given. She gave me a peck on the cheek and I told her I'd pick her up at eight. I was definitely falling for her.

I knew this because I hadn't thought of Dad for so long. I was beginning to understand happiness and how people prioritize their lives. Trouble-makers are the ones with nothing going on in their lives. It seems so simple, but the complication comes with the fact that this happiness is dependent on other people. This leaves you with no control, knowing that everything can be taken from you at a moment's notice. But then again, aren't all lonely people either waiting in anticipation of this person coming along or getting over the break-up of that relationship? Aren't all other emotions a pure smokescreen? Without that smoke-screen wouldn't we still be sitting in caves picking nits out of each other's hair? Mistrust of the human race had brought about medical breakthroughs and catalogue shopping. As ever, I was jumping the gun, trying to box off love. Starting a relationship with the impulse of a teenager but the cynicism of a war veteran.

I looked in my wardrobe and none of my clothes were worthy of a date. They were all bought with lying on a couch in mind: saggy pants, floppy jumpers, and faded freebie T-shirts from my music journalism days. They were handy for pre-sex banter: 'Do you like Nirvana?' My clothes suited the wardrobe more than me. I looked at my watch: it was 4.15. I decided to go out and buy some new clobber.

I headed for another sleepy shopping centre. There was hardly a soul in sight. 'Gios' caught my eye. There were two assistants behind the counter who thankfully were not too nonplussed by my presence. In London, hundred-metre runners do their formal training in clothes shops. There was a black suit in the sale section. I asked to try it on. It didn't quite fit. The trousers were a tad too small, but who was going to be looking at my feet anyhow? The funky music with its heavy beat was doing my head in a little so I grabbed a black shirt and bought the lot, much to the annoyance of the male assistant, who kept telling me purple was in. It set me back two hundred and fifty dollars, which I guess made it a cheap suit. The assistant was perplexed when I said I wanted to wear the outfit home. He turned his nose up and moved his head to the side as he neatly folded my old clothes and put them in the bag. I strode out of the shop feeling good about myself, even though the shirt collar was a little tight and, because of my lack of shoulder activity, the jacket looked like an old Napoleonic war uniform.

Back at the Paradise I sat on my bed and watched the pants ride up past my socks. I don't know who the suit was made to fit but it appeared to be a stocky short-arsed bloke. I catwalked up and down the room, catching glimpses of myself in the mirror. I hadn't realized how big the lapels were. It's always the same when I wear a suit: no matter what the fit is. I am always aware of my nakedness underneath it as if I am masquerading in it and, once caught, I will be stripped and beaten. I took my old clothes out of the bag, took one last look at them and chucked them in the bin. I wanted to lie on the bed but I didn't want to crease my new look. So I sat on the edge and wondered how my date would go.

I knocked on her door at five past eight, not wanting to appear too keen. Bejam opened the door and told me I was looking very priestly. Like I didn't already feel conscious enough of my appearance. She asked me, was it a new jacket? I didn't want Gabriella to know I'd bought it for the date so I lied and said I'd had it for ages. Bejam felt the back of my collar and asked what was the etiquette for leaving the price-tag on in Europe. I went red as the two of them laughed. Bejam handed Gabriella the remains of a spliff and departed with 'I'll leave you two lovebirds to it.'

It annoyed me that I was being spoken about behind my back and that Gabriella felt the need for some herbal assistance for her night out with me. She put the joint out and pecked me on the cheek. She got up out of her chair and I saw she was still wearing her nightie.

She queened, 'What to wear to match my Preacher Man?' and put three outfits on the bed and asked me to pick.

'I'm happy with what I'm wearing thanks,' I joked.

The choice was between a pink PVC dress, a black shift dress and a spaceman's outfit. I looked at her, baffled, nodding towards the full bodysuit and helmet.

'No, you idiot, a punter left that. The dress is underneath it.'

It was a flower-patterned one-piece. I chose this.

'Don't you reckon it's a little virginal, Shea? You're not ashamed of me, are you?' she teased.

'They're just clothes,' I retorted for no apparent reason.

She took off her nightie and dressed in front of me. I'd expected her to be ready at the door so that I would have admired her dress while getting tiny looks at her body during the evening. Now my timing was all thrown off. At least she was being herself. I could see myself already going into date persona. I couldn't help myself but here I was, presentable and polite, my voice aware of its tone. I wished I had her self-assurance or stoned confidence but I guess that is one of the drawbacks of living on one's own for so long. I had no idea what my personality was. She put on some subtle make-up and straightened her dress. She was about to perfume herself when I requested that I'd rather spend the night with her natural smell.

'It's your birthday,' she shrugged.

When she stood up, she was a vision. She only came up to my nose, which of course made me want to be protective of her and I also got to smell her hair all night. She took my hand in hers and they were a good fit. In the corridor she swung our hands and skipped a little and I melted into a seven-year-old. The innocence was blown apart straight away when one of her customers came strolling up the stairs, a balding man in his late fifties, and stood in front of Gabriella, shouting, 'What about our eight-thirty?' He frowned at me.

She let go of my hand, mentioned I was family, and put her arms around fat boy's waist.

'Bejam is doing you tonight.'

He looked upset. 'Bejam! I don't like Bejam. Anyway, I suspect she used to be a boy.'

Gabriella appeased him, 'She's lovely. Anyway, I've taught her a few new tricks.'

He was still having none of it. 'You're my doll. I don't want anybody else.'

I was being ignored and for the first time in my life, I literally felt like a spare prick. Gabriella again pacified him.

'Listen, a week off will make it even more worthwhile. You know the usual, one giant step? Next week, it will be three giant steps for mankind.' She pressed his cheek with her palm.

He smiled. 'You always get your own way.' He knocked her on the arm in friendly fashion, winked and said, 'Houston, OK, we ain't got a problem.' And then, asserting his manhood on noticing me, he pointed his finger. 'Just don't let it happen again.'

I was aware that I was actually jealous. It's not something you can easily control. Gabriella cast off this strange scene with 'Sorry about that. Pay no attention to him. He's a space cadet.' And we laughed. And again we were hand in hand. I don't know if she had an overpowering energy circulating her body but once we were physically touching, all was right.

The taxi into town was a constant big smile from Gabriella and a 'how she hadn't been out for a meal in such a long time'. I was back on track with my romantic delusions when her mobile phone rang. She had another heated discussion with a customer, this time in Italian, and when she was finished she could tell I was feeling hurt. As a grand gesture she turned her phone off. She put her hand on my lap and said, 'Those pricks can get hard inside somebody else tonight.' The taxi driver obviously heard this and shifted a little in his seat.

We arrived at Little Momma's. I paid off the cabby as if it were a normal occurrence. We strolled into the restaurant. It then hit me, the real reason I'd travelled the vast miles. With any luck I would meet Robert Townsend, who I was certain was my half-brother. Somehow it felt right that Gabriella should be with me on this adventure. The waiter brought us to our table. An old-fashioned red-and-white cloth covered our rickety old table. The cutlery was also plain and the candle-waxed bottle took up the middle of the table. Gabriella ordered a bottle of the house red and perused the menu. She read the Italian version – languages were her thing. She boasted fluent Italian and French and a smattering of Spanish. She ordered a seafood platter but I plumped for the chicken. I took what I assumed were quick glances around the room but Gabriella asked if I was looking for somebody. I desperately wanted to tell her the whole wretched tale and knew she would be understanding but I was determined to wait until I met Robert before I dished out any information. I was dying to unburden myself but went back into date mode. I asked her all about herself until the food came, then I kept my head down as I find fish repulsive. It stems from a childhood experience. When eating a fishfinger I swallowed a small bone which stuck in my throat for two days. The discomfort intensified the size of the bone, much like any other fisherman's tale. That put me and the fish kingdom off to a bad start. A summer holiday was also ruined when I was stung by a jellyfish. Another time an eel took a nip at me. It was as if the whole fish population has sent out a circular of my face with 'Wanted' stamped across it. The movie *Jaws* gave me nightmares. I felt no sympathy for Willy the whale and dolphins' only redeeming quality is that they fed off other fish. I wouldn't mind – I haven't eaten fish since the fishfinger incident, but no, they've still got it in for me. I peeked at her platter and I half expected them all to be laughing at me. I don't know how anyone can eat fish. Their eyes are blackly cold and it's a general rule that I don't eat anything that looks evil. I don't go near pine-apples for much the same reason.

We could hear the party next door heating up. A full band was playing standards and Gabriella wanted to go in. I explained it was a private do but I could tell she wouldn't take no for an answer. A bloke selling roses came to our table.

'Happy roses for the happy couple?'

Gabriella waved him away, calling him a parasite. We chatted for another half an hour but there was no spark. We exchanged facts out about each other but it was mainly superficial. She was brought up in a small town sixty miles away from Melbourne and she had one brother. She came to Melbourne to study languages but couldn't get a decent job, which led to her present predicament. Our chat was a disappointment because there would have been more information on her CV. Sensing the conversation was going nowhere, I tried to divert attention away from us.

'Look at all the other couples around us, eating in silence, nothing to say, staying together because they are used to each other. Is that the best we can hope for?'

I think the enthusiasm of the party next door made all the diners realize that their fun times were quenched and eating out was their high point now. Me, I was happy to gaze into a nice person's eyes, in silence if necessary, but I could tell she wanted more. I did that stupid thing and asked if everything was all right. That's up there with 'What are you thinking?' and bear-hugging when drunk for encroaching on personal space. But Gabriella was elsewhere.

'Hey, Shea, that couple in the far corner. Do you think they are happy?'

The couple were in their fifties, dressed up, laughing, holding hands across the table, sharing each other's food. I replied that they were the only couple in the room who seemed content with each other, who still had things to say to each other.

'Why would you say that is?'

'I don't know. They might just be having a good night. Maybe they are a new couple. Or probably nearer the mark, she is his mistress.'

'No, they have been married for thirty years.'

'How do you know?'

'Play the game, Shea.'

'I don't know, they are just lucky.'

'Well, it's bugging me, so I'm going to have to ask them.'

She got up without waiting for a reaction from me and gracefully moved to their table. I don't know what she said but the man was dumbfounded. And as I watched her coming back, he stared at her with an open mouth.

'What did you say?'

'What's important is what he said.'

'Well?'

'He said they were in love.'

'There you go, then, it's as simple as that.'

'No, Shea, it's not. That's a lie. The reason they are happy is he has learned to lie and to live with the lies. And sometimes he even forgets them. Tonight he has forgotten them so he is happy and his happiness has rubbed off on to her.'

'He's still looking over. What did you say to him?'

'I said, tonight he should put a bag over his wife's head and pretend he is fucking me.'

'Jesus Christ, why did you say that? We better get out of here before there's a scene.'

'Don't be frightened of scenes. Anyway, there won't be one.'

I was left jittery, waiting for his come-back.

'Shea, relax, he's one of my customers. His particular kink is he makes me put a bag over my head so he can pretend he is fucking his wife.'

I didn't know what to say. The couple got up to leave. I suppose she could have created a bigger scene but she hadn't given the game away. The guy's wife would have her down as a nutter, while he was reminded of his lies. What Gabriella did was actually brave and principled.

I asked for the bill. The waiter said it had been taken care of by the other couple. Gabriella started talking Italian with him. I didn't like the way she kept pointing her finger at me and he kept looking at me. It became heated and the waiter walked away.

'Is there any point in my asking what that was about?'

'Wait until he comes back.'

The waiter appeared three minutes later with two tickets for the cabaret. The only words he uttered were 'Happy Birthday, sir.'

The red plush curtains hinted at a subterranean masque. Inside there were waitresses circling tables. They wore short red skirts, high heels and white shirts. The head waiter escorted us to a table by the side of the stage. The stage was small, with sweaty musicians still playing their eclectic mix of standards. Twenty or so people danced at the front of the stage. They looked like people who very seldom danced and continually bumped into each other. But to be fair, this was more to do with the cramped space. Little did they know that they were part of the cabaret as they gave the seated guests a visual to punctuate their banter with. I expected the booze to be served at a rip-off price and was going to ration myself but I was delighted to find it was a free bar. My experience of free drink is that you have to down your own body-weight or you're not getting value for money. The waitresses, eyes like mating swans, watched for people to take sips of their wine before refilling to the brim. This makes it very difficult to monitor how much you've drunk and in the morning you wonder why your head's dropping off when you only had the one glass of wine.

The goodwill in the room soon had us tapping along to songs I would have turned off if they'd come on the radio. Gabriella wanted to dance. Now my co-ordination is rubbish at the best of times but pissed I was a fire hazard. Gabriella tugged me into the tiny space. She proceeded to move every part of her body in an overtly sexual way. We soon had more room as the others paved the way for the dancing queen. She wormed around and I was dizzy following her. I can't dance myself, I just try to copy my partner so that in my head I'm dancing just as well but really I'm four seconds behind everybody else. While I thought I was shaking my booty I was in actual fact doing robotics. To make up for my short-comings, I tend to sing along with the lyrics and sometimes, unknown to me, I hold up an imaginary microphone. Soon Gabriella was away on her own, treating whoever came into her patch to a little whoopie whoopie. I slowly edged back to my seat, content to watch her and the delight she was giving. After a time, even the band were focusing on her and eventually invited her up on the stage, where she displayed her talent in a proper context. She moved as though she was being subjected to a series of electric shocks.

The band-leader announced that they were going to have a little breather and asked us not to forget what we were celebrating tonight, the birthday boy. There were big cheers as they asked the host to come up and sing a song. The band-leader sang 'Happy Birthday' to Robert Townsend as a young man was applauded on to the platform. The leader asked him what age he was. Robert, obviously embarrassed, said he was thirty-one today. It was then I had a closer look at him and fucking hell, it could easily have been me. The shock to my system made my surrounds fade into the distance and I quickly sobered up. What was going on? I kind of knew he was my half-brother but to look the spit of me and to share the exact same birthday made me question my own sanity. When I came to my senses, he was singing 'My Way' and dancing with Gabriella. It was like watching myself. I was mesmerized and frightened. The two give-aways that we were different people were the big smile on his face and the fact that he could dance. Well, that and the very notion that a lot of people were in the room celebrating his life. He kissed Gabriella and I then watched him go back to his seat.

There beckoning him were stepdad Andy and a petite lady who, no doubt, was his mother. I was shaking with excitement as if I was adopted and was meeting my real mother for the first time. I was aware she wasn't even a relative and the only connection was by association. The three of them were all smiles and Robert also had a pretty girl by his side. They were opening a bottle of champagne when Gabriella reappeared, making me jump. She was a little out of breath and was shouting about Andy looking like me.

'He has your eyes!'

She summed it up well when she said he was what I would have looked like if I'd taken better care of myself.

I didn't know what to do. I wanted to go over, but what sort of a welcome would I get? I was positive Robert would like to meet me, but was anxious that his mother probably wouldn't want to be reminded. Then again, she might have mellowed towards my father over the years and I assumed that Andy would be indifferent towards the whole situation.

I filled Gabriella in on my dilemma with as much information as I felt was needed. As I'd thought she would, she took it all graciously in her stride. She simplified things by saying I couldn't miss out on an opportunity like this. That is what I wanted to hear. I took a big gulp of red, hoping it would provide some courage. Gabriella was wise enough not to say anything and I realized it was now or never. My head kept jerking to go but my body refused to budge; anyone who was watching would have presumed I was doing chicken impressions. The temptation was to stay put, be aware of my half-brother's existence and leave it at that. What would I gain by throwing a spanner in his works? He had got along fine without me up until now. What if we did chat and had nothing in common, which would probably be the case? I was getting a headache from the speed of thought. So we came out of the same sperm pool. Was that enough? And even if we did hit it off, we would be thousands of miles apart. I don't know. If I did nothing, would I regret it for the rest of my life? What was I worried about? Wasn't it all predestined? The decision was already made. Or was it one of those defining moments of choice?

'Gabriella, have you got a coin?'

She gave me one and I flipped it but it didn't help. The band came on again and I decided to reacquaint myself with his stepdad without saying who I was. I got up and Gabriella squeezed my hand. I turned to her and her face was a picture of concern. I kissed her on the lips and her very presence gave me strength. My legs were wobbly and I knew it was going to be some job pretending to play it cool in this state. I tried to get eye contact with Andy but he was engrossed in conversation. I tapped him on the back and he turned and recognized me straight away and gave me a lovely warm welcome, standing up and patting my back. He angled me towards his family.

'This is the fellow I was telling you about, the one I met in the pub. What do you think? He does, doesn't he, Eve?'

I looked at Eve; her face, already white, lost more blood and she didn't utter a word. She knew straight away who I was. We stared at each other and I wanted to embrace her. Of course, now I realized this was the worst possible day to come into her life. Robert's birthday would always have reminded her of Dad and I was a stupid fucking idiot for not taking that into account. Also, something more pressing came into my mind and it was only at that moment that I twigged that Dad would have been fucking the two of them at the same time. I wondered was it the same day. It made me question was I born from love or did he have his mind elsewhere. It would explain a lot of my personality traits (especially my inability to focus on any one thing).

I looked at Robert. Close up we weren't so alike. Certainly similar, but not clones. Dad's decision to stay with Mum had set the course of our lives. There but for the grace of God went I. If he'd gone with Eve, Robert's life would have been similar to mine and I would have been brought up by Mum alone – or maybe not . . . Of course it also explained that time Dad hit me on my birthday and why he'd always had trouble garnering enthusiasm for my birthdays. It must have killed him thinking of Robert every year. I couldn't help myself and burst out crying, floods of tears. They didn't know what to do. Andy sat me down and gave me some water but I was encroaching on their space and had made them all feel uncomfortable. Robert went to dance with his girlfriend. Andy gently patted my back, saying, 'You're probably homesick, you're a long way from home.' Eve said everything by saying nothing. I wanted to hear her speak but it was as if she had been stricken. I drank the water and calmed down. Andy excused himself and headed for the men's room. The second he was gone Eve vented.

'I want you to get out of here. You have no right to be here. This is my family and you stay away from them. You've absolutely no right, now go.'

I wasn't expecting this. I thought it was a bit strong but it left me in no doubt where I stood. Not knowing what else to say, I half-whispered, 'He's dead.'

'I know and I'm glad and don't think we're accepting his guilt money.'

I could see the anger rise in her, or so I thought, and her mouth began to quiver. She was actually gathering phlegm because she spat in my face with 'That's what I think of your father.'

214

I wiped it off on to the cuffs of my jacket but some of it spread on to my hand. I got up and, I guess on behalf of my father, said, 'Sorry.'

Gabriella, who must have been watching the whole scene, was by my side. I said, in short breaths, 'I'm staying at the Paradise Motel. I'll be there for a couple more days. If Robert wants to see me, please tell him.'

'Go,' she shouted. 'GO!' We now had an audience.

'I had no choice in any of this, you know.'

Gabriella chaperoned me out of the room. We walked round the city as I filled her in on the details. I was scared that I might ever hate someone that much.

I thought we were walking along aimlessly but Gabriella stopped outside a nondescript building, took keys from her purse and opened the door. She explained that she sometimes came here when things got too much for her. We walked up an old stone staircase whereupon she opened another door which had hidden a beautiful apartment with views out beyond the sea. Its decor was that of a plush hotel suite without the coldness those places usually hold. She said it belonged to a rich friend. She didn't have to explain anything else. The bedroom boasted the biggest four-poster bed I have ever seen; it could have slept a footy team. A nearby lighthouse brightened a corner every so often. The bathroom had a Jacuzzi and a heart-shaped bath and en suite there was a small steam room. Gabriella poured out two whiskies. I drank knowing there was no way I could get drunk tonight.

We had a bath together and scrubbed each other clean with loofahs. Even though the spit was long gone, I could

215

still feel it on my cheek. Clean, we took a steam together. I'd never had one before and became light-headed with the heat. I persevered with it, as the sweat that was dripping from my body gave me a sense of well-being. I thought of athletes who worked hard enough to get a sweat going and I felt like a cheat. I suggested we had had enough when I started to feel faint. I was always eager to keep moving. But Gabriella had a fantastic stillness about her. We spent the rest of the night lounging about naked; again, something I wasn't used to. But Gabriella made it feel normal. She insisted I eat some fruit to keep my energy up. It was while eating a pear that one of the downpoints of nudity was discovered, with the juice spilling on to my chest hair, leaving its sticky residue to quench my parched skin.

Gabriella and I lay on the bed, a late-night movie on in the background. We talked mainly about my dilemma and how my father's death was affecting me. Her father had died three years previously, a ponderous cancer which gave everybody time to deal with it, bar himself. She said he had let out a few skeletons but nothing of the same magnitude as mine. She was with him when he died and his last words weren't of acceptance. As she spoke, she relived his last moments and said that her father's last words were 'I don't want to die' and he was gone. He had held her hand tight and as he passed away his grip didn't loosen and she had to prise it off. This talk of death made us cuddle closer, not for comfort but necessity. I still wanted advice as to whether I should carry on my search of Dad's past. Gabriella reckoned I had no choice, that I was being carried by the tide of events and I wouldn't be able to stop until some sort of resolution. I wanted to know if this was the end, if the sum total of his secret life was my half-brother. She told me I'd know when it was the end. I didn't feel I was quite there yet. Without warning she started to stroke my balls. I flinched slightly.

She told me to relax, as it was all part of her tension-free night. She appeared to be enjoying herself but it must have been a busman's holiday for her. Maybe she got off on her own mastery. She started to lick my balls and base of my penis, then painstakingly worked her way to the top. This caused more tension than was needed but it was worth it when she took me full in her mouth. She could sense me fidgeting to get free as I came but she stayed in position and held one finger up, telling me to wait. And then the most amazing thing happened as she got me hard again and, with an even tighter suck, I came again. What most impressed me was that her breathing had remained even throughout. The oddest thing was that it didn't feel like a sexual act. I know that sounds ridiculous but it was more one friend giving the other enjoyment. It helped that Gabriella had no sexual hang-ups and, although what we did was wonderful, it didn't mean we owed each other anything. Gabriella was the first person I'd been comfortable with since my brother. I could tell her anything and know it was OK. We were happy with our silences and, even though I wasn't being what I consider my truthful self, with her I was a better person. It was beginning to be that when I wasn't with her, I wasn't being myself. This I guess is what love is and it was a new one on me. Even with Rebecca I had been kidding myself and I was suddenly saddened at this thought. But so many people who think they are in love aren't. We slept skin to skin, the lighthouse's beam keeping time and giving an atmosphere. I awoke in the morning alone. I worried for a second whether she was downsizing our relationship.

Chapter 20

A light drizzle made the journey across town a merely functional operation. I was hoping to use the fresh air as an incentive for putting a perspective on last night's events. It was only now I was resentful of the spit. I couldn't get it out of my mind. It was a low act and I could only judge it on whether I could ever spit at anyone. I knew I couldn't. I feel bad for the pavement when I spit. I tried to see it from her point of view and I could understand that my presence put her into a frenzy. But what was the spit actually saying, what was it achieving? I'm going to take some fluid from my body and place it on you, mucus and germs, and now the rain was a reminder, thousands of spits targeting my body. I pictured a teenager above the clouds with a control button getting extra points for each direct hit. My fancy clothes, already uncomfortable, were now more misshapen. In London the rain quickens those caught out in its arrival but in Melbourne they were determined to stay at the pace they had grown accustomed to. It was as if I had been speeded up. The cartoon character bombing in and out of people with the agility of a retired ballet dancer.

For the first time, I wanted to get back to London. I missed the London rain. It penetrates better, it means business. And maybe it is poor drainage, but as the muck and the litter drag the feet, puddles amass, giving motorists an opportunity to splash the footsoldiers. Eyes bounce off faces as people buccaneer with their umbrellas, young mothers fight for grid position with their buggies, homeless people have an easier begging day and old women buffet you out of the way with their hunchbacks. But nobody really minds because you're all in it together. You're used to such behaviour from your fellow travellers. It's at this point a cute dog will sidle up to you and shake his wet, dirty fleas over your person and piss on your leg.

There was nothing else for me to do in Melbourne. I had found the Rain and the Wind. The Clouds were the last to be placed. Back home I still had to hook up with Maurice Edwards, Dad's old friend and foe from Nottingham, and get to the bottom of what had gone on between him and Dad, and whether he was the Clouds. That would, as far as I could see, be the end of the journey and it was frightening me that I was coming to an impasse in my life. One more skeleton, one more job for Robin Hood, and then what? Impending fatherhood, a totally uneventful life, darkness, a blank mind, no money. Do I follow in my father's footsteps? Hello, Mum, do you want to get married? My life was becoming a series of shorter breaths. Maybe I could learn yoga and learn to spend the rest of my days in mid-breath, in suspended animation, stuck for eternity in a contemplative state. Frozen in a museum for future generations to stare at.

'Here is a typical post-modern pre-millennial *Homo sapiens* from what we now term the Undecisive Age. The whole race was eliminated because a chemical compound caused by the collective lack of thought imploded. The result: the destruction of a whole race who couldn't care one way or another. Next we have a slide-show of the grimmest last-breath faces of those who believed in heaven.'

I sat in my room back at the Paradise Motel entertaining myself with such scenarios, waiting for someone to knock on my door and kickstart my life once again. I lay down and my brain decelerated from pondering my future to an overriding urge for an avocado. With the impishness of a toddler, I went out and hunted one down. The grocer kept on saying, 'Is that all you want?' Worse was to follow when I strolled into another shop and bought one knife. Back at my pad, I started to peel the thick skin, halving the one piece of food which couldn't decide whether it was a fruit or a vegetable. The fruit world deems it the transvestite of its domain while the vegetables see it as a lightweight embarrassment. I was all for defining this precious provision when I carved away the stone to find the edible part was inedible and as hard as the stone itself. Dad's continual insistence on waste-not-want-not had me playing with the stone for over an hour as I waited for the avocado to soften. Tomorrow I would fly back to England. I would have bought Australian knick-knacks for my loved ones only I didn't have any. Gabriella was but one step away in my thoughts but I kept running from them. I went out and arranged the booking for my flight home the next day.

When I came back, I was heading up the stairs when I heard one of the doors opening. I was hoping it was Gabriella but was annoyed I had been given this leeway to prepare a natural greeting. I took a deep breath and turned into the corridor as if a director had just shouted, 'Action.' There in front of me was the dosser. He was only in his twenties and there wasn't a pick on him. But the most intriguing part about him was that he was wearing my cast-offs. As he passed, he half-grunted at me and I looked back at him: his walk was more of a shuffle, the clothes suited him and I knew I was one step away from his standing in society. This was an eye-opener. All it would take was one night on the tiles, collapsing on the street and then not being bothered to get back up.

The dosser had me preoccupied enough not to see the strange figure lurking at my door. It was Robert. I coughed to warn him of my arrival. He faced me. He had his hair greased back and was smoking a cigarette. We nodded at each other and it did cross my mind that he might turn violent. He was nice enough to placate this fear by apologizing for his mother straight away. I was just about to invite him in when I remembered the pit that was on the other side. My hospitality amounted to offering to share an avocado. I suggested we go for a drink. He agreed. We walked awkwardly, nosing in front of each other like two horses in a photo-finish.

To get the ball rolling, I asked why he'd come to visit. He expressed himself a lot with his hands and from his look it was obvious he was used to hanging out with Italians. His dark-brown eyes hinted at an aggression that wasn't there. Although I was only sneaking looks at

222

him, he was much better-looking than me. He did most of the talking, telling me that seeing me was a shock to his system and that he was just as pissed off as his mother. They never spoke of the past. He was born in England but moved to Australia before he was one and now he didn't see England as anything to do with him. His mother was always looking to the future. We walked on. I followed him and night was already descending. We ended up in a bar which was basically a square room with tables round the sides. It catered for the more discerning drinker and Robert insisted on getting the drinks in. He was on first-name terms with the barman. They did a lot of back-slapping, quick-talking and handshaking. They both had wide smiles, which Robert muted as he walked back to me.

'So, what made you seek me out?' Already regretting I was speaking as if from the pages of the Bible.

He sat down and relaxed in his chair, which he positioned side-on. His posture was straighter than mine, giving him a couple of inches.

'It was your girlfriend, yeah? She came to see me. Kind of put me straight on a couple of things. She's a beaut, that one. You'd do well to hold on to her. Looks and brains, yes?'

He then did that Italian gesture of kissing his mouth with finger and thumb. He looked me up and down.

'So you're my half-brother.'

I nodded. 'Do you want to know about your father?'

'Shea, isn't it? Listen, I don't mean any disrespect but he's not my father. You've met my pop. He was the one who taught me right from wrong. And you know, I get on well with him. It's his little idiosyncrasies I have taken on. Your father and my mother had sex, that's our connection. But you have travelled a long way, so I agreed to meet you. I don't know what you were expecting from me but we're not family.'

I didn't know what to say, my brain wasn't working, but to keep him talking I said, 'I know.'

'And you can understand my mama. You were a physical reminder and she is still dealing with it every day. Your father . . . abandoned her, us. But I personally have no problem with it. I've been rejected before and will be again. What goes around comes around, yes?'

'Did you know that he killed himself?'

'I'm sorry he did that but I can't make up feelings I don't have.'

'That's fair enough . . . Are you aware of the money he left?'

'Yes.'

'Are you going to accept it?'

'You know that was tough. I wasn't going to, out of respect for Mama. But luck doesn't fall into my lap that often and Mama said it was my decision so, yes, I'm going to take it.'

'Will that be hard on your mother, another reminder of the past?'

'She's never going to forget her past and you know she was a little drunk last night. She's quite pragmatic most of the time. I know all the arguments, how he never had anything to do with my life and now he's trying to win his way into my affection but Mama isn't one of those hysterical types who lived with the pride of his having nothing to do with us. The bottom line is, the money isn't a pay-off for forgiveness. Mama will never forgive him, and he's dead so he obviously knew that as well. Hey, I tell you what. Let's drink to your father, yes? To show I have no malice towards your family.'

We raised our glasses and drank. Me to the significance of life our father gave us, he to a dead stranger. I swallowed, wondering if we would have got on in different circumstances. I doubted it. I got the impression he was looking down on me, grateful that he wasn't me and that our flight-paths were so different. One decision would have had us in each other's place. We were just sperms away but we probably were never even that close in the testicles, avoiding each other, warring factions, he the best of his group of sperm in the left sac and me the right. We scuffled with each other for dominance as he was doing now as he bragged about his business and fiancée. Who came out first, me or him? Sibling rivalry. The reluctant brothers. Again I wished my real brother, Orwell, was with me, the brother I would do anything for. I brought the meeting to a close.

'So how are you going to spend the money?'

'I got plans for the business. We might open another Little Momma's. This time I will buy into it, work for myself. It's the only way, yes?'

'Make sure you leave a little so you can buy your mum a spittoon, won't you?'

There was a pause as my attempt at humour died. And then he wagged his finger at me.

'Yeah, sorry, it was just a little joke.' My life was becoming a little joke of which I was the butt. One's

225

sense of humour can often, contrary to received wisdom, be a character deficiency.

I strolled home, deflated by the flatness of the meeting. Gabriella's gesture was all I could think of. She wasn't aware of the onus of responsibility I had put on to her. She was the slightly open window in an exhaust-fumed car, and while I knew it was unfair to lump this on her, as ever, I felt I had no choice in the matter.

I walked by her door and I could hear the murmuring of company. This didn't bother me, the fact that she was having sex. I just wanted to knock on the door and provide for her, ask her did she need a glass of water or a biscuit. I wanted to be capable of that, to become one of those people who work hard at something that they don't like so that they can provide. But I guess Gabriella would argue that's what she was doing. I went back to my room and wrote a note telling her I was leaving tomorrow. I slipped it under her door. I wanted to knock but Gabriella had always said, 'Not on a school night.' I went to sleep excited about going home, curled up in the foetal position, wanting to be beside Gabriella, wanting her to say, 'Stay.' What was stopping me? It wasn't self-pity. But what was I really going back for? Mum was a seasonal visit and an occasional phone call; Orwell was away with the fairies and everybody else was a subliminal message against my will. The responsibility of loving a child was dragging me back. The child would give a focus to my life. I would better myself so that the kid would have a dad to be proud of. Everybody at some point should have a child so they can see a living being whose heart hasn't been broken yet. I drifted into dreams to be awoken before I'd fully slept by Gabriella at the door.

'Come come, tomorrow is now.' And she took my hand. I quickly dressed and she whisked me off. It was gone two a.m. and in the cab I wanted to sleep. The city lights blurred into a continuous line, helping the cabby with his direction. Gabriella took a little bottle out of her bag, opened it and put it to my nose. It was some sweet-smelling salts which made my head jolt. My body started to slowly wake and soon we were down in a basement with a handful of other night people listening to a French girl singing. The singer was accompanied by a guitarist, violinist and double-bass player. She had a husky, lazy voice and even though I didn't know what she was singing about, but it sounded sad, as if she was accepting her lot. The instruments were plucked in slow motion and it was only when they stopped in between songs that I knew how pleasing the mood they had created was. Gabriella smiled at me. There was no need to say anything. We were honorary Parisians for the night and I knew this was our *au revoir*. This was her way of driving me to the airport. I sat there sipping wine, trying not to cry. A lump amassed in my throat and I was amazed that beside me, perched delicately, was a woman who could seemingly read my mind. I wanted to give her my address for when she came to Europe but reckoned that would be tacky.

Her magical presence made me think that when I left tomorrow I would turn around and the Paradise Motel would never have existed. It would all have been a figment of my imagination, put there to teach me a moral lesson. All my life beautiful things have been put within glimpsing distance, only to tear off elsewhere. The elsewhere I was not admitted into, a tease, a test of strength, putting me in my place. But I was clever: I knew the glimpse was the highlight. Gabriella was something else. And I did cry and she pulled me to her chest. I breathed her in fully as she whispered, 'Never regret the future, Shea,' she knew that was what I was doing – catapulting myself back to England, where I knew I'd miss her. With Gabriella it was never going to be a case of what might have been, never 'if only I'd done this or that'. With us it simply happened, we met and what happened happened and I knew if there was any more to it, it would be destroyed. It was best to look at it as a finished painting. The last stroke was when she kissed my tears away and said, 'The next time you're sad, think of me and I will always kiss your tears away.' She held my face in her hands and smiled. Maybe I'd get over this, but the point was, I didn't want to.

Chapter 21

Springtime in London. The sun reflected off the glass buildings lasering dust haphazardly. Builders summed up the season, getting things ready for the false hope of the summer which, again, would mock us. I'd only been away for two weeks but I'd expected insurmountable change. The newspaper offered nothing to get me thinking. Somehow, my culture had survived without me. Back to the flat; it was neat and airy. Mum couldn't resist making it more presentable for me. She left a note thanking me for the use of it. She'd stocked the fridge and cupboards up with enough food to survive a meltdown. It was only with the flat so clean and tidy that I realized how little furniture I had. My post consisted of one letter and a bank statement. I opened the letter.

It was from Ruth Appleby. I only twigged who she was half-way through reading it. I'd always known her simply as Ruth the hairdresser. I liked her surname and it made me want to know more about her. In the letter she told of a new boyfriend who was totally understanding and how he was going to stand by her and the baby and now there was no need for any more contact between us. She signed off 'Yours faithfully' and gave no address. At first, it was a weight off my mind, but with that responsibility gone was there anything else left for me here? I studied the letter again and noticed it was written in a style that nobody ever talks in. I guess she and her new boyfriend concocted it together, paving the way for the rest of their shared lives. I couldn't help but smile at the happy couple raising my child and then not understanding why the kid could never be happy. A constant thorn in their side. Or would the environment beat the genes into submission, would the child live a circular life with no edge?

It was odd that I was already seeing the child as a person with thoughts and feelings. It was strange to be worrying for the baby's welfare when already it had been taken away from me. I was sure I'd have rights but would it be fair to put a kid through that? Her boyfriend I had down as a sap, which was unfair. Regardless of beliefs, it is better to bring a child up with love, something I'm not really accustomed to and I'm too long in the tooth to start pretending otherwise. Was I kidding myself that I had the child's well-being in mind so I could cop out? I'm not capable of raising a child. With me, it would be an experiment, a little follower for all my half-baked ideas. But then again, I was stepping into Dad's shoes by helping a child into the world only never to see the kid again. Here I was trying to come to a decision which was totally out of my hands. Would this easy ride eventually fade to occasional after-thought or come back full thud to shadow my every moment?

I unpacked my case, wanting to feel at home again. The time difference had my stomach jumpy without cause. Have kangaroos got permanent jet-lag? My brain had constipation, waiting for a solid thought. My battered clothes gave my new suit breathing space when I hung it in the wardrobe. I wondered, would I wear it again? I checked through the pockets on impulse, and found a note which was also used as a parcel. I unwrapped it to find two little bronze owls. The note was from Gabriella. It read:

Dear Shea

I will not offer what I cannot give but will look forward to another encounter. But for now, my two little friends will watch out for you.

Gabriella.

I put the owls in my trouser pocket, already transfixed by their touch. I was strangely at ease, as if the owls had magical protective powers. I've always been intrigued by these creatures, the night guardsmen with their penetrating paranoid gaze, going through shit so we can rest in our beds. Their hooting is a calming evocation of our nocturnal order, perched alone and proud like sentries, they have a duty to do and whether they resent it or not, they follow their orders. Having Gabriella's owls in my possession was like having parents again. No, they would never let me get up to any harm and I'd always have someone to turn to. I wanted to be a child again, not so I could be protected, but so I could give my whole family a big hug, where we would gather in a big scrum, clasp each other, pat each other, before we went into battle. As we get older and loved ones die, that missing hug becomes paramount and it wasn't lost on me that here I was trying to say goodbye to Dad with the most convoluted of hugs, that terribly missed hug that never came because we stupidly take these things for granted. Gabriella reminded me what hugging was all about and now I wanted the austerity of the owls to do the same, be a guard against assumptions. It struck me the amount of energy we waste trying to create good impressions for strangers, the mediocrity of wanting all to think you are pleasant enough, this pathetic need to falsely create an affable fellow. That energy could be put to good use elsewhere. Why are people so frightened of not being liked? 'He was liked by everyone' is a slur on a person's character, not a testament. I am emblematic of the mass-produced middle-class sophisticated Londoner. My parents missed the great wars but were brought up by those with hardened memories. I was a bore baby. I was born into the promiscuous Sixties, the tail end of the rock 'n' roll years. My formative years in the Seventies were one long guitar solo, the Eighties were a resting point, the heavy-breather as we looked everywhere and found mini-cultures which we clung on to for dear life, waiting, just waiting for a real movement, a shift which we could bring about ourselves. Politically, Labour were in the same boat until they came up with that fantastic idea to brand 'New' on to our way of life. We bought it in a 'wink wink, we know this is bullshit but if we pretend, you never know, it might make it better' kind of way.

But I had a more pressing concern: my hair – it looked shit. The thing with my hair is, it gives me an hour's notice from acceptable to care in the community. That tiny growth sends it haywire and each individual hair gets into a strop and goes off in different directions, much like a family reunion gone wrong. I don't know if I was kidding myself and using this as an excuse but I went to visit my hairdresser. I walked into the salon as proud as a peacock with the hair of one who had scrapped with a peacock. Ruth was nowhere to be seen. I asked the receptionist where she was. She looked at me disdainfully and rather succinctly told me she didn't work here any more. I knew from her stance that the rest of the staff knew about our predicament and I was public enemy number two. By way of revenge, they set the trainee loose on my hair. I was offered no head massage as this nameless male teenybopper washed my hair and upper body with lukewarm water. He didn't give any chat as he gave me an uneven short cut. With Ruth no longer here, it was going to be hard to trace her. This didn't bring relief or anxiety because I was dealing with new emotions and I didn't know how to tag them.

I busied myself booking a ticket to Norwich, where Maurice Edwards now lived. I also did a draft of the article Robin wanted me to do for our newspaper scoop. I was fidgety with anticipation of Robin's call. I knew it was futile trying to get in touch with him. I would just have to wait. I was trying also not to worry about Orwell. I touched my owls, hoping they would protect him too. He was still alone, battling whatever battle he had projected on to himself. I rang Mum to see if she had heard anything from him. She hadn't and didn't seem overly concerned either. I found out why when she casually dropped into the conversation that she had just become engaged.

I was dumbfounded and my silence brought a panic into her voice and she started talking about her needs. I wanted to congratulate her but it would have sounded hollow. All I could do was lie and tell her I was in a hurry and that I would ring her later to have a proper chat. I hung up and tried to absorb the news. If it made Mum happy, so be it. It was really none of my business but Dad wasn't even three months dead, which made me suspect that there was an overlap happening here. Had Mum been conducting her own affair? Was this pillar of virtue being knocked down as well? Mum and her needs, and how naive was I to assume she didn't have any? Her needs were probably greater than most, having had to suppress them for so long. We never see old people as having sexual needs. At fifty we're supposed to shuffle off into a corner to rest on our laurels, putting our penises and vaginas in the memory box. Why can't two old-age pensioners make passionate love? They are the ones most likely to do it on the kitchen table, the stairs being too much for them. Surely, their love is the most precious, not one to be mocked. Our culture is so aligned to youth, the old are treated like sour milk rather than vintage wine, patronized and tolerated but never cherished. The pittance of a pension the authorities reward them with after sixty-five years of service was brought in when life expectancy was sixty-six.

As I boarded the train to Norwich, I was getting into the idea of Mum's new lease of life; she was rebelling against the system. But who was her new partner, whom she only referred to as 'an old friend'? Did it matter if I liked him or not? It would mean less quality time with Mum, as is always the case when people close to you become coupled up. But this old friend was also taking the responsibility of caring for Mum away from me.

The train's soothing motion suited my natural rhythm. I was surprised how quickly the countryside came into view outside London. I've always loved trains. It brings a meekness out in people. Unfortunately that meekness is carried over with a quiet disdain which followed the privatization of our railways. Now we have a poorer service and the magic is gone, knowing it isn't our loving government transporting us around the country but a bunch of profit-orientated businessmen.

Norwich was experiencing showers as I left the station platform. With the river running through the centre, I could imagine on a clear day Norwich being very picturesque, but before me was a shitty regional town. I sat myself down at a bar by the river and had a quick pint. With my Dutch courage, I rang Maurice from the pay phone. I asked if we could have a little chat. He was surprised but welcoming. He told me to take a taxi up to his house. It was seven p.m. and the early drinkers were starting their ascension. I was never going to make the last train. I wondered if I should book into a bed and breakfast, but I decided to play it by ear and headed straight to Maurice's. The rain was still belting down but luckily a cab was emptying itself of its passengers outside the bar. The driver gave me a lecture about waiting at the official rank before letting me in.

Maurice lived in a little semi on Grove Road, which was near the centre. He welcomed me with a smile and insisted he cook me dinner. Despite his grey hair he looked younger than his years. He asked me what had me in Norwich, assuming he wasn't the reason for my visit. He was taken aback when I told him the truth. Maurice offered information as if it was on a leaflet: he was an architect who enjoyed a simple life. He opened a bottle of white wine from his free-standing rack and added new ingredients to his stew. He obviously liked company but was devoid of it. He had two cats, which constantly rubbed against his legs. We kept conversation to a database until after dinner. Again, it was always when I was asked what I did for a living that I felt such an imbecile. It sounds like a cop-out to say, 'No particular vocation ever interested me.' Even now if somebody told me I could do anything I wanted, I wouldn't know what to say. I think the nearest I ever came to wanting to be someone was when I toyed with the idea of becoming a shrink but I knew that every session would end with 'And you think *you've* got problems?' which kind of defeats the purpose.

Maurice took pride in his cooking and overpowered me with various herbs and spices. On his last mouthful he insisted I stay the night. As I thanked him, I looked at the big pots and pans and could only think of the quiet psychopath Dennis Nilsen. He told me to make myself comfortable in the living room which always, regardless of the sentiment, makes you feel uncomfortable. I was left alone looking through his books and CDs. He had three prints on his wall, all by Rothko the suicidal postmodernist. He joined me twenty minutes later after he'd cleared all other business for the night.

'So, me and your father then.' He clasped his hands as if he was looking forward to his tale. As he began talking, I knew it wasn't going to be a conversation, it was going to be a story.

'I met your father about three days into freshers' week at Nottingham University. We were both out of our depth, trying to mingle, looking at the various societies we could join. I was taking a look at them all from a distance as I had no social skills to speak of. I was what at school you'd probably have termed a swot. I don't know whether it was because I had no friends or because of my love of reading. Anyway, I was looking for a book society so I could hang out with similar types. I walked by the table for the Communist Party where your father was nearly at blows with its president. I shyly nudged nearer and Terence suddenly grabbed my shoulder and said, 'Join this society and together from within we will kick communism into the twentieth century.' I joined up and Terence took me to the student union bar to celebrate. We got drunk and he banged his drum about socialism learning to live side by side with capitalism. His intelligence intrigued me but it was his honesty which I adored. At the end of that night, he was howlingly drunk and admitted that what he'd been preaching was ill-conceived and that he'd simply taken an instant dislike to the president. His name was Stanley E. Bowls. Terence despised him, hated this rich bloke telling him what communism was all about. But the main reason he joined was because he wanted to steal Stanley's girlfriend from him. That woman was your mother. It took him four months but he did it. Your dad always got what he wanted. He was seeing another girl at the time. Her name was Eve. It was nothing serious, but that was what it was like back then. I fancied Eve rotten. I'd never been with a girl. I hope I'm not boring you.'

'Not at all,' I replied. He couldn't have been aware of the significance of his story for me. He continued.

'When Terence started seeing your mum, it caused mayhem in our circle. Stanley went what I can only describe as weird. He became quieter, as if biding his time. There was hatred in his eyes and it was all levelled towards your father. When your dad dumped Eve she was upset and I became her shoulder. Over a six-month period, I went from support to soulmate to lover. I was totally smitten. I lived for her. I've never known the agony of a love that strong. I was so flipped and scared of losing her. This was down to my own lack of confidence. But I was always testing her, seeing how far I could take it, always wanting her to prove her love to me. I was sick with love. I really think some people haven't got the constitution to handle love and I'm afraid I was one of them.

'Terence opened my eyes to a world I had no right to be part of. He gently pushed me slightly out of my depth, continually building my confidence. He took me on many adventures, he even recommended books that I wouldn't have dreamed of reading; you know, books that open your mind rather than tell you straight facts. I went through a total personality change and everything was just dandy for the first few years. At that stage, the four of us, me and Eve and your mum and dad were living together in a little flat in the centre of town. We strode around that town like we owned it, or at the very least had a lease on it. We thought we were the bee's knees in our dead men's clothes. Oh sorry, we used to shop in secondhand shops and that's what we called them. Then one night, it all went wrong.

'There was an organized debate which we ran once a month. It wasn't taken too seriously and we were always a little bit tipsy when participating. One debate was about something like 'The working classes are the scourge of the educational system.' This was a subject close to your father's heart. That night he was up against Stanley and Stanley had done his homework. During the debate, Terence kept on referring to him as Stan, which he hated, but there wasn't a hint of emotion in Stanley's eyes. Terence did a respectable speech on class, more gut feeling than thought-out discussion. When Stanley spoke, he humiliated your father, at first with carefully constructed arguments and statistics on how the working classes were holding everyone back. Then he brought up Terence's actual grades for the year. Your father had been struggling with his course-work and he was embarrassed about it at the best of times. But then, worse was to follow. We always had Stanley down as having a sense of humour bypass, but he finished his debate with an absolutely spot-on impression of Terence who, as you know, pronounced certain words wrong. Seeing a whole room of his contemporaries laughing at him must have really hurt. But what got to him more was when he saw your mother and that she couldn't suppress her giggles –

that made him lose it big-time. He ran out of the room and we were left to focus on a smiling Stanley. Your mother came from money and Terence had been made to feel ashamed of his roots.

'I wanted to go after him but Jean told me to leave him, saying he would be impossible to talk to. She kept repeating that I should leave it until the morning. I was worried he might do something stupid. So we decided that Eve, being the least close to him, might be the one to bring him back to normality. Myself and Jean continued drinking and became a little concerned when we got back to the flat and there was still no sign of them. In the morning, I found Eve sitting at the table, shivering and looking very pale. She didn't want to talk and went into the bedroom. She stayed in this erratic, lifeless state for a couple of days. It was coming to the end of term and Terence rang to say he was taking an extended break to sort out his head. That night was the last I ever saw of him. The next day, Eve went into two days of continual crying. Jean decided she was not feeling well and ducked out of term a few days early as well. Once your mother was gone, Eve opened her heart to me. She'd found Terence in this working-men's club on the outskirts of town. He kept going on about being with his own people. Eve stayed with him, bringing him home when his own people threw him out for being too drunk and ill mannered. As she propped him up, she said he kept reminiscing about their time together and how she was his real love. They sat on a park bench and tried to talk it through. They started to kiss and Terence got frisky and simply wouldn't take no for an answer. Look, I'll spare you and me the details, but Terence basically raped her.'

There was a terrible silence and Maurice started to cry. I felt a mix of absolute horror and a refusal to believe him. I said the only thing I could say.

'Are you sure?'

Maurice spoke a lot slower than before.

'There lies one of the problems. You see, that's what I said to her. Yes, she kept on saying, yes. Her overriding memory was of Terence asking her straight afterwards whether she was on the pill or not. I refused to believe it myself. These were two of my favourite people in the world and the idea of one of them hurting the other repulsed me. It's strange, I could have just about lived with the two of them having sex with each other. So I simply refused to believe her version of events. Of course, that was the end of our relationship. She left there and then. She rang a month later to tell me she was pregnant and for me to let Terence know that he had his answer now. Your mother was pregnant with you at the time. There I was, on my own, in utter devastation and Stanley called round under the pretence of handing back Terence's notes but basically to gloat. What he got in return was first-hand experience of a man cracking up. I poured my heart out to him, told him everything and then collapsed out of sheer exhaustion. I believe Stanley called an ambulance and made sure I got to hospital, where I had a three-month breakdown. You know, your mother never found out, which I guess is what your father would have wanted.'

I wanted him to repeat and clarify everything but what he'd told me was already branded on the inside of my skull. There was nothing I could do or say but I knew I was at the end of my journey. This was why Dad killed himself. Regardless of the state he was in at the time of his death, it was this one event that he couldn't live with. This is the event he couldn't forget. It was this that Orwell was also having trouble living with, that Eve had had to cope with. One act of total selfishness was causing rebounding pain. I felt so bad and it hadn't even sunk in yet. Here was Maurice, a broken man, full of forgiveness but lacking a life. It's what he would have wanted indeed. But the thing that was really bugging me was that I knew Maurice wasn't the Clouds. My journey was complete but I was still in the dark about one of the major players. Could it possibly be Stanley?

The single bed Maurice had laid on for me was tiny and the box-room was akin to a prison cell, a compressed chamber with little in the way of artefacts, only cold dead air filling the gaps. I never have problems sleeping in strange beds and exhausted with the revelation I shivered off to the land of nod. On the way, I tried to picture the scenario Maurice had described but even with faces for all the characters I couldn't conjure up the violation. My mind was a puzzle. Maurice's calmness gave me the creeps. Eve's spitting revenge involved me in the story. But Dad's act didn't disgust me. It disturbed me that I understood him; that beast was in us all. And yet he couldn't live with it. It was not something any decent person would consider doing but wasn't that the point? I don't think Dad did consider his actions, he just did it, indulging all his human frailties, which others might deny. It was barbaric. He used his animal instinct and that's where he was wrong. We sometimes forget that that's all we are. Animals. The highest form, but still animals nevertheless. Sometimes the worst sort: animals with consciences. Or the best, animals with choices. In zoos, it's the gorillas who look at us, studying our natures, and then decide they don't want to evolve any more. They laugh at us. A nation of animal lovers who hate themselves. We live in a civilized society which houses and feeds the gorillas but leaves some unfortunates homeless and starving, begging on the streets. That is the only difference between us and the gorillas: some of us have learned how to busk.

I woke to find Maurice putting a cup of tea by my side. It was only then I realized he was like an overgrown child. I wanted to shake life into him. I wondered what he would be like in a crisis. He told me he had to go to work and I was to make myself at home and stay as long as I wanted. This was very trusting or it could simply have been reverse psychology as it made me want to go straight away. I was frightened I might find some big secret in his house and I really didn't want to know any more about Maurice and his air-hostess personality. We chatted a little more and he was just a little bit too nice. A cloned hospitality experiment that one day would notice he wasn't getting anything in return and when that time came he would leave a lot of carnage. Before he left, he puzzled me with a question. He shocked me because I was about to ask him exactly the same thing. Did I have a girlfriend? he asked. Coming from him, it was like a question uncles asked their nephews when trying to embarrass them. I didn't know where he was heading with this, so I sat up and replied, 'Sort of.'

'D'you think you'll ever settle down, Shea?'

'I hope so.'

'Shea, can I say, these things don't just fall into your lap.'

I didn't know what to say so I just said, 'Right.' Then I asked him a question that I already knew the answer to.

'Have you ever gone out with anyone since Eve?'

'No.'

And he was gone.

I sipped my tea, wondering what all that was about. It still made me question myself, though. Sadly, I don't think I ever will settle but I find it increasingly hard to tell people that because either they lecture you or it brings them down. How can you find the perfect partner without seeing everybody first? These guys who marry the girl next door are either extremely lucky or very lazy. I yearn for my soulmate but I really do believe anyone who has an unrequited love kind of loses interest. Anyone who unearths treasure and then has to give it to somebody else tends to be half-hearted with future excavations. I thought of Gabriella and had a little cry, part loss, part happiness. With Maurice gone, I relaxed a bit more and he made me appreciate my ongoing traumas. It was only when I had a wander around his house that his personality made sense. He was a Scientologist. He had all the books and assorted paraphernalia. I didn't know much about that religion but I knew that you paid for your good fortune in hard currency. I had always regarded Scientology as a tax for the rich.

When I arrived at the train station, on impulse I bought a ticket to Nottingham. To bury Dad I would need to see the actual location of events. I found out from Mum where the flat was and the park wouldn't be too hard to find. Again, when I stepped off the train, the rain poured down. Was Dad trying to stop my search? Was he making things difficult for me? Nottingham was a bustling little town, quite compact, but in the rain it was another shitty regional town. I took a taxi to the flat in Bracewell Street. The flat was above a pet shop. There was a cheap café almost directly across the road from it. I went in there and had an all-day breakfast and stared at the flat. After twenty minutes, two smart-suited guys came out of the flat. Their clothes were stylish rather than work smart. Their hair was conventional but they still looked like students. Maybe it's the walk, the arrogant stride of those first few steps to manhood. And there walked Dad and Maurice, forty years before them. When would their moment come? That moment when they walked into their own shadows. At what point would they become ghosts of their former selves? I asked for directions to the park and walked there wondering when my fatal moment of decline had occurred. I couldn't place one event that I was seemingly in control of. With perfect timing, my pager vibrated.

. . . LJ – the job is on – RH . . .

Yes, of course, that was my moment. Joining an organization which for the good of the people would happily destroy individuals. Put like that, we were no better than any Fascist group. All it amounts to is elitism. One more job to play the media at their own game and then it was all over. I was in the mood for my own personal renaissance. I was tapped on the shoulder and an old woman asked me to help her cross the road. She interlocked our arms and I assisted her. She mumbled about her sight and sound being impaired and since her husband died she was mistrustful of her own judgement. I didn't want to let go of her. I wanted to help her for the day. And I decided to stay with her until she let go.

We reached the park and she talked of her life as if she was orating at her own funeral. I looked at the empty park benches, trying to picture Dad's shameful moment. There were people walking dogs, toddlers trying to walk in multi-layered clothing, two teams of kids were playing football, all wearing replica shirts, mainly of Manchester United, daydreaming their skills to higher planes. A gang of teenagers sat on a wall smoking, exhaling smoke-rings to impress the opposite sex. I sat on a bench, taking all this in with the old lady, whose name was either Iris or Trish. I preferred Iris, so I stuck with that. I watched all these young lives at their various stages, and couldn't remember the park when I was a kid. It was frustrating that these children wouldn't remember these simple pleasures. I wanted to take photos and send them to the subjects in ten years with a little note saying, 'A day in your life when nothing special happened. Be grateful.' I thought of Dad playing in the park when he was a kid,

246

not for a moment thinking he might one day force himself on another person in similar surroundings. Then it dawned on me. I hadn't blocked my parklife from my mind: Dad had never taken me to a park. Dad had certainly paid for his bad judgement but had made us pay also. Those moods he bestowed on us I had taken as the adult state of mind and to stop delaying the inevitable I forced depression and loneliness on to my formative years. Was it to emulate my father? Be proud, Dad. I too am a pain in the arse.

Iris still held on tight and I asked her was she OK? She replied that it was a lovely day. It was still raining. I don't know if she was on the same level, understanding the sudden joy I was experiencing for life itself, or simply commenting about the weather but I was starting to connect. Dad's secret had released me from nagging thoughts. His vile deed was giving me a new start. The kids were scurrying home as God squeezed his thumb on the hosepipe nozzle. Myself and Iris were oblivious to the downpour, holding on tight, wanting this feeling to last. I touched the two owls in my pocket. I wanted to give Iris one of them but I knew there was no need. Because the beautiful thing was that Gabriella had sent Iris to me and I was beginning to reason that Dad had sent Gabriella to me. I hardly noticed the thunder and lightning. Somebody wasn't happy that I'd found some crazy peace.

Chapter 22

For the first time in an age it felt good to be in my flat. Crouch End had rosy cheeks. The residents were taking the chilled breeze of March in their stride. Big thick coats had one button undone, ready at a moment's notice to rejoice in the anticipated spring sun. I was alone as usual, with no prospects, but it was OK, because this was my rebirth. I wanted to chuck out my address book and acquire some new friends but I knew I could build bridges with some of the acquaintances I had discarded. I knew it was time to get a job, one that would fulfil me. I had little in the way of qualifications but the job would have to involve me bettering people's lives in some way and I would need an environment that didn't involve endless chatter. It was a toss-up between doing the catering for a monastery or becoming a librarian. I wanted to enjoy myself because I knew this sense of well-being wouldn't last. Much as people who have had near-death experiences tend to bore us with their 'live life to the fullest' strategy, which lasts no longer than a fortnight, I had to get as much done as possible while I could still access this added energy I had been given.

I had to get my assignment from Robin Hood today. I had already drafted our damning report on the proprietor. But my main worry was still Orwell. Where was he? – he still hadn't been in touch. I rang Rebecca. She was coping better, trying to pull her shit together. From her tone of voice, she was resigned to losing Orwell. I got the distinct impression that she didn't want me to call. I think she wanted all the Hicksons out of her life. I could understand this and kept the conversation brief. I rang Mum to congratulate her properly on her engagement. Of course, during the pauses, I kept on wondering how she would react to Dad's secret. She was wasting no time and told me they had set the date for the wedding for May 3rd. It struck me straight away that this was the workers' holiday. We both agreed that I should meet her fiancé and then she rather vaguely suggested the weekend starting April 2nd. I didn't understand Mum's hurry but she was taking further steps away from Dad. Within five months of his death she would be married again.

I arrived in Turnpike Lane once again. The bus journey had me dozy. Robin was in a buoyant mood and quickly ushered me into his study. As usual, he got straight to the point. The editor of the *Daily Angel* would be made to stand down after we told the truth about Mr Rumininger. He himself would be forced to sell and Robin had a little extra plan that would mean the paper would be in dire financial straits. We were to place our article with our mole in the newspaper on Thursday, 1 April. Our mole had come up with the ingenious idea that we could pass it off as the paper's April Fool joke. Robin was informed that it was the chief-sub and the designer who were the last to see each edition and they were, at that point, always more concerned about the look of the pages than about the content. Our mole had a story placed for that edition which he would pull at the last moment and replace with our own. This all seemed well sorted out and I was excited by the plan but I pointed out to Robin that I didn't see where I fitted into the equation. Surely the mole had it all in hand.

'*Au contraire*,' Robin mused. 'This is the first job involving our mole. You are a senior member. It's up to you to see that everything runs smoothly and if the chief-sub smells a rat, you'll have to deal with him. And more importantly, I want to give you, as a goodbye present, the opportunity to leave our calling card on the editor's desk.'

This sounded fine in theory but I didn't know that, if there was a confrontation, I would be able to deal with it. I had many questions. What about the security cameras, wouldn't they pick me up?

'Yes, my dear boy, and you should smile at them. You are doing nothing illegal. That's the beauty of it.'

'What about our mole? Is he not going to get caught?'

'He knows what he's doing.'

'How do I get into the building?'

'The mole has booked you in for work experience.'

'I'm a bit old to be a work experience boy, aren't I?'

'We'll say you're our mole's brother. Just relax, Shea, everything will be fine. Everything's taken care of. I'll give you instructions of the timetable the day before.

You're simply there in a supervisory capacity. This is your glorious out. This is an achievement you can be proud of.' He went to shake my hand. 'This is probably the last time I'll see you.' A strange smile emitted from his mouth.

He handed me the box of Black Magic and we said our goodbyes. My hands were all sweaty and I was nervous about the operation. This newspaper was a big organization and I felt out of my depth. I didn't like how relaxed Robin was or his sudden willingness to let me leave the organization. I wished I had somebody to talk this over with. Where were you, Orwell? He'd know the set-up at the *Angel*. He'd spent his early training there before he went freelance. I went home clinging to the Black Magic, knowing we were going to destroy more reputations. My arm started to go all tickly and tingly. Safely in my flat, I shoved the chocolates in my drawer. My equilibrium was overtaken by mellow pains up and down my arm. In all probability it was just bad circulation but my brain was registering the start of a heart attack. The slight panic made my breath heavy and laboured. I worked myself into a state until I was hyperventilating. I lay on my bed breathing through my nose. The black pollution that had collected there was making it a chore. I tried to relax and pulled the covers over me. But all I could think of was the sharper pains, the suffocating air and all the women I had deceived on this very bed.

The base of the bed was a steel frame with eight planks of wood holding up the mattress. It would have been more honest to hit my lovers over the head with one of the planks rather than pretending I was in love with them. I've never understood men who dutifully use women for sex. Me, I always kid myself that this is the beginning of something special. But were all those women purely retaliation for Rebecca's rejection? Was I stupidly thinking she might somehow through telepathy know that other women wanted me? And then, having gone through this pathetic rigmarole half a dozen times, I had lost sight of its purpose and it had become all about the pure ego of a woman wanting me, as if that was going to help me get over Rebecca. If only I could have followed through with masculinity and admitted I just wanted sex. But no, I mistook cowardliness for sensitivity, prolonging the pain for me. Rebecca lived like that with me for two years. I suppose I have to admit she only stayed with me to have an 'in' with Orwell and then he threw away what I desperately wanted. At least with Dad he brought about his own downfall.

Sex had messed up his head. How could he have possibly ever made love again? Rapists can get anything up to ten years in prison. Surely his penis had served that sentence. Me, I feel my penis is on probation, never breaking the law but doing some wrongs. Maybe I should send it out to do some community service. The freewheeling love of the Sixties spoilt it for the rest of us. Finger food spoiling the appetite and what legacy has that left us millennial types with? The act of love is dead and all we can do is to separate sex and love. Sex is lust but love is all those other things, the sharing of moments, washing each other's clothes, feeding each other, having secret reference points. Even Bill Clinton has endorsed this way of life. At least he shows his human side. Tony Blair tries to act superhuman when you know he was the boy in the class who was the loner, who tried to join in with all the other groups only for it always to end in embarrassed silence. This is our leader: not one who leads, but one who tries to catch up. The man who doesn't quite fit in but who we don't find too offensive. Where are his human qualities? Lead by example, man. Let us all know we are in the same moral boat. If he wants another term in office, he better start shagging some interns. I slowly got to sleep, half dreaming of Utopian society, half expecting a heart attack.

The morning had my breathing back to normal. The skies were cloudless but somehow foreboding. The wind rattled my bedroom door and I decided it was time to throw out the assorted memorabilia in my wardrobe. I came across love letters from Rebecca, photographs of people I have a hazy memory of, badges of punk bands I'd long forgotten about and tons of research notes for a project I'd helped Dad with one summer.

I could never understand his obsession with the weather. I guess he loved the fact that it was out of our control. He despised those thoughtless multinationals that were fucking with its natural order. His proudest achievement – along with the James Hunt project – was putting forth a nationally accepted reporting system for the bigger companies' use of carbon dioxide. He was on the ball about global warming long before the politicians tried to get the green vote. And he became increasingly frustrated when few would heed his prophecies of doom. I can't remember at which point he gave up his serious crusading to become a weather man but it must have hurt. Or was it the same old story? At a certain age you take on different priorities, realizing the fight is hopeless. I threw all the notes into a carrier bag and decided to recycle Dad's wasted project. I contemplated keeping the love letters but in one of those not-making-a-decision moments, I just chucked them out with all the other mementos of false memory.

Crouch End was pottering about. I arrived at the recycling post to find that the containers were brimming with others' waste. How many other tales of failed relationships did this container hold? It was sighing with its responsibility as I left my memories leaning against it. I walked by the library and decided to go in and ask for a job. I took in my surroundings and decided against it. It wasn't a place of learning; it was mainly old duffers reading the free papers on desks reminiscent of my school days. The main problem was that it didn't smell like a library: that austere antiquarian aroma was missing. In fact, the library had no smell. I took a round trip of Crouch End in search of a job.

Cafés and pubs were out because I didn't want to hang out with piss-heads and gluttons. The first real prospect was the Church, Dave Stewart's recording studio. But did I really want a job there? Having to listen to a band's upbeat mix of their new crap song and then having to pretend I liked it in the hope that they might share their drugs with me; I'm a little too old for that. The two hairdressing salons were out as I was *persona non grata*.

Then there were a couple of New Age shops. That would be the easy life, but no, I couldn't sell gullible people phoney trinkets. What about the second-hand record shop. That would be nice just listening to music all day, devising my own charts of what sells, making up new systems. But again, it would be too depressing, watching people down on their luck, selling their precious collections for a pittance. Seven-Eleven: the primary colours and overpricing would do my head in. Dunn's the Bakery: the smell would be overpowering and I'd feel sorry for the cakes that didn't sell. Victoria Wines: I wouldn't be able to hack the alcoholics who pretended they didn't have a problem. Our Price would put me off music for ever, seeing the half-decent records gathering dust as Boyzone clocked up sales the bakery would be proud of. The Electricity Showroom: I would be out of my depth in, recommending appliances I didn't know the foggiest about. Oxfam speaks for itself. Prospero's Books: now I could fit in there. I touched my owls for luck, took a deep breath and asked to see the manager. He was a jumper-wearing, bespectacled, short-haired man called Patrick. He was a couple of years younger than me. I came straight to the point.

'Have you got any jobs going?'

He surprised me with, 'There is a short-term position coming up. Do you want to come in the back room for a bit of a chat?'

We appeared to hit it off straight away. I was honest about my lack of experience but also put forward that I was well read and informed about authors. He joked about Delia Smith being their best seller and that it was complete bull that Crouch End was crawling with beatniks. The mainstay of their custom was bored house-wives. One of his staff was taking four months' paternity leave and he said he was willing to give me a week's trial. I was as elated as a boy getting his first paper-round. The money wasn't great but it would do. He said I could start the first Monday of April. On the way out I bought Douglas Coupland's new book. Patrick, in an act of good faith, gave me staff discount. At home, I put the book on my shelf, along with others which I intended to read one day. But for now they would serve their purpose of looking pretty, a row of thoughts I could dip into at any time. It was comforting to know that.

I sat down feeling I deserved a rest, as if I'd already put in a day's work. Satisfaction of work had me buzzing. I would be a nine-to-fiver; I would eat ready-made sand-wiches and discuss the news with my fellow workers; I would be tired at night and appreciate leisure time and have a proper appetite. Oh, the future: Thursday and my freedom; Friday, meeting the love of Mum's new life; and on Monday I'd be assisting people with their literary needs. I felt good because I felt normal. Here I am, thirty-one years of age and I'm so behind the rest of the human race. This euphoria I should have experienced when I was twenty-one. Ten years I wasted just thinking. That's all behind me now. This is year zero. From here on I will be existing, just enjoying the simple pleasures. I looked out at my new world and all was right with it. The sky wasn't sharing my new-found happiness which hadn't budged all day. I remember what Dad used to say about that, which always put the willies up me. He insisted that when the sky was still, it was because it was scared stiff, storing all its energy up, hoping it would be able to hold its ground against what it knew was about to besiege it. He was seldom wrong.

Chapter 23

I awoke to the sky's rumblings. The sun was speckled orange like the aftermath of a Vietnam film's napalming. It was soothing as the clouds broke and shattered into tiny pieces. It reminded me of how insects react when you lift a stone. Lightning flashed and a dog a few doors along howled in all directions having no moon to focus on. I must have stared out the window for at least half an hour. The sky was in continual movement. I turned on the radio. Some zany cunt was shouting as if he was at an all-night disco. The newsreader told of a huge fire in a department store in town; they suspected that the early morning lightning had caused it. I eventually got the weather report for London. Hedging their bets some-what, they said we would be experiencing isolated showers with sunny spells. Tomorrow was my big day. This would be my last day as a layabout.

I was slightly nervous about the newspaper job and was hoping it would be cancelled. But when the post came, Robin had sent my instructions. I was to meet my accomplice at four p.m. outside the CrossBar in King's Cross. He was then to inform me of our schedule. I was just contemplating a day of nervous unease when Rebecca rang. She wanted to see me but wouldn't say why. I didn't care what she had to say, there was no way I was going to Hounslow again. We compromised and arranged to meet at the National Film Theatre café on the South Bank. I spent the morning reading the *Daily Angel* and there was plenty there to fuel our little prank. Their commentary was smart-arsed and insular. Their Arts pages sneered but still devoted space to their targets.

It was pissing down now so I ordered a mini-cab to the South Bank. Mini-cabs are a lottery. You don't know what kind of service you're going to get. I didn't mind as long as they were quiet. The English drivers usually take pride in their old bangers. The Irish talk, the Jamaicans play music, the Indians adorn their cars as shrines to their god and family, while the Nigerians are genuinely entertaining. I got an Irish guy. Thankfully visibility was so poor because of the rain he had to concentrate on his driving. This one was very keen on checking his brakes every thirty seconds or so. He was also one of those drivers who hated traffic and kept repeating that it was doing his head in and to avoid it took me via every sidestreet adding fifteen minutes on to the journey time. All drivers hate traffic but I think all mini-cab drivers hate driving – they see the job as some sort of penance. I arrived at the South Bank ten minutes early and when I got out of the cab the driver lost any chance of a tip with his 'You don't get many blacks around these parts.' The rain had eased a little so I took a little stroll along the river. The South Bank is glorious even in the rain. The huge pavements are a luxury which every street should have and the outdoor art makes sense here.

I always think I'm over Rebecca until I see her. She'd had her hair cut short like it was when we first met. She was wearing a black top, tartan skirt with black leggings. I told her she was looking great and hoped that it didn't sound like a come-on. We sat down. She ordered a mineral water but I fancied a Guinness. There was little in the way of small-talk. Her face was still puffy with sadness but she was coping. She took a sip of her water as if to clear her throat and said, 'Orwell visited me last night.'

I sat up, giving her my full attention.

'He looked terrible. He was fidgety and nervous.'

'What did he have to say?'

'He apologized for the way he acted and said very little else.'

'Do you think you might be able to reconcile things?'

'There's no question of that. He's a different person. The beard's back, he's hiding again.'

'Does he need help? Do you know where he is?'

'No.' She looked me in the eye and said, 'I got the impression that I wasn't going to see him ever again.'

I told her about my similar call and it really did feel like he was clearing the decks before disappearing. But where to? Rebecca and I took stabs in the dark like third-rate detectives. She was still very much in love with him and concerned for his welfare above her own happiness. God, how I envied him. I think if I had Rebecca by my side, I could surmount all obstacles. I wanted to bring up our past again but knew it was futile. I wanted to tell her of women who, between us, we had let down. I'm sure she knew she only had to say the word and I would be her slave. But this was far from her mind as her parting words were 'I just hope it's not at Orwell's funeral that we meet again.'

We pecked each other on the cheek and I was disappointed that the new improved me hadn't made itself known to her, though at least I could say my new outlook was for my own benefit, not for anyone else's. Fearing I would never see Orwell again, and remembering how she had given me the picture of Sophia, I gave Rebecca one of my owls. I hoped Gabriella would look after her too.

Wednesday, 31 March. I was shitting myself. I put the box of Black Magic on the table and stared at it, contemplating all I had done for the organization. Today I would see it through. I wondered what our final draft for the paper would be and how Robin would sign it off. We'd never bothered with a name for the organization because Robin thought it belittled our battle if we were seen as another piddling little self-aggrandizing group, rather than 'an organization' that had everybody's interests at heart.

I jumped on a bus to King's Cross but couldn't relax. I needed fresh air but the other passengers unnerved me with their calmness. I got off the bus and started to walk. There was a wind gusting which was twirling around my stomach, the velocity clipping at my bones. The cold pressure was numbing the bare parts of my body but I was still sweating. The pavement was practically empty as London was now expecting severe weather. It's hard to make sense of a gale in the city. It tends to attack you at corners. The buildings ward off most of its power and it's just the assorted rubbish flying around at head level that reminds you of its density. I wanted to be beside the seaside watching crashing waves battering the pier, beautiful and relentless. I love the way the wind mocks us with its whistling, the unpredictability of its direction fascinates me. It has the skill of a Brazilian footballer and is there to remind us how insignificant we are.

I came to King's Cross. Rush hour was about to start its descent and train stations across London were bracing themselves. I had the wind behind me now and it was shoving me towards my destiny. It was catching me from below, trying to lift me and I half expected to see a dozen Richard Bransons battling for balloon space. How I wished I was above the clouds, soaring and weightless.

I approached the CrossBar. There was no sign of anybody. I was two minutes early, two minutes to contemplate ducking out, taking a network train to the end of the line. I spent this time watching the commuters coming out of the Thameslink, the gale welcoming them to London by taking off their hats and flinging them out of reach. From the opposite direction, I could sense I would soon have company. I turned around and there standing beside me was Orwell.

'Shall we do it, then?' was his greeting. He started to walk ahead leaving me no option but to follow.

I caught up with him and shouted, 'What the fuck is going on?'

'I'm your mole. You don't need to know anything else.' He spoke dispassionately, almost robotically.

I pulled him towards me by his forearm, 'How long have you been involved?'

'Look, I was approached and it seemed like the best option.'

He walked ahead again, which gave me time to consider this strange outcome. There was something wrong. Why hadn't Robin told me about Orwell? He didn't seem surprised to see me. Why was he throwing away his career? I caught up with him but he didn't give me a chance to say anything.

'Right, Shea, leave all this to me. You're here purely as back-up. I don't expect to have any problems. I've done these last-minute changes before.'

'Look, Orwell, are you involved with Robin Hood?'

'Relax, Shea, this is a one-off. I was in a position to do you a favour. It's no skin. Anyway, the *Angel*'s had this coming to them. They're just a bunch of power-crazy profiteers. They're not interested in giving us news. I guess we all have our price.'

'Orwell, once we have done this, can we have a proper talk?'

'Yeah, sure.'

We walked to the entrance of the *Daily Angel*'s building. Just as we were about to go in, I stopped Orwell and gestured that I wanted a hug. Without pausing, he held me tight and we embraced for at least twenty seconds. Nothing was said but it put life into me and I felt good because it was me and Orwell against the world again.

The receptionist smiled at Orwell and didn't bat an eyelid when he signed me in. We went up to the fifth floor where the freelances had makeshift offices. He explained to me that he had to get the lawyers' approval of the original story. It was an exposé of a circus's cruelty towards animals. He left me alone in the office. The rain was shoving itself against each window of this greenhouse of a building. The elements were at play as thunder clapped and lightning lasered the sky. I counted the time between the thunder and lightning. It started at six seconds but got as near as three. The lightning was three miles away, probably a bull's-eye hit on my flat. The fluorescent bluish light began to flicker annoyingly as I pondered my lot looking out the window. It was as if London was blinking. There was an adrenalin-fuelled rush around the office as the sub-editors made the last-minute changes to the pages.

I watched the newspaper's editor, Jeremy Case, sprinting around making split-second decisions. There was about twenty minutes of mild hysteria before only a handful of staff remained. I watched as the rest made to leave. Orwell came back and told me the lawyer had given him the go-ahead. He had told his chief-sub that he was still tinkering with his copy. It was now just a matter of biding our time. A little after seven o'clock they started hassling Orwell for his copy as they wanted to put the paper to bed. It was soon just us two and the chief-sub in the offices. Orwell got into the computer and filed out our new feature and then we waited for the chief-sub to question him. Orwell told me he had got on particularly well with this guy and that he trusted Orwell. As Orwell said this, the sub came up to us with furrowed brow.

'What's all this about, young Mr Hickson?'

As brazen as I've ever seen him, Orwell casually said, 'It's been approved.'

'You're joking,' the sub rebuked him.

'Yes, I am actually. It's our April Fool's joke.'

'Oh, I get you.' And he was gone.

Orwell smiled and then without any remorse said, 'It's a pity really. He's one of the good ones. He'll be sacked tomorrow.'

'What about the editor?' I asked.

'He's a goner too. Mr Rumininger has a German sense of humour.'

I was pretty excited and disappointed that there was no immediate action.

'So what happens next, Orwell?'

'The first editions hit the street at about ten-thirty and then of course it will be taken out. But then the other papers will lead with it in their second editions.'

I asked him where the editor's office was so I could leave my little package. I placed the chocolates on his desk with a little 'Good luck with your new career' note. We then decided to go for a drink. He was in ebullient mood. We dashed to the nearest pub as the weather wasn't letting up. The wind and the rain were in the midst of a nervous breakdown. The tiny run had soaked us through. Orwell got the beers in and I had so much to say to him I didn't know where to start. I filled him in on my latest adventures and casually mentioned that I'd found out about Dad. He sighed.

'He was a piece of shit. I can't believe that he did it.'

'When did you find out?'

'Round November.'

'Did he know that you knew?'

'Yeah, I confronted him about it.'

'And how did he react?'

'Shock. He talked about it being a long time ago and how he couldn't forgive himself so he didn't expect forgiveness from me.'

'He didn't try to deny it all, did he?'

'No. It's strange but it's usually the victim who lives in denial. It's easier for them to pretend it didn't happen. Obviously the impact was lessened for Dad over the years.' He paused for a moment and then came out with 'But his dead memories have been transposed on to me.'

'Orwell, how can you possibly blame yourself for any of this?'

He interrupted me. 'You know what the weirdest thing is? It's that he could live with his actions but not with the knowledge that I knew. Isn't that strange?'

'And you shouldn't feel remorse for that.'

'I know I shouldn't. I tell myself I shouldn't but I do. I loved Dad. But when I found out it made a sham of that love, and it got to the stage where I don't think I could love anyone again.'

It was hard for me to take in the seriousness of what he was saying because he said it in such a ho-hum way. I tried to assuage him.

'But Orwell, we have each other, we love each other.'

He hugged me again. I had to loosen his grip, as a couple of heavy drinkers were offended by the gesture. Orwell got another couple of pints in and a short for himself.

'So what's next for you then, Orwell?'

'I don't know. The umbilical cord has been cut for me. I guess I can go anywhere.'

'I'm going to visit Mum and her fiancé tomorrow. Why don't you come up with me?'

'I don't think so.'

'So, tell me. How the hell did you get involved with Robin Hood?'

'He used to write to me to tell me that he admired what I did and that we should fight corruption together. Eventually I met up with him and I was intrigued by what he had to say so I agreed to do this one job for him.'

'And he told you I was involved?'

'Yeah, he said you'd been assisting him for years and he thought we'd make a good team. And we did. It was smooth running. It was nice to be able to do something together. It's been a long time. It's been a long time since I did anything with anyone else. You see, you're lucky, Shea, with the organization. It must give you a rush.'

'Come on, you're a great journalist. I'm so proud of you. I've often been jealous.'

'Nah, they were only words. What did I achieve? Circulation went up. I was just lining those bastards' pockets. You were right with your direct action. It's the only way.'

'Don't let Robin Hood delude you. There's a big ego at work there. I don't want to get all big brother on you but I've been through this phase of looking for a focus. We always go to outside sources. If you're going to find any peace, it will come from within.'

'Shea, if you love me and respect me, you'll let me do my own thing. When I was growing up I tried to emulate you and it took me years to find my own personality. All those bands I tried to like, clothes I tried to wear. All those traits. I was a little clone of you but I forgot to find out what I liked. And when you went away I was scared but at least I faced up to myself and I didn't like what I saw so I hid behind others. Dad, Rebecca . . . I guess I'm sick of hiding.'

'But the beard. Why grow that again? You're hiding under that.'

'It's the last line of defence. I don't like the world in which we live. I don't like how we all pretend it's OK. I could never become one of those moany cunts down the pub who drink for freedom. And I can't do anything to change the way it is. I don't want to become one of those types who hide themselves in a family and let that become all-encompassing.'

'What are you going to do, then?'

'I'll get by.'

'Orwell, I feel the same as you. We've been given this hyper-gene which demands more out of life. Maybe it's Dad's way of balancing up his own morals. But it's not our fault. Never lose sight of that. It's not our fault. We've all done things we're not proud of. But that's the human condition. Please don't take all the world's woes on yourself. Christ, you could have a brain haemorrhage at a moment's notice. It's only recently I've started to enjoy the simple things.'

'I know what you're saying, Shea. I've enjoyed them too but I find them repetitive.'

It was hard arguing my case with Orwell because I agreed with what he said. He took on these sentiments with more valour which troubled me. We sat in silence. His eyes were blank and he was drinking more heavily than usual. He spoke on. His talk was of hopelessness and, worse still, acceptance of that hopelessness. The last orders bell went. He downed two quick shorts and then with the excitement of a Boy Scout suggested we go over to the office and read the first edition.

Outside the *Daily Angel* there was pandemonium as reporters from other newspapers were snooping around. The rain had stopped and the wind had moved on. The office was brimming with subs who had been called back to work. We went to Orwell's office and read the paper. And there it was for the nation to see on page six. The banner headline of the article read, DAILY ANGEL PROPRIETOR IN ILLEGAL EARNINGS CONFESSION. The story focused on Rumininger's fencing of stolen Nazi gold and art. This had been an unsubstantiated rumour in the business world which everybody had known about but nobody was ever able to prove. The report tailed off about the information being unearthed by an unnamed organization. The organization's duty was to seek out truth in all corners and this was just a warning to all and sundry of its intentions . . . 'Sick of Big Brother watching you while sweeping his own dirt under the carpet? Well fear not, because we are a bigger brother and we are watching. The spine of our society is stooped. Together we can strengthen and straighten it. The enemy is not the wolf but the one disguised as the grandmother. Remember at all times from whom you are getting your news. Don't take this as fact. Please question every report you read. This is not news. It's a view of the news.

270

Committees sit with other interests in mind, trying desperately to maintain the status quo. Your forty pence helps them stay in this position. Buy wisely.'

Orwell was giddy with enthusiasm and kept re-reading the passage. He asked me, what did I think? I didn't want to bring his buzz down but I told him that I admired what Robin had said, even though I thought it was written in the style of a student. I thought it would have been subtler to put all the information in the form of clues to their crossword. It wouldn't have been as immediate but, long-term, it would have become folklore. Regardless, the other newspapers would be able to quote verbatim without fear of a lawsuit. It would create quite a stir but I questioned whether it would change anything. Money buys you power, that is the bottom line, and it's a sad fact of life that money stays with money. Dad had had trouble coming to terms with what he should have been proud of: England is an inherently classist society. If you're born in the gutter there are few ways out. Showbiz freaks and sporting heroes, all there to entertain the chattering classes.

I could feel that Orwell knew I was making sense but I remembered when I thought I could change things. A piece of your brain comes alive, similar to being in love and it is blind, so I left him to his dreams.

He spoke as I had years before and for a moment I wanted to be dragged back in but I had come to the understanding that doing your bit was only enough for certain people. Dad caved in. I've caved in. I just hope the rubble softens Orwell's fall. I have not given up but I would rather take my place in the human race, whether I like them or not. My future was a steady job, personable friends, an occasional spark of happiness and, some way down the line, a stab at sharing my life with another. Maybe it's an age thing – at thirty-one I find all my energy gone. My youth has vanished, taken from me overnight, snatched. Teenage girls push past me to make eyes at distinguished fifty-year-olds. Ear hair offers me protection against the cold. The Cardigans are not a pop band but items of clothing. Old men nod to me in the park and I've started taking an interest in other people's gardens. It's the sporty types I feel for. They're the ones who have the crises, watching their bodies physically decline. I have never exercised and therefore miss nothing. The year thirty-one could well be my year. I have no regrets for my missing youth but would have liked a warning. It would have been nice to be able to celebrate the last day of my youth. Maybe I did. I looked at Orwell and his ridiculous beard, still on his slow come-down. I didn't want to spoil it for him. I stared out the window. Night was meshing its colours. Orwell wanted another drink. I had some wine at home and suggested he come with me. I was delighted when he agreed. I missed our late-night talks.

Outside the building the reporters were still trying to gather new information. They ignored us, which was a reflection of the state of today's journalists, their reckoning being we weren't wearing suits so we couldn't be important. We jumped on a night bus which took us as far as Archway. The kebab shop was packed with dehydrated clubbers, whose testosterone was craving cheap meat. We decided to walk the rest of the way. The Archway Tower was blocking the undecided sky. Orwell, still bubbling, raced on ahead. I had trouble keeping up with him. I knew a shortcut but he insisted we go via the bridge high over Archway Road. We paced up this road, which was pretty much the start of the motorway. I tried to talk but the articulated lorries vibrated past in a steady flow. The cold air was going up and down my legs, slightly numbing my feet. We took the steps up to the bridge, which left me out of breath. Orwell wanted to take in the view from the bridge. I persevered even though there was very little to see. The spiked black panelling obscured what there was. Then Orwell came out with a bizarre statement.

'Do you think our lives would have been much different if Robin Hood had been our father?'

I didn't know what to say and assumed that Robin had him under his spell.

'Orwell, Dad had many faults, but he was our father. Nothing is going to change that. There are certain things in life that we just have to accept.'

'Why?'

'Because that's the way it is.'

I was shivering with the cold and put my hands in my pockets. I felt Gabriella's owl.

'Are you not cold, Orwell?' Hinting that I wanted to go home.

He was perfectly still. 'No, I'm warm, very warm.'

I took the owl out of my pocket and handed it to Orwell. He stared at it. I thought maybe now that Rebecca had the other one it might bring them back together. I remembered what Gabriella had told me and I repeated it to Orwell.

'A friend gave me this owl to protect me. She was lovely, Orwell. You'd have loved her. I know this may sound stupid but I feel as if it was Dad who sent her into my life, because she put me straight on a few things.'

A light rain dropped. Maybe Dad didn't want me telling Orwell this.

I continued. 'She said that all our lives are a mass of lies but we somehow learn to live with those lies and sometimes we even forget them. They are the moments we should cherish.'

'Shea, do you think that's all there is to life?'

'It's a theory, Orwell. A lot of the rest of it is pure decoration.'

'That doesn't bode well for me, then, does it? You know I've got an excellent memory.' He laughed and joined him. 'You think you've got problems? What about the Memory Man? His life must be a nightmare.'

We laughed more heartily at the absurdity of it all. Orwell started to shout.

'I want to be a goldfish. They must be the happiest creatures alive.' The rain came down heavier as we both danced about pretending to be goldfish. We kept circling each other. Every time we were head on, we would ask each other our names only to turn around and then start the conversation again. It was part goldfish impression, part raindance. We interlocked hands and swung each other about, taking our joke to the extreme.

'Did you remember to do the lottery? Our numbers came up.'

'No, I forgot.'

'Ah, as long as you're happy.'

Orwell started singing that Simple Minds song, 'Don't You Forget About Me'. I joined in with 'Who?' We stopped eventually, exhausted. Soaked through but elated. Natural smiles on our faces. Orwell looked intently at his newly acquired owl.

'It's beautiful. Owls are our great protectors. But are they good flyers?'

'When they remember to be.'

We smiled at each other again. Orwell put his arm around my shoulder and said, 'I've really enjoyed tonight. You're right, you know. What is the point in worrying all the time? You're right. I could have a brain haemorrhage at any moment.'

'That's the spirit.'

As I went to put my arm around his shoulder he said, 'I'm about to have one now.'

He climbed the panelling, awkwardly got his balance right, kissed the owl and jumped upwards. My soul followed him down while my body stood frozen. There was a thud followed by the honking of horns. I didn't look down. My legs were going from under me. So I sat on the pavement, trying to cover my ears and eyes. I wanted to join him so badly for that final embrace.

I knew I would not experience a happier time in the rest of my life if I could hold him once more. I wanted to rush down the steps and hug what was left of him but I was just so fucking annoyed. Why did he do this? Why did he do it alone? Why didn't he take me with him? Had Dad called for him? I could have grabbed his legs. But no, that would have been selfish. I would have been saving him for myself. It never entered my mind that I should save him. Why? Because I love him. I love him so much that I wanted him to do what he wanted to do. It wasn't a cry for help. It was a decision. His final decision. I cried because I wasn't there for the last five seconds of his life and I should have been. If he'd loved me, he would have told me. We could have flown together. Or at the very least I could have been down there for him, beckoning him on, a smile on my face for my dear brother. We could have shared one more precious moment together. But no, my duty was to help clean up the mess.

Chapter 24

A squad car took me to the Whittington Hospital, which was only a minute's drive away. They wanted me to go to the hospital to identify the body. The policeman sat me down in casualty while he dealt with the formalities. Then he beckoned me forward silently and apologized for what he had to ask me. And then quietly said, 'Which side of the bridge did he jump from?'

I looked at him, puzzled.

He explained, 'The two sides of the bridge come under different jurisdictions. If it was the south, the coroner has to come from Islington and the north is Haringay.' Maybe Orwell was a snob: he jumped into the Borough of Islington.

He wrote down the information and thanked me. He led me into a room where my brother was laid out. He explained I only had twenty minutes because the body had to remain refrigerated so that they could do a proper post-mortem. He was bagged up in clear plastic with just his head out. Haringay council would have probably put him in a bin-liner. There was a glass screen between us which I wanted to smash. Without focusing on his body, all I could think was that they were going to put him back into a fridge. The smile was gone from his face and I already missed it. I could still picture his childhood face. The nights I couldn't sleep I would spend hours watching him sleeping. This always made me feel safe. He always slept soundly, never any movement. He would find a position and wake that way. Me, I pushed and shoved my way through the night. I could wake up in the morning in a different house. I was left alone in the room with my brother. He slept soundly and I watched. My parents were in the other room, Mum's snoring reaching into ours. Beside my bed was my poster of Queen's Park Rangers football club. I never really liked the team but I supported them to get Dad's goat because he was so fervently anti-royalist. Beside that poster was one of Freddie Mercury but my biggest poster was of the Queen herself. I'm not into the monarchy myself, but with the Queen's poster and my childish imagination, I used to pretend I lived in a giant letter and many of my dreams were about being posted to exotic places.

Orwell had a giant poster of Tottenham Hotspur above his bed. He also had a poster of the cast of *Happy Days*. God, he loved that programme. We used to watch it together. I thought it was passable but he geared his day around it. The second the theme came on, he would sing along and his eyes would dart around the screen as he tried to take in all the information he was given. He even wore a little black plastic Fonzie jacket. His innocence was remarkable and I sometimes teased him about it even though I was secretly envious of him. On Sundays the family would all sit down and watch television gether. It was either *Little House on the Prairie* or *The Waltons* and soon myself, Orwell and Mum would be crying and Dad would spoil it with his rationality.

'It's just the weepy music they put over it, that's what's making you cry.'

He never understood that we wanted to cry. We didn't care why. Of course, in time I became like Dad, as did Orwell. This growing-up lark, this holding on to your emotions, that shit comes out in other ways, sometimes in bad forms. I remember analysing *Happy Days* one day with Orwell and how bizarre it really was. The Cunninghams, a moralistic middle-class American family, allowed a wild drop-out who fucked a different woman every night to rent a room above their garage. This same man, well into his thirties, was then allowed to dispense his advice to all the teenagers in the area and where did he lure these kids when he wanted to help them? Into the men's room of the local hamburger joint. All very suspect. I think after that I spoiled the programme a little for Orwell. That and the fact that every time the Fonz appeared, I always shouted 'Paedophile!' I wonder if the Fonz had turned up at the bridge, would Orwell have got his sense of innocence back?

The policeman told me I had to leave but I could see the body again in a couple of days. I kissed the glass quietly. I didn't want to wake him up. This story had all started with me stupidly wanting to wake Dad up. But I wasn't going to take any risks with sweet Orwell. I had one last look at his non-functioning body and then looked around the room to see if he and Dad were having an after-life punch-up. Wouldn't it be great if at your

279

death you are given all the answers and you full
understand peace and happiness and joy while we o
earth continue to struggle with these words and use the
out of context on greetings cards. I took a deep breath
closed my eyes and left my brother. I kidded myself tha
I was strong, but as I closed the door behind me I bur
into tears. Rather than covering my face and disappea
ing from public view, I strolled out with hands by m
sides, body upright, with pride for my brother.

Outside I decided to go straight to Mum's rather than m
own flat. I think it was for fear of catching a glimpse o
my own little fridge. I wished I could have taken Orwe
and put him there, though. I bought a couple of new
papers in an attempt to take my mind off the event. *Th
Times* had the *Angel* fiasco splattered all over its from
page. The *Angel* had obviously dropped its story from th
second edition and was leading with the big departmen
store fire. It was arson and there staring back at me wa
James Fentelli. He had been arrested for the fire. One o
the shop assistants must have really pissed him off.
guess we all have different ways of letting off steam. I
some ways I admire his grand gestures. The rest of us le
people tread on us and apologize for the intrusion.
    I managed to catch a train that was just leaving. It wa
full so I had to sit on a seat that faced London. I watche
life's big picture through the window as an afterthough
The train was moving forward but I wasn't given th
chance to study the future, to prepare for it. I was seein
images as a quick, last glimpse before they were take

way from me. Sleepiness made the experience even
oggier. The blood was trying to circulate around my
ody but it wasn't getting past the hot bubbling stomach.
plashes were reaching my brain and hands. A life-force,
reeping around my body. My skin was tight and
cratchy. The air-conditioning was blowing hot and cold
ir, a minute torture made all the more painful because I
as the only one experiencing it. I no longer had a family
o hide in. I was the lone gunslinger, surveying the wreck
y family had left behind. I had no horse to ride off into
e sunset, no journey to embark on. Yes, I was always
n the move but to nowhere in particular. Here I was on
y way to Mum to wish her the best for her new life and
o inform her of another death. The other passengers
ent about their business.

I wanted them to show me their own devastation. I
atched two kids playing snap. Each time they crashed
eir hand down and shouted, 'Snap!' I could feel another
ne of my brain cells doing the same. Their giddy,
ugared excitement was carefree and I wanted to warn
em about their futures. The grubby dirty-haired young
overs who used each other as cushions. I wanted to warn
em too. The tourists with their maps, the buddy-buddy
usinessmen. I wanted to tell them all. But why should I
oil their little moments of forgetfulness? I didn't mind
ow they got there, be it through chit-chat, a crossword
r a knitting pattern. But it was comforting to know they
ad made it there. Why did it feel like I was always on
uty? The guard showing people around the gallery of
fe. All the fun gone for me but getting a kick out of
thers' enjoyment. Why was I so concerned with when

they would next come across the agony of their ow
existence? They were doing fine without me.

Wasn't my role that of the fixed ex-lover, there purel
to remind others of their failings, a walking exhibit c
where your life might go wrong? Whatever happened t
those blokes who used to parade up and down Oxfor
Street with their doom-laden placards? Did they jus
become happy? Or did they see us subtler versions doin
their job for them? Did they swap their 'The End of th
World is Nigh' signs for 'Golf Sale Now On'? I knew
would be OK if I had a like-minded soul by my side
Where are you, Gabriella? If I could lick somebody else
wounds. Maybe that's why I joined Robin Hood's gang
That's the only reason anyone joins a club. Not that the
have an all-encompassing passion for it but so that the
can talk to others about something in common, but
even saw through that.

My parents brought me up with love and protected m
by swamping me with cuddly toys. My deep love for m
teddy bear was my first love and I think I went on t
judge all other relationships by that high standard. Wh
didn't my parents warn me that human relationship
were not that simple? Fuck it, I've only realized this now
I've never got over my teddy bear. Rebecca is not m
unrequited love, Teddy is. Why couldn't Mum have tol
me that Teddy was eventually going to leave me? B
handed down to Orwell. As a child, you go from tha
pure love to the television's version, where it all work
out, then you're thrown into the real world and it isn
like the movies. You begin to think you're a failure. M
mistake is that I believed everything I was told when

was a kid and, as all these lies, one by one, got found out, was left with nothing to believe in. It is my duty to get in touch with Ruth. I can't let my child make the same mistakes as me. I should butt into the child's life as a caustic reminder that things don't always work out. I am the only male Hickson left. Our legacy must live on. Maybe I could hijack kindergarten groups and instil some truths. Turn up at children's parties and tell them exactly how it is. Hello, I'm a teddy bear's witness, can you spare a few moments of your time? I joke and yet know it makes sense. Elvis was being truthful when he asked could he be our teddy bear.

I arrived at the New Forest. The sun was out but dark clouds protected it. I approached the house; it looked tilted from a distance. Smoke was coming from the chimney and I hated having to be the one to disturb this peace. I touched on to the gravel driveway with a foreboding which made me walk slower. Mum wasn't peering out of any window as was normally the case. I rang the doorbell and turned away slightly, not wanting to look her in the face but also by way of trying to compose myself. I heard the door opening and my heart started beating faster. I turned round and actually did a double-take. There standing in the hallway was Robin Hood. I was dumbfounded. More so, when he casually invited me in.

'What the fuck are you doing here?'

'That's no way to talk to your future father-in-law.'

All I could keep saying was 'Fuck off.' Eventually I got round to asking where my mum was.

'Oh my dear boy, she's out getting in a few last-minute provisions.'

283

I stared at him but it wasn't registering. He couldn'
really be there. This was some warped magician's trick.
was suddenly freezing and went towards the fire. H
followed me in and congratulated me on last night'
work. I just wanted to get rid of him. I never wanted t
see his sorry self again but here he was, smiling at m
smiling through me.

'Listen, there's been a family tragedy and I woul
really appreciate it if you could just get out of my life fo
the moment.'

'I am family now, Shea. Anyway, we've got so much t
catch up on.'

He was trying to freak me out and I had to sit down.
went to Dad's armchair. The seat was sunken. Tha
fucker had been sitting in it.

'Is Orwell not coming?'

'Orwell is dead.'

Even though it was me who was saying it, it was als
the first time I really heard it as a bold statement. M
throat went dry.

'Suicide?' Robin Hood said. I looked up quizzically.
thought he might, that poor soul. You Hickson boys, yo
just haven't got the fight in you. You're like a house c
cards.'

Ready for a fight. I asked, 'What did you do t
Orwell?'

'Come, come. I don't do things, I instigate them
Orwell wanted a trumpeted farewell. I'm very obligin
and I helped him achieve this.'

'Do you get some sort of a kick out of trying to contr
people's lives.'

'I see a lot of your father in you.'

'Leave my father out of this.'

'But he's such a big part of it all. Shea, now that we're family, I think it's time you knew my real name. I'm Stanley E. Bowls.'

In my haze, it took me some time to cotton on to what he had said.

'Stanley . . . ? Oh God.' I stared at him. He was the one who went to university with Mum and Dad, the one who humiliated him at the debate. He was the Clouds. It all made sense. He sat down with that big stupid smile on his face. He was the fucking Clouds.

'See, Shea, I didn't like your father. He didn't know how to behave and yet he thought the world was his for the taking. He had ideas above his station. So I made it my hobby to put him straight on a couple of things. Unfortunately, he took it worse than I thought and in the end it destroyed him.'

As I took in every bit of information he was steam-rollering at me my breathing became more agitated. He kept on reversing over and over me. I wanted to hit back but for now all I could do was listen.

'You and Orwell were his world and I took you away from him.' That explained the Robin Hood books. That was Dad telling us he knew but also that it was somehow OK. I couldn't let this bastard get his own way.

'You could never take us away from our father. We're not puppets in your stupid game. I love my father. You don't even know what that means.'

'Love? Yes, indeed. But with me, Shea, you'll do exactly what I tell you to.' This was said with improbable

285

venom. He spoke to me as an evil stepfather would to ten-year-old. I suddenly had a moment of absolute clarit in which I realized he had no hold on me. He was not m leader. I am my own leader, we all are. He had taught m that. This gave me subdued strength.

'And I suppose you used Mum in your game as wel He's dead now, you've got what you wanted. Why don you just leave us alone?'

'There lies the twist, young Shea. Yes, initially I did us your mother. We go back such a long way. We alway kept in touch and grew to like each other's company an then one day we found this acceptance grew into a lov of sorts. You see, your mother told me about your littl fact-finding mission. I could have saved you a lot c trouble and, like Orwell, I could have told you all abou your father.'

There was no hint of emotion in his face. Then h cockily continued, 'But the least I can do for you is to fi in the blanks. Myself and your mother were going to g together anyway. Jean had grown tired of your fathe long before he did himself. But he was that typical smal minded animal in the sense that once he was losin something, he desperately wanted it back. He wa making it very difficult for me and Jean to get on wit our lives.'

'This getting on with your lives . . . how long have yo been seeing my mother?'

'The word is "affair". Is that so hard for you to say You found out all about your father, why should yo mother be any different? But in answer to your questio which I think you deserve, it's been pretty full on for th

286

last five years. It's weird that, pretty much ever since you joined the organization.'

'Did you make my father kill himself?'

'I told you, he was pig-headed. Nobody told your father what to do.'

'Yeah, but did you force his hand? You knew about the rape.'

'Maybe, but more importantly, he knew about it. He was more concerned with your mother finding out.'

'You threatened him with the photos.'

He simply nodded.

'OK, so if you wanted my mother, why drag me and Orwell into it?'

'Simple: because you would have resented me and that would have reflected on your mother. So it was easier to have you on my side.'

'But that's backfired. I'm never going to be on your side.'

'Oh you will.'

'What makes you so sure?'

He looked at his watch and then went over and turned on the television. The news had just started and they were concentrating on one story: the deaths of seven people in the offices of the *Daily Angel*. A crude device had been left there, a bomb timed to go off at ten a.m. It was an evil attack, primed to explode when the office was at its busiest. No organization had taken responsibility. Stanley turned off the TV and looked to me.

'That trip to Libya came in very handy. You did a very good job carrying that bomb in for me. You're looking at a minimum of thirty years in prison . . . that's if you get caught.'

287

All I could think of, as anyone in a crisis does, was stupid religion and I wished there was a heaven and hell so he could suffer but throughout all the pain, sadness, tiredness, mental instability and body wreckage, the brain slowly beeped as if it was keeping me alive. Just slow beeps telling me I was right all along. There was no ordered sense of right and wrong. Mum had lied to me. And this man whom I had put my trust in had let me down. Everybody had let me down. I wanted to join my brother and father. A trinity of failures. I was truly alone. I fell deeper into my chair, knowing I might never have the strength to get back up. Why had Bowls done all this? To take revenge on my father? For his love for my mother? Or had his father done something to fuck him up? What was his story? Does all this relate back to a throwaway moment in the Garden of Eden that aligned itself to me? Stanley wasn't cherishing his moment of forgetfulness. He was enabling the rest of us to have none. I had taken him as my teacher, I had learned his way. Or was I spoiled from the moment that Dad overpowered Eve? I wanted all thought to go away. I saw Stanley's bitter face, smug and cruel, lines of corrupt deeds written all over his face. He was a clever man who used his skill on small-mindedness. That was the waste and then he became blurred as my tears welled up and I felt genuine sadness for this pathetic figure, trying to prove his manhood time and time again. And then the tears were for my brother and my father, unable to live with what their lives had amounted to. Then I cried for myself and I wanted my teddy bear.

I peered out the window for respite but there strolling up the driveway was Gabriella, and my body started working again. She was going to make everything OK. She was going to save me from this mess, and as she got closer my strength came back and then she waved at me and put her key in the door. She rushed in but from the door to the lounge, she turned into my mother. She kissed Stanley on the cheek and asked me was I OK. Poking out of her shopping bag was a fresh trout, one eye closed, winking at me, mocking me. I sank back into the chair, falling. My body sinking, all my organs collapsing into the pit of my stomach. I'll make us all a nice cup of tea and Mum was in the kitchen. Stanley followed her out to break the news about Orwell. I looked at the fire, still sinking, the log was nearly a cinder and the wind was funnelling down from the chimney to help blow it out. I sighed heavily but the air wasn't reaching my lungs. Dad's chair was a perfect fit and it was now my turn to take the baton. Stanley brought me in a cup of tea and I sipped from it. Soon my cup wasn't half empty but half full. And I knew the pretence of my life would linger on. I had nothing to live for and then I remembered I really liked blow-jobs. I'd nearly forgotten that.

Staring at the window I watched a police car parking and rather than fear being arrested I saw it as escape. I watched Stanley trying to compose himself and I knew that he could never control me. To do that I would need a will, but mine was gone. He knew this and as I smiled he became more worried. I had accepted my lot, so what difference would another thirty years of confinement make to me? I was free for the first time in my life, no four walls could contain that. I opened the door to give myself up. The senior policeman of the two asked for

Stanley. I showed them in and they promptly handcuffed him and arrested him for murder. His 'Gentlemen, surely there's been some mistake!' echoed around my head. I was taken in for questioning.

In the squad car, I simply admired the scenery, ignoring Stanley's occasional protestations. I suddenly twigged that the sun was on my side, bathing me in its glory while throwing shadows at Stanley.

The two officers remained silent. They seemed edgy and ready for trouble and I remembered Mum's sad face as they took the two of us away. And, yes, there is an after-life, because Orwell was still protecting me. He wasn't going to let anyone bully me. He'd seen through Stanley.

The police had received a letter from Orwell detailing all the organisation's crimes and strategic planning, which implicated Stanley in the thick of the action. Orwell had substituted my involvement with his to clear me of the bombing.

And here I sit in this cell writing this sorry tale. Stanley was given thirty years, which means he will die in prison. He tried very hard to bring me down with him, but nothing would hold.

I got two years for my involvement with the organization. Every mediocre television personality can rest easy in their bed, but, then again, so can I. This time is given to me as a clearing-out process, a tease, a build-up to a life that I can at last cherish. My little window gets the sun most mornings and now I'm enjoying a good book.